PENGUIN METRO READS
BLOOD SONG

Juggi Bhasin was one of the first television journalists in
India. He joined Doordarshan News in 1987. He has many
landmark news reports to his credit, including the demolition
of the Babri Masjid in 1992. He has also been a senior anchor
for Lok Sabha Television.

Juggi can be contacted at juggibhasin@gmail.com.

Also by the same author

The Terrorist
The Avenger

BLOOD SONG

JUGGI BHASIN

Penguin
metro reads

An imprint of Penguin Random House

PENGUIN METRO READS

USA | Canada | UK | Ireland | Australia
New Zealand | India | South Africa | China | Singapore

Penguin Metro Reads is part of the Penguin Random House group of companies
whose addresses can be found at global.penguinrandomhouse.com

Published by Penguin Random House India Pvt. Ltd
4th Floor, Capital Tower 1, MG Road,
Gurugram 122 002, Haryana, India

First published in Penguin Metro Reads by Penguin Books India 2014

ISBN 9780143419747

Typeset in Sabon by R. Ajith Kumar, New Delhi

Printed at Repro India Limited

www.penguin.co.in

How can I write a story about the courage of a woman and not acknowledge the true-life grit of the two most important women in my life–my wife, Sonu, and my mum, Inder Mohini? And as always there is the young man cheering them on from the sidelines–my son, Karan.

Prologue

She knew it in her bones that today was the day that everything she knew of her life would change for ever. She felt like a bloodied infant emerging from a secure womb, traumatized by the world outside. She had thrashed around and shook the steel cage with an energy she never knew was curled up inside her like a sleeping demon. She had surprised herself with her resistance and it had brought her some respite. But her teeth still clattered and her body, stripped of all clothing, shared the fate of a windswept leaf tossed around in a current of cold air. Her mind raced in all directions. She had an overwhelming urge to see her face one more time before whatever was to follow. She knew then, as any girl in her kind of situation senses, that after the passage of the event her face would change forever.

In a situation like the one she found herself in,

it was best to let the mind wander. She saw herself standing on the train station platform, next to the Southall signboard written in Gurmukhi. She was the girl who would always be waiting for the 7.22 to take her to Paddington. She looked in closely at the girl. Her head would always be bent and she would never make eye contact with anyone. She reached across and carefully removed the chunni draping the head. The face slowly looked up and she felt like an explorer who after walking for days, lost in a forest, comes across a single, wildly growing exotic flower, in a carpet of green. The eyes were large orbs of tremulous brown, the lips bit into each other with uncertainty and a crease of worry moved between the unclipped eyebrows as if the girl had been caught with her secret. A train on the opposite tracks passed the girl standing on the platform. The sun had come up and she caught a glimpse of her face in the window of the speeding train. It looked horribly disfigured, the ruddy light and the windowpane playing tricks on what she saw.

Then suddenly the dream was broken. Somewhere close by in her hole she heard the boys laughing, and driblets of carousing talk reached her ears. She could no longer shut her mind and her ears to what they were saying. She knew then that the time was close at hand. And then an overwhelming fear gripped her. This could not be happening! This was London, the centre of the universe, a safe city. She was not the kind of girl who would risk being mugged in unsavoury street corners. She was a faceless middle-class girl living in a faceless red-tiled house. Girls like her never found a mention in the *Sun* or the *Daily Mail*. She closed her eyes tightly. Wishing, praying and hoping for all of it to go away. And for a brief time, she felt that the terror of her situation could not affect her. She was free and far away.

She saw herself looking in her bathroom's sink mirror with her nightdress unbuttoned. Her left breast stood exposed and she looked in wonder at its perfectly rounded reddish-pink areola. A day earlier she had sneaked down after eleven to the TV set in the drawing room in complete darkness. She had muted the sound and put on an adult film streaming in on the cable. She carefully observed the European girls taking off their undergarments. She looked in the mirror in her bathroom and she smiled, a little consciously. Her circle of honey was better than theirs—better rounded and more firm. She blushed; she knew that behind the unthreaded eyebrows and unwaxed arms hid a girl of peerless beauty. And she knew there would be a day when the world would stop to look at her . . .

She opened her eyes , knowing that the steel cage gave her no respite. The biting cold claimed her and then a wave of complete panic hit her. She could no longer shake it off and pretend that her little escapades of the mind could shield her from what was about to follow. She began to tremble violently and curled up in the dirt and grime; her body continued to shake with unrelenting spasms. Her cries were muffled; it was as if a small animal was in distress. Someone heard her cries in the hole and a single corresponding laugh, as though a hyena had strayed in, rang out.

She turned over and began to kick the cage in complete terror, resisting an imagined attempt by an unseen entity forcibly dragging her in the opposite direction by her feet. Desperate, she covered her breasts and her vagina. She felt as though an unseen body was mounted on top of her. The next few seconds were the most terrifying of her life. She thrashed on the floor with manic energy, grunting, making indecipherable sounds, her hands like claws protecting her vagina from all ingress. Her lungs were bursting for the lack of air as she let out a scream that like a projectile shot across the hole, bouncing off the walls and spinning violently inside the underground, its trapped energy finding no release. And then she was free of the unseen presence and she stopped and lay still, covered in a film of sweat. She looked up at the ceiling and wondered why in God's name had her parents named her Simran.

She remembered as a little girl when her mum would put her to bed at night and tell her that she was blessed to be called Simran. 'The recitation of your name invokes Baba Nanak. What can be more auspicious than that?' Simran would then snuggle up to her, secure in her mother's warmth and assured that there was order in the universe, that someone above her was watching out for her.

She was not sure of all that now. The man with the hyena-like laugh spoke across the hole. Taking pleasure in his strength and her vulnerability he called out, 'We are coming for you Simran. Si! Si! Simran! Simran! Simran! We are coming for you, my pretty, innocent Sikhni! You can run but you cannot hide, Si! Si! Simran! Simran! Si! Si! Simran . . .'

1

Some time back

Simran was a poet at heart. When she walked, her natural inclination was to drift amongst the clouds, in a time and space she had created for herself. She had built her own little universe by stretching the limits of her imagination almost like it was an elastic band. She wanted to give expression to the thoughts that filled her mind.

She was struggling with the first few lines of the poem that she would eventually write one day and savour for herself. The words were not coming. A million thoughts filled her head and then there were the everyday cares and responsibilities she could not run away from. But today was different. After putting in six months as a probationer she would finally get her letter of confirmation at the post office. She had spent time at the post office as a kind of Jill of all trades, sorting out the mail, helping with the tax forms, even taking sundry inquiry calls on courier issues and postage. She had kept her head down, listened to and followed instructions, and generally conformed to what the whites at the office said about her: 'That quiet, hard-working Sikh girl'. She quickened her pace during the short walk from her house behind the market on Uxbridge Road to her place of work at the post office on King's Street.

The South Asians in her office, she knew, held a contrary opinion of her. They avoided her and, for some reason, most had taken an instant dislike to her. She was aware of the epithets they used to describe her. She was called everything from a *jhalli* to a 'white-arse-licking, dumb Sikhni'. She had never quite understood why some of her countrymen had made themselves prisoners to the useless us-versus-them debate. 'Get on with your life!' she wanted to tell them. But the words would not come to her when she witnessed their bad behaviour. All she knew was that the younger lot in the office was even worse. They would often voice opinions and focus keenly on incidents that would strain the mesh of race relations.

Simran now broke into a run, knowing that she could be late for her big day. One of the neighbours, Mrs Satwant Kaur, taking down the washing from the clothes line in the front yard in violation of the rules, smiled indulgently at her. Simran did not respond. She knew the meaning behind the smile. Mrs Kaur was one of her staunchest critics at the never-ending 'dinner get-togethers' within the community.

'I feel such pain to look at Nirmal's daughter,' she would say to anyone who cared to listen in their close-knit community. 'She buys the worst suits from the second-hand sale at Little India. Her face looks as if the gardener has not mowed the lawn for a week. And that stupid cap she wears with the flappy ears. I wish I could call her by another name but then she is not a jhalli for nothing . . .'

Simran bounded up the steps and she saw Mrs Ashley waiting for her in the lobby area.

'Dear girl, thank goodness you made it on time. The super, no less, is here to give you your letter. Come on then now, off we go!' Simran held up her cheek for Mrs Ashley's morning peck and both women disappeared into the warren of management offices behind the work area.

*

The red-tiled house at the end of the lane behind the market was Simran's refuge from the world, filled with hope but also fear. Her heart would soar whenever she'd see her brother, Bobby. He was in person everything that she ever hoped to be—an idea that could only be put down in words, pen to paper. At six feet, of lean build, he carried his athletic frame with the ease of a ballet dancer. He had laughing, crinkly eyes. The first bristles of his beard were breaking out and she knew that all the girls in the neighbourhood only bothered to talk to her because of him. They all wanted a part of Bobby. But Bobby divided his affection between his sister whom he loved with a passion and the world of RnB music, with a Punjabi *tadka*.

So Simran couldn't think of anyone but Bobby with whom to share the happiest news of her life. She looked at her watch. It was close to six. Throwing her purse on the living room sofa, she sprinted up the stairs to the first floor, straight to her brother's room. The door burst open and Simran, framed in the doorway, produced the coveted letter with a flourish.

'Ta! Ra! Ta! Ra! Miss Simran Kaur Banga is hereby confirmed as an employee of the post office after a successful completion of her probation period. Ta! Ra! Ta! Ra!' she announced happily.

Bobby who was strumming the strings of a guitar leapt out of bed. 'Yay! That's the way to go, sis!' he exclaimed, kissing her and then gathering her in an embrace, lifting her high up in the air. Both siblings yelled their lungs out and danced in the room; their mother, fearing the worst, rushed into the room. Bobby picked up the guitar and celebrated Simran's accomplishment with impromptu, mad lyrics and they forced their mother to sing along to the ditty which made no sense to anyone. Mrs Nirmal Kaur laughed and joined in for a bit. Then she was suddenly reminded of dinner and her strict husband, and she rushed down to the kitchen again. Breathless, both sat on the bed and read the letter once again. Simran couldn't stop smiling. She snuggled up to her brother and he stroked her wisps of hair, in a moment of quietude. 'Well done, sis!' he whispered. 'You are finally on your way. This is the first step.'

Simran looked up at her brother and she felt all her worries and insecurities seep away.

'You made it possible, Veerji. You keep pushing me on, extending my boundaries. Left to myself, I was only good for making *karah-prashad* offerings at the gurdwara on Sundays with Mum and her friends.'

'And even there they wouldn't have allowed you to actually do anything, except wash the dishes!'

'Yeah, yeah . . .' She nodded with a smile.

They caught each other's eye and laughed; Bobby, gently stroking his sister's pale, white fingers, asked her, 'So, have you written the first few lines?'

She shook her head. 'No,' she replied. 'The words are coming but they are flowing in a gush. I can't select the right ones and make sense out of them. But I am closing in.'

He kissed her fingers. 'Keep trying,' he spoke softly. 'You and I will change the face of this forgotten place in the UK. The world will sit up and take notice of us: the sister an alchemist with words and feelings, and the brother an RnB star with his own radio station and a million-pound contract. We will fly in our own company jet, sip champagne and on our way to Ibiza, while you write poetry, I will make out in my suite with a blonde air hostess!'

Simran rolled on the bed, clutching her sides as she could not stop laughing. 'Is that all you're thinking about?' she asked.

Bobby winked at her.

Their little celebratory party broke up as their mother announced dinner from over the banister. There would be no 'eating in the rooms' today. Simran felt the old stab of fear when she heard that.

Alone in her room, she took off her clothes and went in for a wash. In the blue light of the bathroom, she looked at the areola of her breast in the mirror and gently squeezed the nipple, circling the areola. She felt a tremor of pleasure course through her body. She had a feeling that things were finally coming together for her. The knot of fear that she'd always felt would now loosen and the anxiety about the future would now be washed away. Things had finally begun to happen. She turned on the shower and let the fear within her pores drain away. She alternated between a hot and cold cascade and, bit by bit, she started to feel completely relaxed as the sediment of oppression residing within her was cleaned out of the sluices.

When she emerged, wrapped in a towel, she looked at her handbag excitedly. After a moment's hesitation she pulled out a long box from the bag. She felt that she had earned the purchase. Mrs Ashley had bought it for her at a discount. It had been their secret. She opened the box carefully and looked at the epilator. Then, after she'd read the instructions, she adjusted the blades and set it against the hair growing on her forearm. No more would she be called uncouth and ungroomed.

'Don't press the switch!' came her mother's firm voice from behind her. Simran froze and the fear was back in her life again, just like that. She hadn't known when her mother had come into the room.

'You know the ground rules,' her mother said with ice in her voice. 'Not a millimetre of hair will be cut or shaved in this house. No one will be allowed to pollute this house!'

Straight ahead of her she saw the reflection of her mother's face in the mirror. Her mother looked transformed—she was no longer the caring, indulgent mother that Simran so desperately wanted to believe in. She wasn't even the woman who had danced with joy with her children moments ago. This was a woman who was carrying out orders from the other fearful entity who resided in the house. Gone was the simple, unsure village woman from Amritsar, who had immigrated with her husband in late 1984 seeking political asylum. The eyes were almost robotic. There was no flicker of pain, empathy or any other emotion in them.

'Your father is waiting downstairs for both of you at the dinner table,' she said coldly. 'He's already on his fourth drink. Don't keep him waiting. Come quickly.'

2

Balwinder Singh Banga sat in the largest and most comfortable easy chair in the drawing room sipping Black Label whisky. The heyday of that alcoholic beverage was long past, but Balwinder stuck to it, because ever since he was a teen, when he had started to drink, Black Label had been an aspirational drink. This was a man who had come close to losing his life in the purges carried out by Pratap Gill's men in the killing fields of Punjab in the late eighties. Now he was determined to hold on to what was dear to him, besides the whisky of course. He had to inject sense into that rebellious son of his, who in his mind had fallen prey to the ills of Western lifestyle. His daughter followed the straight and narrow but at times she would say or do something that was totally inexplicable. Maybe he had to increase his watch over her—observe carefully what all she did in her spare time. And as for his wife— well, she was a settled issue. He sipped the whisky and stroked his flowing salt-and-pepper beard.

Simran came down the stairs with dread in her heart. She heard the soft strains of the Japji Sahib (a hymn) on the Bose speakers. Fear gave way to anger as she could not comprehend the old, blasphemous habit of her father—combining bouts of whisky drinking with incantations of religiosity. She wondered whether he even listened to the mellifluous strains of the Japji Sahib or if all that was part of a larger plan in which her mother would create a mise en scène down below for him, to abet the beast forever lurking in his heart to come out. She trembled at the thought of how the dinner would end. 'Not today, Wahe Guruji, not today,' she silently prayed. 'Please let it not happen on my big day.'

Her brother was already at the dining table, scanning an old issue of *Rolling Stone* magazine and her mother was piling up the table with their father's favourite chicken dishes. There was deathly stillness below and it struck Simran that like in a puppet theatre the marionettes had scuffed the stage with their two-bit acts and now everything had become still for the king to make his appearance. And what would the king do? He could be pleased with the stage having been set for him; in an improbable situation he could even be amused, and if the sun had risen on the wrong side he could even laugh. But more likely than not he would end up picking a fault and then his temper would rage.

After his fifth drink, a red spot had appeared in Balwinder's eye and it made him look dangerous, almost rabid. The scar running between his bushy eyebrows and his forehead, gifted by Gill's men decades ago in a police cell, looked inflamed, as if it would burst. At that point in time Simran hated her father more than anything in the world. The fifty-plus man wearily got up from the easy chair and announced, 'Let's eat.'

They began eating in silence and Simran could so easily see from which quarter trouble would come. Bobby was quickly wolfing down his meal, keeping the magazine plastered over his face, eager to make a quick getaway from the table. He had perfected that stratagem, ever since he was a child, to escape the raging battles at the dinner table. Simran could see the familiar signs of anger stirring up in her father. She took a reluctant initiative. She placed her confirmation letter next to her father and told him, 'I got the letter, Pitaji. I thought you would be happy to know.'

Balwinder looked a little befuddled at the peace offering. He nodded and pushed away the plate decked with generous helpings of spicy chicken curry.

'Girl, you got the job because of the loyalty of this family to the British. In our own small way, we have been doing yeoman service for the British. Do you think the British don't know that? They keep an eye on everything. Even during Maharaja Ranjit Singh's time, the British knew that it was the Sikhs who really mattered in tilting the balance of power. Not like the Indian government, which has always oppressed us! The things they have done to my *quom*, my people! The bastards . . .'

The silent alarm bell had started ringing for the others gathered around the table. They were no longer skating on thin ice. They were sinking under the weight of a surface that could no longer hold them. Nirmal Kaur pitched in with a diversion.

'Bobby, I tried something new. Instead of the usual carrot halwa, I prepared apple pie. It's good to try these English recipes once in a while. The neighbours have an apple tree growing in their backyard . . .'

Balwinder's fist came crashing down on the mahogany table.

'Don't interrupt me, woman, when I am putting sense in the children's heads! You have to yaw-yaw your stupid mouth precisely when you should be shutting up to listen. After all these years you still behave the same as that illiterate village woman I brought along to this country . . .'

Bobby flung the *Rolling Stone* magazine and got up, trembling with rage.

'Look at you calling my mother names! You

are nothing more than a wasted old drunkard who concocts a new fiction every night to feed your insecurity. It would be the end of days for the British Government to have anything to do with the likes of you. They would probably give you a free ticket to get your ass back to the country you came from, which you keep cursing. Today is your daughter's big day but how does that matter to you? She got a permanent job by dint of her hard work and not because of some mythical debt you are paying and you force us to pay. Instead of applauding her, you had to get drunk and become bestial with all of us. Fucking lunatic I have for a father!'

Bobby's fiery intervention brought out the raw face of the internecine battle, from which there was no looking back now. Balwinder looked choked and ready to burst. Simran suddenly had a vision of how things were unfolding. It was like a scene from Kabuki theatre. The faces of the main actors, plastered white, concealed the well of emotions lurking underneath. But in a sharp move, all the Kimono-clad protagonists unsheathed their swords at the same time to cut and maim each other with utter savageness.

Balwinder, foaming at the mouth, took the plate loaded with chicken pieces and flung it at his son. Bobby ducked and the plate exploded behind him into a million fragments against an artefact mounted on the wall. Nirmal rushed in the way between father and son and Simran shielded her brother. But the acid began to drip from Balwinder's tongue.

'You bloody *bhand*, I raised you for a day like this. Bastard bhand sits the whole day in the room, fiddling with my money and patience! Nirmal, you have given birth to a bhand, who one day will land at the *kothewalis'*, those filthy prostitutes, and he will end up fiddling their bloody instruments, eating and spitting paan!

Simran could no longer restrain herself. She pushed her brother behind her as she turned to face her father.

'Pitaji, there no kothewalis in England! I think you are completely confused. Why don't you go up and sleep and leave everyone in peace!'

Nirmal Kaur with surprising strength pushed her husband on to the chair before he could attempt another charge at the siblings. Simran's unexpected defiance had somewhat deflated Balwinder.

'See, Nirmal! Corruption runs through the veins of this house. The bhand has finally got through to his sister. Even she shows her eyes to me.'

There was a moment of respite after that and it looked as if the storm had passed. Then in a sudden move Balwinder picked his slipper up from the ground and repeatedly beat his own face with it. Simran watched in horror as her father's saffron night *patka*

came off and his salt-and-pepper mane came undone
from the customary knot and a trickle of blood sprang
out from his forehead. Nirmal Kaur flung herself on
her husband and snatched the slipper from his hand.
Everyone was shocked to silence. Balwinder began
to weep.

'Oh, the ignominy of rearing children who grow
up to spit on you!' he wailed. Nirmal Kaur consoled
him and she turned to face her children. Her eyes
were blazing.

'Upstairs to my room, both of you! I want a word
with you both.'

She pushed them up the stairs, came in behind
them and closed the door to her room from the
inside. Like a madwoman she opened the drawers
desperately searching for something. Finally she
found what she was looking for. She took out a
kirpan with a blue sling. She put the sling around her
and she drew out the kirpan. She held it between her
eyes. Her eyes glittered with an intensity never seen
before by her children.

'So let me tell you who we really are, my children.
I am an illiterate woman from a village in Punjab but
I am also a survivor. I am a Jat Sikhni and the Kaur
in the middle is my badge of honour, my strength!
And your father was a proud farmer tilling his land,
earning a decent living, before Gill's men picked him

up and locked him up in a cell under false charges for helping the Khalistanis.'

Nirmal Kaur deliberately nicked her finger against the sharp end of the kirpan and a thread of blood began to run down the handle freely. Simran moved forward to help her mother but she hissed:

'Stay away, child, listen and let the blood run! It is a story conceived in blood. Those were the days when practically every young Jat Sikh was being picked up by Gill's killers in uniform. They spared no one. District by district, village by village, all the young men and sometimes even women were being lined up. The chaff and the grain were being pounded together with no distinction. The special police officer of Amritsar district took a particular dislike to your father. He arrested him on frivolous charges, then they beat him up as if he was a street dog. The police officer took pleasure in ripping his nails off. He would hit your father on his private parts with a leather belt with a steel buckle. Even today, after decades, your father passes blood in his stool. In less than a week he destroyed the proud man that your father once was.'

Nirmal Kaur licked the blood flowing from her finger.

'Your father was perhaps a day away from certain death. That night I paid a visit to the special police officer at the police station. I did things to secure his release that my Wahe Guruji will perhaps never forgive me for doing. The SPO told me that I could take him home for one night only. He had drawn plans for shooting your father like a mangy dog in the fields the next day. And that was the night that changed our lives.'

Nirmal Kaur stopped for a moment and then she cut the air around her with swipes of the kirpan as if the ghosts from the past were standing before her.

'I never learned to read and write in my life. But I learnt a lesson only life teaches you. You have to know where you come from. People wrongly think that the Sikhs are fighters. No—that is not true. We are survivors. We have always faced oppression in our history. It is our fate. But unlike so many others, we have not turned our backs to it. We have faced it head-on and we have survived.'

Nirmal Kaur wiped the blood off the kirpan and sheathed it. Her voice lowered.

'That very same night your father and I escaped into the fields from the police dragnet spread all around the village. We knew a travel agent in Delhi who put us on a train to Madras. From there we took a sailing boat all the way to Singapore. And then we applied for political asylum to the United Kingdom.'

Nirmal Kaur was suddenly completely bereft of all

energy. She sat down heavily on the bed. The kirpan slid away from her hand and her eyes looked vacantly into space.

'Your father is not an easy man to live with. I know that. I have known it for a long time. He has been afflicted with so many wounds that it is not possible for a lifetime to be enough to heal them. Try and reach out to him. Try and understand where he comes from. Can you do that, my son?'

Bobby dug his hands deep into his pockets and then he looked up squarely, meeting his mother's eye.

'I hear you, Mum. And I empathize with what both you and he have gone through. But I belong to a different generation. I was not even born when the Khalistan movement was raging in India. How can you expect me to understand it? I find it strange that every night my father rants and raves against India, but he makes a living by selling Bollywood DVDs in his rental shop. We live like Sikhs here but cannot go back to the country of our origin. I have plans, Mum. I want to leave this cold and foggy country and settle somewhere in warm climes, perhaps in our *kothi*, our bungalow, in Amritsar and open my own studio.

'I am sorry, Mum. You immigrated to the UK and this country has taught me to think independently of all biases. You did not. I find it immoral to live in a country and practise the values of another culture, of another time and place. There, I have said it to you.'

Simran looked at the crushed face of her mother. She knew this was not the end of the matter. A storm was building up in their lives.

3

The nights had become cooler and winter was knocking at the door. There was a chill in the air and Simran wanted to draw the smells, sounds and colours of summer one more time before the trees were stripped bare of life and the grass turned a muddy brown. It was a Friday evening and she got off a little early as most of the office had emptied out for the weekend. While the others headed for the nearby pubs for draught beer she decided to take the long walk home, cutting across rolling parks. The light outside was still good and her cap flapped on her ears as she tucked herself into her coat. She started to walk through pools of riotous green along the deep, sonorous shades of giant trees and through acres of parkland that rolled peacefully along the circuitous, not-so-well-known roads.

She looked beyond the railing of the parkland and as far as the eye could see, there were acres of autumn flowers, trembling in the gentle wind. The world, it seemed, had become a sea of many-coloured dahlias, white snakeroot, lilacs, lilies, begonias and sweet pea, all jostling against each other to preen their short-lived beauty.

Simran closed her eyes and looked up at the sky. This world pulled her away from her dark existence; it gave her legs which enabled her to climb above her miserable universe and look at a life that was neither scarred nor ugly. She continued to walk the shaded path, the first lines of her poem appearing in her head, like the trilling of a song by a gifted singer. At the bend she saw a lanky youth under a tree embracing a girl, kissing her with passion. She felt embarrassed and happy for the young girl. As she came up behind them, she froze. It was Bobby, kissing a girl she had never seen before!

Almost as if on cue, Bobby turned and he was laughing and smiling at the same time. She had never seen her brother look so much at peace, without a care in the world. 'Hey, fancy meeting you here!' Bobby said and held out his hand for her and her heartbeat quickened. The girl was wearing a black headscarf, a purple top and tight jeans.

Her ears were bursting as she heard Bobby say to the girl, 'What a day this is turning out to be! I am caught up in a time and place with my two favourite ladies! Amina, this is my sis, Simran . . .'

Simran clutched her brother's hand—fearful for him—the rolling vistas of green suddenly looking devoid of life and colour. Simran politely smiled and whispered to her brother, 'A word with you alone, please.' Brother and sister walked away to the next tree. Simran had a terrified look on her face.

'Who's the girl?'

'Amina. Amina Sharif. I just told you.'

'She's a Muslim.'

'So?'

'Are you crazy, Bobby?'

Bobby drew in a long breath and he looked above the trees. The world was completely still, expectant. The girl in the headscarf looked closely at brother and sister. Bobby held his sister's face with tenderness.

'One life—that is all,' he said, shaking his head determinedly. 'And I am not going to waste it on those two relics in the house. The world has so much to offer us. Who cares if she is Amina or Dolly Sandworth who was with me in junior school? All that matters is that I love that girl standing next to the tree. Do I care whether she ties a scarf and I a turban? Really, what's in a bloody name after all? *The Encyclopedia Britannica* on the history of the Sikhs and the Muslims and what they did to each other is just a book. We are living, flesh-and-blood creatures. I believe in us and not what they would like me to believe in.'

Simran's face became tear-stained. 'Veerji, Veerji, it's not as simple as you think. Please don't do this.'

Bobby held up his sister's face in the weakening light. 'Yes, it is. And I have made my choice. I should have told you earlier. On Sunday I will be leaving the house. Amina and I will be going backpacking across the continent. Once we come back we will take it from there. I will probably get a hair chop during that time. I am preparing you for that.'

And then suddenly, without an earthly reason, the light completely faded across the parkland and it became dark and cold.

*

The red-tiled house in the back lane was a beehive of activity that Friday evening. Balwinder had invited his closest friends for dinner—the Dhillons and the Majithas. The local hire for help, Anna of Romanian descent, was there in the kitchen along with Nirmal Kaur, rolling out the entrées, the main course and the dessert. In the drawing room, Balwinder stood deliberating in front of his liquor cabinet and then finally, reluctantly, he took out a couple of his finest malts and his usual tipple, a Black Label bottle. Close to seven, Anna finished her work and Nirmal Kaur packed her off with a tip; she went upstairs to check what Simran would be wearing for the evening.

Simran sat on the dressing table stool in her room, looking out of the window with a stunned expression on her face.

Her mother came up to her and stroked her forehead. 'Whatever is the matter? You are not dressed yet? The guests will be arriving shortly. Hope Bobby will come down for a short while. I don't want any unpleasantness today between father and son. Go talk to him.'

'He is far away,' Simran replied simply.

'Well, get him back then, girl, there are social etiquettes that have to be observed . . .'

Simran firmly held her mother's hand and looked her in the eye.

'You really have no idea, Mum, what's going on under this roof? Or do you pretend not to? I have never been able to figure that out. It's like you have put a cloak over this house so that we cannot see what is within. But everything is rotting inside, Mum. Bobby and I are suffocating under this cloak of hypocrisy and self-denial.'

Nirmal Kaur firmly held Simran's arm and shook her. 'What is behind your cruel words? You speak as if you have taken leave of your senses. I can feel something is terribly wrong. Tell me the truth or I will ask your father to step in.'

Simran shook with fear at the mention of her father. She knew her father would block Bobby with force, if need be, if he stumbled upon his plans. She was left with no choice but to take her mother in confidence. She shivered when she told her mother the truth.

'Veerji plans to run away this Sunday with a Muslim girl. He said he will also chop off his hair. Mum, please accept his wishes, please help him. The world has changed, Mum. Be happy for him. Let him go and let him discover a life for himself . . . Please, Mum . . . Please . . .'

Nirmal Kaur snatched her hand away with a cry. She looked accusingly at Simran as if she was a co-conspirator. 'Never! As long as we are alive, never!' Then she turned away and went downstairs, repeating to herself as if she was under a spell, 'Sache Padsha, forgive our trespasses, forgive our trespasses, Sache Padsha . . .'

She went up to Balwinder and stopped her incantation. She looked at him and debated for a moment whether she could keep the truth away from him, for everybody's sake. For a split second she did not see the man or what he had eventually turned out to be. She saw a man from a long time ago, with fear in his eyes, desperate for the well-being of his wife and himself. She then knew that they were bonded together for a lifetime in pain. If he had become a raging beast today, then once, long ago, he had also been a caring husband and a sensitive man. She knew then that she could not keep the truth from him. She wouldn't be able to, and the more she delayed it, the worse it would get for her.

Upstairs, Simran heard a sharp crack that originated from below.

She jumped and clamped her hand over her mouth. Her eyes had widened in terror. Almost at the same time, the doorbell rang. The guests had arrived.

Balwinder uncorked the Black Label bottle and drank lustily from it. His eyes were bloodshot while his hands trembled. Nirmal Kaur looked at the shattered glass vase, the pieces scattered all over. Balwinder had given his reply on hearing the news from her. She knew everything in the house had gone to pieces. But there would always be someone there to pick them up. She tugged at her husband's party kurta. Her eyes implored him. 'Please hold yourself. The guests are here. Maybe we can still retrieve the situation. We will talk to him in the morning. If word of this gets out, there will be a scandal in the community.'

The doorbell rang again. Nirmal Kaur went to the door, full of excuses for the shattered vase. The storm funnelling up in the house paused at the interruption but it continued to build up inside Balwinder's heart.

He drank his whisky, thought about what his son planned to do and at the same time talked local gurdwara politics with his friends. As the whisky diminished in the bottle, he could no longer separate the hate from the anger churning in his mind and the innocuous subject he was discussing with his friend. He poured a stiff malt drink for his friend and sneered. 'Drink up, Ranjit, because you are not going to like what I tell you next.'

Ranjit Singh, already plastered with drink, readily accepted the challenge. 'Bring it on, Baloo. All your life you have never won a game, a drinking bout, money at the card tables, in fact nothing ever, against me. So go ahead and try. What's bugging you?'

Balwinder now drank straight from the bottle. 'I always doubted your family pedigree but even for you, what you plan to do is the limit. I don't know of any cheap man other than you in the community who plans to introduce chairs at the Singh Sabha Gurdwara. Do you call yourself a true Sikh? People will be entering the gurdwara premises with shoes? Is that your idea of catching up with the times? Have you gone mad? I curse the day I supported your nomination for the gurdwara management board's elections.'

The women picked up the first signs of approaching trouble and they quickly began to arrange the table for dinner.

But Ranjit Singh was fuming by now. 'You supported my nomination because that was the only way you could put an end to your own irrelevance.'

Downstairs, as words sharpened and battle lines were drawn, Simran shut her ears and lay curled on the bed with her head between her legs. In the other room, Bobby also tried to keep the noise away in the only way he could. He began to loudly strum the guitar with the appropriate rendition of the Linkin Park song 'Numb'.

Suddenly the drawing room exploded with more shattering glass and screaming and a call to arms. Ranjit Singh and Balwinder Banga were at each other's throats. The turbans of the two men had come off and they began grappling ferociously, slapping and punching each other. A liquor bottle broke. Someone stepped on the broken glass. More screams. A trail of blood opened up on the floor and began spreading into a big brown blotch. Bobby raced down the stairs to separate the men raining blows on each other. Upstairs, Simran stood shivering in the dark, feeling the current of violence lashing all around in the room, in the house, in her life.

4

A short while later the guests departed, swearing never to have anything to do with the Bangas again. The house looked as if it had come in the path of a hurricane. There was blood and shattered glass all over the floor. Chairs were upturned and some priceless crockery, smashed to smithereens, lay strewn all over. Balwinder's nose was bleeding and a glass piece had pierced his foot. But he brushed aside Nirmal's attempts to apply antiseptic and plug the wound. Bobby had gone back to his room and bolted it from inside. Simran assisted her mother in cleaning up the mess. Balwinder took out another Black Label bottle and drank heavily from it. His eyes became glazed and hate overpowered him.

Later at one in the night when everyone had gone to sleep, Balwinder kicked away the emptied Black Label bottle and got up unsteadily on his feet. He looked around the room and for some reason he remembered the time when he had met a junior official in the home ministry to press forward his case for political asylum. The officer had told him that relations with India were excellent and they were not likely to do anything to damage relations between the two countries. It was a polite way of telling him that his demand could not be accepted.

But Balwinder did not give up. He had been given time for a short stay in the country and he used the time to galvanize the Sikh community in Britain and get in touch with human rights groups. His story was highlighted in the papers and pressure was applied on the government to give him asylum. He remembered the day when he was praying at the gurdwara and the news reached him that his wish had been granted. He had done that then, all alone, in the face of impossible odds, against all hope. Now the storm had reached his home. It was his sacred duty to bring his son back to the righteous path.

He bellowed to his wife to come down. She scrambled down, fearing the worst. She saw that he was completely inebriated yet strangely in control. She knew this was a supremely dangerous moment.

'Come up and sleep, ji. Whatever you have in mind we will handle it tomorrow. It is good to wake up fresh to new challenges,' she said.

'Don't patronize me, woman. Fetch the children.

I will settle it right here and now!' he retorted.

She had inured herself to his raging moods. But his utter calmness completely unnerved her. She went up and with great persuasion urged Bobby and Simran to come down and listen patiently to their father.

A short while later, Bobby and Simran stood before their father bearing the ordeal for their mother's sake. Bobby looked sullen, ready to pick a fight. Simran had walled up within. She could sense it in her bones that an irreversible process would be set off tonight. There would be no turning back for someone tonight.

Balwinder Banga bluntly came to the point. He appeared to be calm when he spoke.

'Bobby we have a word in our tradition for all those who do not comply and keep the faith. They are called *tankhaiyas*. They are literally outcasts from the community. No one talks to them, no one has any business dealings with them, and they are not allowed to set foot in any gurdwara in the land. They are apostates of divinity and short of being stoned, they are left to rot in their misery, loneliness and deprivation.'

Balwinder Singh paused, measuring his words, hoping that he was reaching across to his son with his message.

'Such a fate awaits you, Bobby, if you are seen having anything to do with that Muslim girl. From this night onwards not only will you have nothing to do with that girl ever again but once and for all you will stop all your bhand activities. Tomorrow morning I am going to throw away that guitar, your music system, drums, CDs and all the tools that have made you a diseased person,' he said in a measured, clipped tone and then became silent.

Time ticked past.

Bobby replied, 'Said your piece? Now listen to me. This tankhaiya nonsense is a creation of hopeless, frustrated old men like you who only get their kicks by squeezing the aspirations of their progeny and those people who want to escape your vicious system. As far as the Sikh religion is concerned, from what I know, it is one of the most humane, liberal religions in the world. We are not your slaves, Father! And you should know that I have rights in this country . . .'

Balwinder Singh laughed like a maniac. 'Really? Rights, you said? What are you, a helpless infant? Should Social Services send a counsellor to take care of you?'

Balwinder Singh leaned forward. His face was contorted with rage.

'Let me tell you how it plays out on the ground in the real world. After you come back from your holiday with that girl you won't have a roof to spend the night under. No one in the entire community will put you up for even a single night. No one will loan you a single farthing. No langar at the gurdwara for the likes of you, I promise. The doors to the house in Amritsar will be closed to you, forever. You think there are no poor people in this country. The next time you travel in the underground look around a bit more carefully. You cannot miss them. You will find them sprawled in the darkened corners of the U, looking at you with their yellowed teeth and hollowed cheeks, high on acid, singing in their cracked voices, holding their hats for pennies. I promise you, son, you will be joining their ranks very soon. And that would be a first. To find a sardar with that lot, with a grubby, unwashed face, not having eaten for days, chewing on a piece of bread thrown by someone, using dirt-filled nails. A bhand singing their songs in a Punjabi-accented voice. Go right ahead, son, and live that life, but, before you do that, leave everything I have given you, behind.'

Balwinder, with surprising tenacity for a man reeling from the effects of excessive alcohol in his system, sprang from his chair and began to tear the night T-shirt off Bobby. The outrageousness of what Balwinder did stunned everyone. He tore the T-shirt off his son, stripped him and then he opened the door leading into the house and pushed Bobby out into the freezing cold. He slammed the door shut. The fight went out of Bobby as he stood shivering in the night outside the porch. At twenty years of age he had developed sensitivity and a language to express his deepest emotions but his skin had not yet thickened to face life in the raw. Simran felt her limbs could no longer hold her and, struck with the turn of events, she simply sat down and stared into space. Nirmal uttered a low scream and flung herself at her husband's feet and begged him to give their son a second chance.

There was a maniacal light in Balwinder's eyes. He took Nirmal by the scruff of her neck and pulled her up. 'I want him to be humiliated. I want him to suffer. He has made me suffer for a long time. I have reached the end of my tether with him. He's out. He has to go.'

Nirmal was gasping from the stranglehold. But she kept on repeating, 'Let him in only for this night. Tomorrow morning, I will pack him off. Only this one night . . . let him in . . . I beg of you . . . if you have ever cared for me.' Tears were streaming down her face.

However, Balwinder Singh did not care to respond. His anger had been quenched and, feeling the release, he let go of Nirmal and walked upstairs to his room. Nirmal rushed out and embraced her son who stood outside the door shivering, with silent tears streaking down his face. She brought him in and Simran's heart sank when she saw her brother. It was a different young man who had walked in. The fight had gone out of him.

The next day Nirmal Kaur woke up unable to

decide if she was having a nightmare in which someone was screaming as if their lungs would burst. She sat up in her bed and heard Simran screaming in the next room as if the world had come to an end. In a split second she was transported back to her village in Punjab—the village where she had once fallen into a well. She sank under and it felt as if someone was pushing her down into the inky, opaque waters with great force. Her ears were bursting and she could no longer see the light as she went down. She began to take leaden-footed steps out of the room to the door at the end of the aisle. The door was wide open and she knew that the worst had happened. Simran was screaming and pounding her bloodied head on the door, uncontrollably, as if she had severed herself from all that was sane in the world. Balwinder Singh sat cross-legged outside the door, staring vacantly into space. By this time Nirmal Kaur had reached the bottom of the well—everything was shut out for her and there was complete darkness below. But she still had to make an attempt to see.

She stood outside the door and saw her handsome six-foot-tall son swinging like a slow-moving pendulum from a saffron scarf tied to a hook in the ceiling. His neck was broken, face discoloured and he looked at all of them with wide eyes, as he swayed in a rhythmic arc. He had savagely cut off his hair as would a madman, before he had climbed the chair leading to the scarf. The bloated face was masked by hair with split ends. Simran then, one last time, let out a never-ending scream that crashed against the interior of the house without any release. She then collapsed on the ground. Balwinder Singh got up and told his wife, 'I will bring him down and you will cover his face with a cloth. The neighbours must not see that he cut his hair before he took the final step.'

5

Thirteen days after her brother had taken his own life, Simran sat in the Singh Sabha Gurdwara, along with many other ladies from the community; the men sat on the left side, all of them dressed in white. She watched the head priest conduct the *antim ardas* (final prayer) held in her brother's memory. She looked at a large glass-encased photograph of her brother kept not far away from the Guru Granth Sahib. She thought in the end it all got reduced to a smiling face in a photograph. No one could even begin to understand the pain masked by the smiling face. She was sure no one wanted to. It was important to maintain the facade and extol the virtues of tradition and continuity.

The head priest completed the final prayers and then speaker after speaker rose to say words of praise for Balwinder. He was described as a shining example, a pillar of strength of the community. Balwinder's friend Ranjit Singh was perhaps the most effusive. He

43

shed tears as he spoke of his old friend.

'Balwinder and I go back a long way. He has always been a leader of men. He has made enormous sacrifices for the Khalsa *panth*. We live in troubled times. We live in times that test us, our faith and our way of life. Corruption comes in many forms—debased Bollywood films, a never-ending supply of drugs on our streets, tense relations with other ethnic communities here in Southall and not to forget the debaucheries associated with the Western lifestyle. All these and more corruptions are affecting our youngsters, making them stray from the righteous path. Bobby was troubled by some of these ills. We know that. But Balwinder persisted till the end to bring him back into the fold . . .'

Simran sat alone in the ladies section away from the rest with her back to the high marble walls. Her throat felt dry. She felt numbed by her loss, fearful at what was coming her way. She knew she was changing and she wondered whether the alien emotion of anger that spiked and ebbed in her was a good thing or not. She had never before been angry at anyone in her life. And then, from nowhere, that emotion had crept up on her, like a guerrilla stalks his prey. All she knew was that she felt cleansed when she was filled with rage.

The speakers were done eulogizing Balwinder. They wanted to use the solemn occasion to speak about their own brand of politics.

A speaker spoke up, 'When we talk of the ills affecting our community we also have to talk of the outside influences responsible for them. I talk here, brothers, of our government's act of giving a visa to that butcher general who carried out Operation Blue Star. He moves in this country with complete freedom. He comes and goes when he feels like it. We have to put a stop to this. I say that we must get together and petition our government to deny him a visa the next time. Tomorrow if someone has a go at him they will blame us. End the rot before it spreads. You know, when I see his face I think of the hundreds of innocents killed in that savage operation. Their faces come up before my eyes.'

Cries of 'shame! shame!' resounded in the large precincts of the gurdwara. Simran got up and walked out in the cold air. She breathed keenly, drawing in huge lungfuls of air. She felt refreshed from the oppression of words that had been assaulting her inside. She was all alone in the outer precincts of the gurdwara. She walked up to a row of taps, removed her dupatta and splashed cold water on her face. Her body shuddered as she felt a light touch on her face. She looked up into the smiling, sly eyes of a young man, her own age, with stylishly wavy hair, wearing a road-gang leather jacket, zippered up. She could see the beginnings of the contours of a tattoo inching up his neck, the lower part suggestively hidden below the collars of his jacket. She got a mild shock when she made out that it was a naked woman.

'Ash Kool,' the young man introduced himself. She raised a questioning brow. 'Well, Ashish Kohli,' he said, shrugging his shoulders. 'But who cares—after all, what's in a name? You have to be Simran. You probably won't remember me from back in school. I was the last guy, in the last row, in the last bench but I was the first to leave school midway because honestly there are more interesting things to do rather than study.'

He grinned, pleased with his own goofy humour. Simran, without saying a word, turned to go back to the gurdwara.

'Hey, hold on. So sorry for your brother. Had met him a couple of times at local gigs. He was a great guy. Had potential, you know.'

Simran stopped in her tracks, on the stairs leading inside the gurdwara. Ash Kool held out a white handkerchief as a peace offering.

'Uh, you could use this to wipe the water off your face. Shall I do it for you?'

He took a step towards her and she crept back quickly, a little off-balance, and she stared at him fiercely. She looked at him, meeting his gaze, and then she wiped her face with the end of her chunni. As she stared at him, she felt an odd sensation of excitement and fear. She knew immediately that he was a waster, a kind of a sophisticated derelict. But she was surprised and struck at her continuing engagement with him. He had tried to provoke her and she knew he had succeeded. She had been drawn towards him as one would stand near a deep, large well in excitement and fear, measuring how deep the well went. Maybe he was all real bad but at the very least he was definitely the guy on the motorcycle speeding on a flower-strewn road to nowhere, without a care in the world, with a girl holding him from behind.

Simran shook herself from her reverie, feeling nauseated that she saw herself as the girl at the back of the motorcycle on the occasion of her brother's antim ardas.

She could see that the gathering inside the gurdwara had broken up and people were slowly streaming out. She saw her father standing in a corner, accepting condolences one last time from all those walking out. Her mother came out of the gurdwara, her face pinched with grief. Then she suddenly looked in her direction, intently. And something inside Simran snapped.

She turned to look at Ash Kool and listened to his pitch.

'There is a local gig we do on the first floor of the Balle Balle pub. It's called "Banging with Bhangra".

It's loads of fun, dance and music. We meet up next Friday at seven. Why don't you come? I will keep a ticket for you. I think you could use a break.' He smiled expectantly.

She could see her mother looking at her worriedly now. She turned and rearranged the chunni around her face. Then she smiled slightly at Ash Kool. She climbed up the stairs and walked across the precinct to meet her mother. She felt terrified at the step she was about to take. But she had made up her mind. She would neither listen to her gut nor think it over. All she wanted to do was climb up to the highest point of a mountain and plunge into the abyss below, floating freely, letting the wind guide her path. Something within her was urging her to take this flight.

She faced her mother who took her aside. Nirmal Kaur asked her, 'Who was that *mona*, that non-Sikh, you were talking to? We have already lost Bobby to this ill wind. Be careful, very careful.'

Simran did not respond to her mother or give her comfort. She looked blankly through her. She stared into the distance. She could never have imagined that a day of such mourning would end on a happy note for her. She had broken away, like a speeding cyclist at a bend, from the rest. She walked away to a volunteer offering amrit, took a cup and drank from it as if she had been thirsty for a long time.

6

'You are not going out at this hour!'

'Yes, I am,' said Simran with finality, facing up to her mother. She had an odd feeling that her mother had begun to draw from a reservoir of anger that had always been the upkeep of her father. But she was more surprised at her own continuing defiance of her mother. It was almost as if she had found a new voice after Bobby's antim ardas.

Her voice had an edge to it. 'There is nothing wrong in going for an office party with colleagues. I will not be chained and confined to this house. I earn for myself and frankly I am fed up sitting here in the evenings, listening to the same old drivel. I need a break.'

And with that, Simran lied to her mother for the first time in her life and broke away from the invisible cordon that her parents had set up around her.

Nirmal Kaur looked exasperatedly at her. She felt as if, almost overnight, her girl had become a stranger to her. She tried her final weapon. 'Shame on you, Simran! You seek merriment outside within days of your brother's death? Is this how you honour your brother you claimed to love so deeply?'

Simran looked at her own self in the mirror one last time and wiped off some of the excess lipstick with a tissue. She removed the chunni from over her head and wrapped it around her neck like a scarf.

'Veerji is dead and gone, Mum,' she replied, looking in the mirror with blank eyes. 'And don't get me started on how we all got there. All I know is that he would be so happy to see me do what I am doing now. He lived his life like a free bird and you tried to chain him. But he broke the yoke. I don't think you knew your son at all. And you know even less of me. You can't make the same mistake twice. I won't allow you to do it.'

The voice died in Nirmal's throat as she watched Simran pick up her bag and go down the flight of stairs.

As she walked out of the red-tiled house, Simran trembled at her own insouciance in front of her mother. She was being propelled by an influence she knew not the origins of. All she knew was that she did not want to look behind her. She quickly covered the distance to the Balle Balle pub. Night had fallen. The lights were blazing on the first floor and the diffused sounds of Punjabi RnB music filtered downstairs. A steady stream of youngsters her age made their way up a black-painted banister to the first floor. She looked at them and her newly minted confidence melted away. She stood apart from them, dressed in a Punjabi suit. The difference between them and her was not merely one of Western attire. She was like a fish in a pond that had drifted to the high seas. And there was no anchor out there in the vastness to guide her.

She lost her nerve and turned to go back. Ash Kool appeared in front of her. He took her hand and whispered seductively, 'I knew you would come. Don't let all this intimidate you. You look stunning tonight. Come up with me.'

He led her up the staircase, nodded to the bouncer standing outside and she stepped into the new world. She felt flushes of fear and excitement course within her as she walked in and took a first look at the new world. It was a world created out of a smorgasbord of pounding music, flickering strobe lights and rappers on stage belting out an infectious mix of Punjabi–English underground foot-stomping lyrics. Her mouth was dry with fear now as she saw familiar faces from the neighbourhood, both boys and girls, looking at her with amusement, and some with curiosity even. She tightened her grip on Ash Kool's hand and fiercely whispered, 'Please take me away from here. This was a mistake. I can't bear the way they look at me.'

Ash Kool smiled, parted her hair and whispered close to her ear, 'If you can't beat them, then join them. I know you have it in you. I will get you something to calm your nerves.'

He left her and for a terrifying few seconds she stood in the middle of the dance floor, all alone, unsure where to look.

Soon Ash Kool was back with a drink.

'What is it?' she asked, the fear inside her pounding away into a splitting headache.

'Coke and rum. And don't resist it. It will calm you down. Drink it up like a good girl.'

'But I don't drink.'

Ash Kool brought the drink up to her lips and coaxed them open. 'You never used to apply lipstick earlier, correct? And one day you did. It's the same experience.' He was laughing. She relaxed a bit. There had to be a first time for everything.

She swallowed the drink and he led her away from centre stage to a seat at the back, in the shadows.

'Okay, maybe it is too much for you, this first time. I understand. Just soak in the atmosphere from the back. No one will disturb you. I will join you in a while.'

The alcohol soothed her somewhat and she was grateful to be plucked away from the limelight. She settled more comfortably in her chair and the ever-present fear inside her began to subside. After a while she began to enjoy what was going on around her. There was a lot of energy, music, fun and laughter in the room. And slowly she began to notice the deviance lurking in the corners—the eyes glazed over after a hit, the exchange of monies and the black and white streetwalkers who in ones and twos had crashed the party. She surprised herself by reaching for a couple of more drinks and she felt good and connected with what was going on. Ash Kool never really disappeared completely; he would make an appearance every now and then to check on her. She was quite sure he inhabited the netherworld between people like her and the other world of drug addicts, pushers and prostitutes. But she did not care. She was drifting in the chasm, floating in it with perfect balance and for once in her life she wanted an outside force to take her along paths she had never visited before. The band on the stage raised the music to a crescendo and then killed it for an announcement by the party host. Tally (Talwinder) Singh called everyone to the dance floor.

'Oh! Yo! All you lovely Punjabi kudis and Jats! This is the night we get to see your moves! Yo! Yo! Kick ass with Tally Singh and his beats! Let's see you lovely Punjabi ladies perform the *giddha*—yo! Straight from the Punjab heartland! The real desi, raw stuff! Come on, my beauties, to the floor! Special prize for the *soni* with the moves! Yo!'

And with that, giggling, laughing, keyed-up women came up centre stage one by one and showed their moves. The room exploded in a cacophony of Mexican-style cheering, clapping and whistling. Simran looked at girls her age perform a UK-style truncated giddha, in the wrong attire with the wrong moves. None of them were able to match the explosive rhythms of giddha beats. Almost all were unwilling to drop their city pretence and fully embrace the rustic and raw passions of that folk dance form. Simran suddenly wanted to show them what she was made of, show it to the sons and daughters of those who conspired with her father to put down Bobby. And if Bobby was watching from above then he would be delighted to see his sister take them head-on.

'Veerji, for you, wherever you are!' she said to herself and got up.

Tally Singh was looking with despair to see if anyone else in the room could liven up the stage after the string of flaccid performances. He saw a hand go up in a corner of the room. Ash Kool saw it too and, completely surprised, he whispered in Tally's ear. There was complete silence, broken by some titters, as Simran moved up to the centre stage. The others moved back. Tally introduced her, 'And now we have the final wild card of this evening. It's none other than the authentic girl from Punjab in a Punjabi suit and all—ladies and gentlemen, give way for Simran Banga! A round of applause for her!'

No one chirped, let alone clap, and then someone let out a catcall from the back: 'Jhalli takes centre stage!'

Everyone laughed at that and then the chants of 'Jhalli! Jhalli!' slowly built up to a deafening roar. But the ragging held no meaning for Simran and she was oblivious to all the catcalls and insults. She tied her chunni around her waist and stepped into the ring. Her eyes were trained on the drummer who sat on the stage with his *dholki*, testing the taut drum skin. The man on the synthesizer flicked through his notebook and chose a *boli* for the accompanying dance. Their eyes met. The musicians suddenly felt that this girl would match them word for word, beat for beat.

Tally Singh alone began to clap rhythmically and Simran like a gazelle responded to the beat and her feet began to move in sync with the lyrics. Her body began to gyrate and the dholki player stepped up on his drum with a smile. The man on the synthesizer belted out the first of the bolis and Simran, clapping in unison with Tally and Ash Kool, spun around in a circle. She picked up her pace as she moved round and round in circles to the frenetic beat and then she surprised everyone by arching her back completely, head almost touching the ankles, eyes glued to the drummer and all the while moving in circles at that speed. A flurry of loud cheering and clapping broke out and even her critics reluctantly joined in. The dholki player now energetically stepped up the beat again and Simran grabbed Ash Kool, who was standing just outside the circle, and brought him in. They both held hands and then Simran spun Ash Kool in circles by the length of his arm. She picked up dizzying speed and the room became a blur for Ash Kool. A roar went up in the crowd and they joined in with whistles and loud cheering. And then, without a warning, Simran let go of Ash Kool and he went spinning to the side, crashing into the tables. But Simran did not miss a beat and her step and she completed her rhythmic dance to the crescendo of the boli and a clash of cymbals.

The room exploded with applause and Ash Kool, bruised from the crash, got up and smiled and joined in with the rest. Simran was bathed in sweat and Tally Singh gushed eloquently about her. He handed her a glass figurine and her prize—a paid voucher for two people. It guaranteed free shows and rides at the London Eye.

'You want to say something?' asked Tally Singh, giving her the mike. Simran thought for a moment and then she shyly held up the figurine and said, 'This is for all the jhallis of the world and my brother, Bobby.

He would have wanted this for me.'

There was more cheering and whistling and Simran ran out of the room and Ash Kool followed her. He caught up with her at the bottom of the staircase.

'Hey, hang on! The fun's just beginning. It's not even ten.'

'No, Ash, I have extended my curfew. I had a point to prove tonight. It's time I got back.'

Ash Kool made a face and then laughed sportingly. 'Well, the winner takes all. Can I at least walk you to your house?'

Both skipped the road leading from the main car park and took a less familiar pathway that cut through open fields and a quiet neighbourhood. It had grown to be cold and Simran shivered, her light cashmere sweater offering her little protection. Ash Kool took off his jacket and wrapped it around her shoulders.

'Thanks,' she said, acknowledging the gesture. He rubbed his hands and said, 'You were a revelation tonight. The way you moved. Your moves were, well, stirring . . .'

'Say the word,' she laughed.

'Okay, your moves were hot, you were sexy. I could not take my eyes off you.'

He grasped her hand and she could feel the heat radiating from him. A tree with its branches bent with age came up and he deftly guided her under it, away from the road. He pushed her hands back and kissed her, his tongue exploring the corners of her mouth. He pressed himself against her and she could feel his erection. She smelt a nauseous mix of tobacco, cheap booze and stale breath. She struggled against him as his hand went up her kurta and below her bra and grabbed her breast. His fingers played with her nipple and circled the tip of her areola. An image opened up in her consciousness. She saw herself caressing her areola in the bathroom mirror in the bluish light. She felt an odd mix of fear, revulsion and animal excitement. But this was way too soon for her. She pushed Ash Kool away and let out a low scream.

'Stop it! You disgust me! Don't ever touch me again—not like this!'

He stood panting like an animal that had been denied what it was looking for and he held out his right hand in a peace offering. 'Okay, I crossed the line,' he responded. 'But the truth is I was charged. I could not take my eyes off you throughout the evening. I should probably have jerked off in the men's loo but I held back . . . for this . . .'

She looked up, her face stained with tears. 'You are disgusting. You had to spoil this day for me.'

He came up to her and held her. She did not resist this time. He whispered in her ears, 'That's why you like me. Because of who I am. Admit that. I am an experience like no other in your life. Hanh?' She looked into his eyes. 'It's okay. I understand,' he said in a calming tone. She pushed him and walked away. It was time to go home.

She felt confused and offended and somewhat desperate after what he had just told her. She questioned herself as she walked back home. Any kind of answer to the jumble of thoughts raging inside her eluded her. It had been a night of joy and victory and then confusion. She came up to the doorstep of the red-tiled house and she felt the old fear crawl back in. She pressed the doorbell.

Her father was slumped in a corner, drunk out of his mind. She looked at her mother standing in the passageway. She had never seen that look in her mother's eyes before. Her mother spoke to her quietly, with great viciousness. 'I blame you for Bobby's death. You had influence over him. If you had wanted you could have prevented him from straying from the path. But you encouraged him. You led him to his death. You did that because you are essentially corrupt and debauched from within. I hate you for taking my son away from me.'

She looked at her mother, stunned, unable to grasp the great change cleaving through the house, tearing apart father from son, mother from daughter, wife from husband. She wondered whether Bobby's death had ripped open the cloak that had hid so well how all of them had walked along the edge of insanity for such a long time.

She walked up to her bedroom without answering her mother. Tonight she had no answers to what was happening around her but tomorrow was another day.

7

Simran celebrated her win at the Balle Balle club in the company of Ash Kool, on a Sunday morning at the London Eye. The city, the world and even her own doubts looked transformed from the top of the giant Ferris wheel. She connected to the child within her, and the freedom of being up on top of the world, as it were, unlocked a deep desire within her. And it was simply to have fun, eat ice cream and not look back at her retinue of fear and doubt that always accompanied her.

After the ride they both raced to the horror show museum nearby. For the first time in her life she felt she could laugh away the demons, the ghosts and the apparitions of her own making. Both cracked up at the games, at the monsters and their acts on display in the museum. Simran walked out feeling refreshed. She felt she had let go of the demon constantly riding on her back in the dungeons of the museum. She

licked an ice cream cone and both walked across the
Golden Jubilee Bridge to cross the Thames River. She
stopped somewhere in the middle and looked out at
the span of the river curling along the embankments
dotted with tourists.

'Can I steal a kiss from you?' asked Ash Kool. She
laughed and shook her head.

'Is that what you think about all the time?' Her
eyes radiated with happiness. 'All in good time, Ash.
But thanks for today.'

'For what?' he asked, genuinely puzzled. She did
not reply and she ran across the bridge and he raced
after her. She stumbled near the grassy embankment
across the bridge and took a tumble. She cut her foot
on the asphalt and sprayed the green grass with her
blood. He knelt down and took her bleeding toe in his
mouth and sucked on the flow. Her face was flushed
and she looked animated. She watched him as he
fussed over her wound. He stopped the blood flow
and then tore off a strip of his shirt and bandaged her
wound. He kissed her feet and she did not protest. He
helped her up and put his arm around her and helped
her walk the distance to the Underground.

'Do you still intend to stick to your curfew?' he
asked.

'Yes,' she replied enigmatically. 'Walk me to the
station. It's been a perfect day. Let it end that way.'

They went down the steps to the Underground at Embankment Station and joined the hordes of tourists passing through the turnstiles to catch direct or connecting trains. He stood with her on the platform from where a train would take her to Paddington, where she would change trains bound for Southall.

'You won't be coming home?' she asked.

'No, you carry on,' he replied, looking into the darkened cavern from where the train would emerge. 'I have to meet someone workwise. Sometimes I do put in some work, you know.'

She smiled at that and he grinned in that innocent, rascally way that she knew was his signature calling card. They heard the pneumatic rush of the train coming in from the cavern, the passengers edged closer to the tracks and the train rushed past, slowing to a stop farther away, near the neon signage. The automatic doors opened and she flung herself on him and kissed him passionately. Then she withdrew and looked at him intensely. He was at a loss for words, looking at her with wonder.

'Thanks for helping me get in touch with me,' she said as a parting greeting and then she disappeared into the crowds moving into the carriages. He stood on the platform as the train shot past him and in the last carriage of the train he caught a glimpse of her looking above the bobbing heads at him. He was struck with the look in her eyes. The platform had emptied out but he continued to stand there, looking into the cavern on the other side of the tracks into which the train had disappeared. Finally, he forced himself to look at his watch. He felt as if a draft of cold air had swept in from nowhere and a perfect late-autumn day had come to an end. He walked back heavily to another platform in the station from where he would catch a connection to Marylebone. The man had said he would be waiting for him there.

He sat in the Tube and took a couple of interconnecting trains to confuse or shake off anyone who might be following him. A little later than the appointed hour he reached Marylebone Station and hurried to the designated platform. Sunday tourists milled about the narrow stretch and he looked around for his contact. He saw him sitting alone, on the last bench on the platform, wearing a working man's cap that was popular in parts of Eastern Europe. A train entered through the tunnel and there was a scramble for seats in the carriages. Very soon the jostling crowd departed and it was all quiet on the platform. He sat next to the man wearing the hat.

'You are late,' said the man in a thick East European accent.

'Sorry,' mumbled Ash Kool, 'I got held up at a station.'

The man turned to look fully at Ash Kool. The Punjabi boy's blood would run cold whenever he would look closely at the Albanian. Kreshnik Hoxha had piercing green eyes but he looked unreal because he had practically no eyebrows. He had thin lips that never really opened and he spoke slowly and with great emphasis. The Albanian smiled mirthlessly. Ash Kool trembled inwardly.

'You look worried, Ake,' said Hoxha. 'Tomorrow is the big day. You should be excited.'

'It's Ash . . .'

'No, if I say Ake then it is Ake.'

Ash Kool kept quiet. Kreshnik put his arm around Ash Kool. 'You don't answer me. We have a date tomorrow.' Kreshnik let out a low laugh at his own joke. Then his eyes were slits. 'It's all arranged. You get me worried by your shut mouth. Shall I call it off?'

Kreshnik began to stroke the back of Ash Kool's neck. A trickle of tourists began to converge on the platform, waiting for the next train. Ash Kool had trouble breathing but he spoke up.

'No, we will go through with it.'

'Good boy,' said Kreshnik, stepping up the pressure on the neck. Kreshnik began to stroke more vigorously and suddenly Ash Kool could no longer breathe. The Albanian applied just the right amount of pressure not to strangulate Ash, but sufficient to completely immobilize him and make him see stars. The platform had filled up by now and there were people standing all around the bench and Ash Kool was in excruciating pain, choking, unable to speak and completely at the mercy of the man sitting next to him. To a casual observer it would appear that the man in a strange cap and the Indian kid were gay lovers. Kreshnik certainly looked the part. He parted Ash Kool's wavy hair falling on to the ears and he slowly began to whisper, 'In Albania, I dispose of a human being in many ways. But we are in London—the most sophisticated city in the world. So we do it, what do the English say, elegantly. I will throw you on the tracks and watch the train run over you.'

Kreshnik said that and he licked Ash Kool's ear. Then he quietly laughed in his ear.

'But why would I do that? You are my friend now. You are my gateway to Southall. I do that to vermin who double-cross me. But you a good, decent Indian boy. Correct, no?'

Kreshnik released the pressure and Ash Kool drew in precious air denied to him and coughed violently. The train came into the station and the carriages disgorged the commuters while many others got in. The train left and the platform emptied once again. Ash Kool had tears in his eyes and he was shivering as he looked up at the Albanian who had stood up and was smiling once again, mirthlessly.

'I wait for your call tomorrow then, Indian friend,' said Kreshnik. 'Bye-bye.' He tipped his funny cap and walked out of the station.

8

Ash Kool looked at the butchery named Prime Chops tucked away in a leafy part of the street and, for the hundredth time since morning, he rehearsed in his mind what he would have to say to the man inside the shop. The familiar chalkboard was kept outside the shop as usual. A child's scrawl or perhaps a grown-up man's lack of education was on display on the board. All the names of the articles kept in the shop, be it pork or mutton ribs, or *halal* and *jhatka* meat, were misspelt. Jhatka was misspelt as 'Jackass' and Ash Kool could only wonder whether Andrew Hall in his advancing years was developing a morbid sense of humour.

That was highly unlikely. The six-foot ex–professional pugilist and Jamaican emigrant ran a tight ship with an iron hand and a no-nonsense business acumen. He dealt with meat ribs during the day and funnelled cocaine pouches and crystal meth, through his foot soldiers, in the night. Ash Kool stood outside the shop and for a moment the thought flashed through his mind: Who was worse of the two—Hoxha or Hall? He wearily trudged into the shop. He would find out soon.

Sam, the Nazi with a shaven head, was at the counter, pretending to be engrossed in sales figures. Klute from the Cayman Islands, without the money of course, was stacking up prime ribs in the shelves. From the rear door, Tattohead, hailing from an earlier generation of skinheads, made an appearance. He smiled, showing his yellowed teeth to Ash Kool. There were more tattoos on his body than there was pale white skin. They all pretended to be hard at work. Ash Kool looked at the deadliest small army of vicious thugs and crack dealers collected under one roof. He knew what he would be attempting to do would not be easy. But then he had run out of options.

'Where's the man?' His voice croaked.

'Inside, Indie,' replied Tattohead. 'He's counting the carcasses.'

Ash Kool felt a stab of fear and went in through the rear door to the narrow passageway that led to the refrigeration at the back. It was gloomy inside and he could see the door to the refrigerated section partly open. He heard the hum of the assembly line as the carcasses moved in a kind of elliptical path. Hall stood within the ellipse with a sheet and a pencil stub in his hand. Ash Kool caught glimpses of the bull head and powerful shoulders of the one-time emigrant from Jamaica. The man was in a good mood.

'AKool! My man! Good to see you in these parts. Surprise visit this, eh? Thought we were catchin' up in the night at the shelter?'

Ash Kool steeled himself but the words tumbled out, unprepared.

'Don't step into the shelter tonight, Hall. You and the boys will be walking into an ambush.'

Hall switched off the assembly line. The freezing storehouse became deathly quiet. Hall stood behind the carcasses.

'Says who?' he asked.

'Says I,' responded Ash Kool, his voice quavering in pitch. 'A man called Kreshnik and his boys will be looking for you.'

'I heard of that man, ya boy. Who tipped him off about our meet-up at the shelter every night?'

The seconds ticked past as there was complete silence. Ash Kool finally croaked, 'I did. I sold you out.'

The left hook came so fast for him that Ash Kool had no time to process that Hall still had some of his earlier quicksilver moves from the boxing ring. Ash Kool felt for less than a second as if his brain had imploded from within. Then he passed out.

He woke up to the hum of the assembly line and a splitting headache. As his vision cleared he saw the floor sweep past him, close to his eyes. Complete panic gripped him. It took him a moment to realize that he was moving on the assembly line upside down along with the carcasses, stripped completely naked. His feet were bound to steel hooks on the line. He managed to lift his head up and he caught a glimpse of Hall sitting in a chair in a corner with a lead pipe in his lap, surrounded by the boys. They all looked at him with curiosity, as if he was a worm hanging down.

On a gesture from Hall, Sam stopped the assembly line. Hall slowly walked up to Ash Kool. The boy from Southall braced himself. The lead pipe came down on his buttocks and he screamed in pure agony. Hall continued to beat him till his backside looked like one of the carcasses.

Done with that, Hall looked at the others and said, 'Say hello to my little Indie friend.'

The gang laughed and on Hall's bidding, Ash Kool was brought down and made to sit on the stool. He cried in pain as he could hardly sit on the stool with his lacerated buttocks. Hall allowed him to recover and then took over the questioning.

'Now that the hellos are over, AKool, the obvious question for you is why is a rat like you still not dead meat on the assembly line? You care to answer that?'

Ash Kool spat out some blood; he brought up his legs on the stool and covered his face, between his legs, with both hands. He mumbled from somewhere between his refuge.

'I might still be useful to you, Hall. I know the community here. I am your point man to get in touch with them.'

Hall looked at the others and they all burst out laughing.

'Indie boy is smart. Yeah, you got that bang in the centre, Indie. You could have your uses. Let me be the judge of that. So if you want to live, then tell me, my man, what's Kreshnik's play? And don't hold back . . . You know I am good at finding out that sort of thing.'

Ash Kool tentatively raised his head and looked at Hall. The he began to gush.

'Kreshnik is the future, Hall. He and his fellow Albanians and Romanians are taking over the city's streets. His stuff is the best and the most genuine in the market. He gets it directly from Afghanistan. It comes via Tajikistan onwards to the Baltic republics and then it is shipped to markets in western Europe. Only last week a boat carrying over 100 Ks landed in Marinas port in Scotland. They have customs officials on their payroll in a number of places. He's offering deals, bumping off the old-timers and bringing in his troops from Eastern Europe. After the free trade agreement between this country and the eastern states, influx to London is not an issue. He and his men are ruthless in ways one cannot even imagine.'

'How much did he buy you out for?'

'No, he does not deal with fixed amounts. He was prepared to give me twice the percentage you give me for every deal. He was ready to upgrade me to a level higher than a foot soldier.'

'How many Ks are we talking about?'

'About 30 Ks are being transported by road tonight. He's zeroed in on Southall as low-hanging fruit. There's been reluctant drug abuse here. But if he comes in, he will flood the streets.'

Hall sniggered at the suggestion. 'We will see about that. The West Indian brotherhood is not dead as yet. And if we can combine with the Pakis then we will see who rules the city. Where's the drop?'

Ash Kool began to breathe a little easy. 'The drop is at the shelter,' he said. 'No one in town goes to that abandoned World War II bomb shelter. His plan was to eliminate all of you tonight at our daily meeting. After he bumps everyone off, he starts distribution from there. The sun would have risen on a new boss, tomorrow.'

Hall snickered. 'Sweet. If I had to do it I would not have done it differently. So, now the million-fucking-dollar question, Indie. Why in blazes would you have a change of heart? Why not pitch your tent in the light of the rising sun?'

Ash Kool began to tremble. He withdrew even more into his rathole. His pitch began to flow.

'Hall, I made a terrible mistake. Yeah, I was greedy because I am always short of cash. I got bills to pay, man. I have to look after my mum who needs a nurse to get through the day. I was desperate, man! Kreshnik is on a recruitment drive. In my greed I did not bother to check out the man. Yesterday when I met him I was convinced the man should be confined to a nuthouse. He's nobody's friend. He would have put me on the tracks as soon as his load sold out in these parts. He's short-term, man, not like you. He's only loyal to his other East European buddies. You are not like him. Look at it this way, man, you got a rainbow coalition going . . . black, white, brown, yellow . . . Serious, man, I made a huge fucking mistake . . .'

'Shut up, fucker!' snarled the West Indian as he got up. Everyone stepped back. They all knew this was a moment of decision. Ash Kool's life hung by a thread. Hall grabbed Ash Kool's hair by the roots.

'No second chances in the business, they say. So why should I spare your life, fucker?'

Ash Kool blurted out, 'Because I will be your slave, man, for the rest of my life. I will deliver my community to you. Street by street, house by house, boys and girls, each and every one. You will not regret this buy-in.'

The eyes of the two men met. Hall looked deep into the eyes of his street soldier. He gave his verdict.

'Okay, you can borrow some airtime from me, my man. But I will fine you for crossing the line. There will be no appeal on that. You have six hours to pay me 10,000 quid as fine. Since you crossed me, I will claim a body part from you. I give you a choice. It's your pecker or your toe. What's it gonna be, Indie boy?'

Ash Kool began to wail that he could not meet both the conditions. On Hall's nod the others grabbed him and he thrashed wildly in their grip. Hall brought out a meat cleaver. Ash Kool screamed pitifully, 'The toe, the toe, and not my pecker, for fuck's sake . . . Ahhhh!'

A spray of blood shot up on Hall's butcher's apron. Ash Kool passed out in pain as he saw his toe wriggling in a corner. When he revived he found that his foot was bandaged, and Hall was waiting for him. He was all businesslike.

'Indie, you will keep the eight o'clock deadline with Kreshnik. You will meet them as scheduled. After that you hand me the quid and you go home. If you put on another act or give another excuse, I will shoot you with your other friends.'

Inside the shop he heard Hall's army fit their TEC-9 submachine guns with silencers. The light was fading fast and soon the trap would be sprung. This was the life he had chosen. Today he had to pay a price for it.

9

Kreshnik Hoxha was a child of the mean streets in the cities of Tirana and Lazarat in Albania. His earliest recollections were from a time when as a child he would stand in the freezing cold in the dole queue begging for free bread. He quickly graduated to stealing the same bread from the United Nations trucks trundling into Tirana to feed a starving citizenry. He would trade the stolen bread for cigarettes and whisky because he learnt early on that the Albanian currency was worthless and he could only barter his way out of trouble. He soon established a reputation as a sharp, if not ruthless, smuggler and soon the marijuana capital of Europe—Lazarat—beckoned him to try his luck there. He effortlessly moved into the drug trade. He opened new drug routes to western Europe, especially England.

When the European Union cracked down on Lazarat he started sourcing the weed and other hallucinogens from Afghanistan. He would look back with pride and some contempt at how quickly he had taken over the trade in England with a combination of shrewd positioning and utter ruthlessness. He made his first mistake when he thought that Southall would be a cakewalk, especially after he had forced Ash Kool to do his bidding. In his underestimation, Hoxha forgot the first basic rule of his trade: There is always someone out there more desperate and determined to snatch the piece of bread that you want.

Kreshnik Hoxha kept the eight o'clock appointment with Ash Kool. It was the last appointment in his life. Andrew Hall proved to everyone, which is if anyone had any doubt, that he was the drug overlord of Southall and Ealing Borough. Kreshnik and his men walked into a trap in the shelter and Hall and his men opened fire from all sides with their silenced machine guns. No one for miles around heard anything, though a late-evening jogger did say that she thought she saw spits of orange fire from a distance. Six men lay riddled with bullet holes and the floor became shiny with newly spilt blood and gore. The bodies were dragged to an inside room and stacked one on top of the other. The van carrying the 30 K load was taken apart completely and the loot was transferred to hundreds of plastic pouches, all bound for a new deserted warehouse outside the borough limits. The time had come to literally bomb the bomb shelter but one more gap had to be plugged before that.

Hall called Ash Kool and told him, 'A good ending to this business. Now it is time for my payback. Where's the quid?'

Ash Kool tried to reason with Hall. 'I delivered for you, Hall, did I not? You crushed Kreshnik and you will walk out of this blasted place a few mil richer because of the stash. What's a few more hundred quid to you?'

'It's the principle, Indie boy. I won't ask again. I will line you up and shoot you and throw your body with the others in the room. Then I will firebomb this place.'

Ash Kool finally got the answer he was looking for. There was no difference between Hoxha and this monster that stood before him. He had been a fool to switch allegiance again.

He replied calmly, 'Okay, I understand you. I will get it from the house. You trust me to go back, don't you?'

Hall gave his assent. 'Sure, Indie boy. But remember, you can neither run nor can you hide from me. I will be waiting here.'

It was freezing outside as Ash Kool emerged from the bomb shelter. He covered his head with the hood of his leather jacket and broke into a run, unmindful of the dismembered toe, determined to get away as far as possible from the hideout. He picked up speed and for a moment he felt he could run away from his life and disappear to a time and place where no one would bother him. The adrenaline coursed within him and the night air was full of possibilities. He was soon out of breath and, unable to decelerate, he tumbled and rolled over, next to a fencing girdling a large field. The stump of his severed toe bled from the exertion. He made no attempt to get up and vacuously stared at the night sky. Then his whole body shook with sobs. He looked around helplessly but there was no one around for miles. He was all alone and he understood what it meant to feel abandoned.

'My entire life is a lie,' he talked to himself. He looked around, desperately hoping that someone would come for him and pull him out of this situation. But he could have been the last human being left on the planet. He had no choice but to fend for himself. The cold had begun to seep through him and it cleared his mind. His tears dried up and he began to talk to himself again.

'I can't look for truth at this time of the night. We are all the sum of our lies—some big and the others small. What I need is another lie to help me pull through this night.'

He smacked his hands and the solution presented itself before him. It came to him as the cold but inescapable truth. He thought about it for a moment and then got up and made the call.

Simran's fingertips were poised over the keys of her laptop and the entire opening stanza of her poem was within her reach. It would be a poem about beauty—but a kind of beauty scarred by conflict. Everything in life was an interpretation she understood. She never really got down to filling up the screen with her thoughts because her cell phone began to hum urgently. She responded to the incoming call.

'It's late, Ash, what could be the matter at this time?'

Ash Kool was wheezing at the other end of the connection as if he was unable to breathe. 'Simi, I am in a spot of real bother. I need your help. There's a very obstinate man who is making things really difficult for me. Could you meet me outside the house? I need you to help me talk to him. He's not listening to me.'

'What have you done? Why is this man chasing you?'

'Some stuff. It doesn't matter now. Just come!' he pleaded urgently

'Are you crazy, Ash? You know my home situation. It's time you gave up your dissolute lifestyle. I can't be jumping into your affairs. Whoever it is, I will talk to that person in the morning.'

'Listen, sweetheart, this can't wait. I am so desperate . . . I might just do something to myself if there is no resolution tonight. Please, Sim! This is not an empty threat. If you care for me, if in your heart you have ever loved me, step out for a while. Come out through the back door in the kitchen. No one will notice. I will walk you back to the house in no time.'

The back and forth continued till Simran gave in and put on her coat and stepped out of the back door.

'Where's the man?' she asked as Ash Kool quickened his step and she caught up with him. 'And what's all this about?'

'The place is a little out of town. Trust me on this. I will tell you all about it when we reach there.'

Ash Kool grasped her hand and walked her across the neighbourhood, through the fields, to the rotting sheds and abandoned buildings on the outskirts— which stood in the night like ghostly silhouettes telling a story of neglect and despair. Ash Kool took her along a trail cutting into the fields from one of the sheds. They walked through knee-high wildly growing grass and Ash Kool took her deeper into the fields, all the way to the bomb shelter.

Outside the bomb shelter, Simran freed her hand from his grasp. There were worry lines on her face.

'This is insane, Ash. This looks like a derelict place. Everything is dark and dingy. I am turning back right now. I am convinced you are holding something back. This place is making me very uncomfortable.'

Ash Kool took Simran's face in his hands and lightly kissed her.

'Do you seriously believe I would let any harm come to you? Please, this is important to me. We will be through with it soon. Follow me down the steps.'

Simran looked around her in the desolation and the dark. She suddenly had a desire to break free of Ash Kool and run away from the place, back to her house. She shivered a bit in the cold and she thought, 'Run back?' 'To what?' her heart asked. To that house bereft of love? To turn her back on a boy who cared for her? A boy who was damaged goods but still was the only friend she had in the whole wide world. Let her parents feel her void too! Ash Kool grasped her hand again and tugged at it. She looked at him in the dark. She could barely make out the outline of his face. It was just as well. You could not take a leap of faith with your eyes open.

They went down the steps and Ash Kool opened a rusted iron door leading to a sit-out area. It was pitch-dark and Ash Kool took out his lighter and snapped it open. In the dim light, he began to feel the wall in front of him for an embedded lever. He found the lever and turned it and a door the size of a trapdoor, but installed vertically, swung open. She first heard the drip of leaking water coming from above and then to her surprise she saw old, rusted train tracks lit up by yellow light. As her eyes accustomed to her new surroundings she saw that they were inside an old, abandoned railway station which must have doubled up as a bomb shelter during the War.

They stepped inside and she saw that the platform was reasonably well lit by bulbs encased in wire mesh. Up ahead the distorted shadows of some men were dancing on the tunnel's roof. They approached the men and Simran's blood ran cold. She saw men with sunken cheeks and murder in their eyes looking at her very carefully. Ash Kool was no longer in step with her. He had fallen behind her. Suddenly he pushed her from behind and she fell on the tracks in front of a man sitting in the middle of the tracks on a chair.

She could not believe her ears when she heard Ash Kool say behind her, 'As promised, here's the quid, Hall. And she's worth a lot more than the ten thousand.'

10

Unknown hands grabbed her, forced her up and pushed her in front of a gnarled, old man with watchful eyes, sitting on a chair. It felt as if someone had pushed her out from a secure shuttle in deep space without a lifeline. Her body was tingling with fear and anger as she rose in front of the gang leader. Hall's hands shot out and caught hold of Ash Kool's neck, who had come up to him. His eyes were bloodshot.

'What is the meaning of this?' he snarled. 'And who's this bitch? I am looking for my payout, not a broad from your community!'

Simran looked at Ash Kool, shaking with uncertainty and fear. She in an instant realized that everyone, including her parents, Ash Kool, just about everyone, had used her for themselves. Something snapped inside her. A steely resolution set in. She was not going to go down without a fight. Gathering all the strength she could, she slapped Andrew Hall hard across his cheek. The impact actually staggered Hall for a moment and he looked stunned at the suddenness of it.

And then the tide turned against her.

Hall let out a cry like a wounded beast. 'You fucking bitch!' he screamed and slapped her back.

Simran's ears were ringing but she did not cry or scream. Completely maddened, she continued to spit and kick at Hall and the geriatric signalled to his men.

All four descended on her like a wolf pack. They seemed to know the drill. Two men from either side forced her arms outwards and the other two parted her legs and held them firmly to the ground. Then they tore off all her clothes even as she struggled and writhed under the assault. Her anger seemed to only amuse them. She tried to scream and a large hand closed around her neck tightly. Her eyes widened in fear but her anger at her violation was greater. She looked fiercely at the gang, each and every contour of their leering faces etched in her mind.

Hall's eyes were deadened as he came up close to her and then he spat on her. 'My men and I are going to make you very filthy, very dirty, you whoring little bitch! No one has ever dared to look me in the eye before.'

Her voice was hoarse, the words garbled but strong. 'Well, I am looking at them now, you grandfuckingfather, pervert!'

Hall smiled and his face looked wolfish in the weak light.

'You are fucking right, Indie boy. She's worth more than ten thousand quid. I might even get excited when I finish with her. Payback time, Indie girl!'

And then Simran felt the complete horror of her situation. The strength went out of her and her knees buckled. Her throat was completely dry but she managed to spit one more time weakly. Hall was struck by her defiance. He held up his hand. He continued to look at her with hate in his eyes as he asked Sam the Nazi.

'How do you get the best pieces from a piglet?'

Sam lisped the answer: 'You slow-bleed the piglet. The fear sets in. Wait a while. And then you hack it. You get the prime juicy stuff then, eh, Hall. But it's illegal stuff, you know.' The others laughed at the joke.

Hall simply nodded. He spoke slowly, his eyes not leaving Simran for a moment. 'We follow the same principle, boys. Put her in the cage. Let her squeal and spit her heart out. And then once the fear sets in and it is out of control, we will bring her down. And then we will take turns.'

Simran was forced into a cage attached to the wall in a room next to the rail tracks. In the same room six other bodies torn by bullets had been stacked up like lumber logs. She finally began to lose consciousness and as the door closed on her she caught a glimpse of Ash Kool standing in the doorway. In the weak light, he appeared to have shrunk to half his size. His carefully cultivated carefree look was gone. He looked like a demented pigeon which after a collision loses its sense of direction and starts crashing against each and every object. It was an image that would not leave her for the rest of her life.

'Si Si Simran! Si Si Simran! Si Si Simran!' The periodic, ritualistic chanting initiated by Hall's gang rose to a crest and then fell like a witch's chant. It was followed by long stretches of deafening silence. For four hours, till the very first streaks of daybreak broke across the night sky, the pattern continued. In that span of time, Simran experienced each and every emotion, ever known to man or woman, in a cage. At the end of it all she was completely drained, emptied of any thought or feeling. She felt as if she had lost her sense of touch and smell. So, finally when the cage door was opened and she was carried out, she saw the blurry faces of hungry men which made no sense to her.

She felt as if she was viewing a distorted film on a projector from a great distance. The faces and expressions of the characters in the film were twisted and exaggerated in all sizes and proportions.

She was laid down on the cold, dirty floor and held down, her mouth stuffed with a rag. A very old man climbed on top of her. His body was wrinkled, battered and ugly and he was having a difficult time in getting it up. A whistling then grew in her ears alarmingly and she suddenly heard the laughter and cries of a pack of hyenas tearing at a kill. The wrinkled old man in the picture bent down and disappeared from her line of vision. Rough hands grabbed her hips, her legs held apart. A sharp, shooting pain tore deep within her. It seared her abdomen, grew upwards through her throat and sliced its way through her head as if someone was cleaving it in two.

A silent scream grew and raged within her, seeking a release. She wanted to spit out more than anything else in the world. But all egress was denied to her. She was choked, forced to look up at the dim ceiling, completely unable to move. She felt her insides being ripped open, the pain intolerable and continuous, the laughter and the cursing and the jokes adding a serrated edge to the thrusting of her violation. It felt as if all this would never stop. The blur of faces mounted on top of her would change but the pain would not. Her ears were ringing and a rotting smell invaded her nostrils and her world had shrunk to forcibly looking up at the ceiling. And then suddenly it all stopped. Or so she thought.

She saw four ugly men laughing, buttoning their trousers, buckling their belts. Then Hall entered her line of vision once again. He had dragged Ash Kool by the neck to her.

'Now you will fuck her. And we will watch,' he ordered.

A roar went up in the room. Ash Kool with great tenacity freed himself from Hall's grasp.

'I won't do it!' he screamed. 'I can't do this!'

He tried to run away but Hall caught him and forced him back. He hissed in his ear. 'I will slice you up, Indie boy, if you don't complete the rites of passage. I know how to collect a debt. A family that fucks together stays together. Now get to work.'

And then Simran saw the face that had whispered eternal love in her ear descend to her. The face was no longer a blur. Simran forced herself to look into his eyes. His face was sharply defined, the torment etched on it vividly, the shouting and the jeering in the back clear as a whistle to her ears. She saw the face coming up to her during its descent, barely inches away from her, hesitate for a fleeting second. Their eyes met and she now saw clearly what he really looked like. Then he was on top of her. She shook again and after some time she knew it was all over.

She painfully got up and vomit filled her mouth as she saw the blood flow out of her vagina, trickling down her legs. She began walking the short distance between the tracks and a door leading out, a blood trail following her, smearing the rusted tracks.

She was almost near the entrance from where she had been led in, when Hall's voice rang out sharply. 'Burn her and firebomb this place. It's time to end this pantomime and destroy the evidence.'

She stopped at the entrance and Tattohead took out a cigarette and lit it. He did not extinguish the lighter. The flame flickered, waiting in uncertainty.

For the first and last time in his life, Ash Kool appealed to Hall in the only way that could influence his decision. 'If you burn her,' he said slowly, with great emphasis, 'then you and these three and me, all of us, will go to prison for the rest of our lives. Let me explain to you how that will happen. The entire community in Southall knows this girl is going out with me. When they find her burnt body, which they will, the police will come after me. Some people know I work for you. That link will be explored. Within a day all of us will be in custody. Let her go. She's finished for life. If I know my community well, we don't advertise rape. We brush it under the carpet and carry on. That will be the case with her. I guarantee you that.' He looked at Simran.

Simran looked through him and, without waiting for Hall's approval, slowly and painfully began to walk out of the door. A draught of cold air came in from the outside and she felt cold, a bit more human as she walked out. She came out of the bomb shelter and walked up the steps and stepped into the fields.

The world was waking up and the sky was charged with a bloody streak. She walked through the fields as if the path was etched in her consciousness for years. Behind her there was a controlled explosion and a small fireball escaped into the sky. Simran continued to walk through the fields, across the sheds, the abandoned plants, through the rolling countryside and then across the neighbourhood towards a red-tiled house, the last one in a row of similar-looking houses in the lane. As her house came up before her, a stray thought filled her mind completely. Whose pain was greater? Hers or that of her brother who had climbed a chair to end his life?

11

From a distance a hysterical Nirmal Kaur saw her daughter walk towards her. She could not believe what she thought was an apparition coming at her. She saw her daughter, walking stone-faced towards her in the morning sun. She was completely naked and her hair was dishevelled. Her body was caked with grime and dust and she covered her breasts and vagina, walking in a straight arrow, disconnected to everything around her. Nirmal saw the blood trail, freshly flown, between her legs. She then knew what had happened and with both hands she violently and repeatedly slapped her face and head in the traditional *pitna*, mourning. Balwinder Singh, standing next to his wife, sank to his knees. His night turban, a yellow patka, came off.

He whispered, almost to himself, 'Cover her, Nirmal. The neighbours must not see her in this state.'

The opening stanza of Simran's poem was buried deep in the recesses of her mind and remained unwritten. As the Bangas recovered their senses, they resolved that not a word of the gang rape would ever be made known, either to the police, the neighbours or the community.

It was the end of the road for Simran in Southall. Her bag was packed with some of her stuff and her father bought a one-way ticket for her on a British Airways (BA) flight bound for Amritsar. She was entrusted to the care of Nirmal's sister and her husband, who for years had lived on remittances provided by the Bangas. Since they also lived in the Bangas' kothi in Amritsar, the day had finally come when they were called on to pay some of that debt.

They were sworn to secrecy about what had befallen Simran and the family. They were told to look after Simran in their quiet little village, just a kilometre off the main road leading into Amritsar. When the dust would finally settle down on the entire matter, they were to find a suitable boy for Simran and get her married. And then they would be more than adequately compensated for keeping quiet.

A conspiracy of silence and denial was brought into play. From the car park outside Heathrow Airport, Balwinder Singh heard the rumble of a BA flight taking to the skies. The flight and Simran Kaur Banga were soon out of their airspace and mind frame. Nirmal Banga slapped her forehead one last time as she got into the car and cursed, 'The witch has finally left. She ate up her brother and then she bought infamy on our heads. We had to see this day because of her loose morals. I hope that is the last I have seen of her.'

Balwinder Singh sat in the driver's seat, a little slumped. He sat there lost in thought and then he switched the ignition on and said to no one in particular, 'I think I need a drink.'

Amritsar

Simran's head rested against the windowpane at the back of a speeding Suzuki car, as it left behind a trail of billowing dust clouds on the road leading from the airport to the forgotten village of Kasba Chardi Kala.

In a heartbeat the brown and red-tiled antennae-wired monotony of Southall and suburban London had been replaced by the dusty, green-and-mustard flatness of the Amritsar countryside. A man enveloped in a quilt and somewhat slouched passed them by. The remnants of the early-morning mist hung around the undergrowth in the fields. Tractors chugged at a slow pace in the fields sweeping past them. A farrago of images filled her mind. Some of them were revolting but others were quite confusing and almost all were enervating. She was walking down the road on a cold autumn day and Ash Kool had taken off his coat for her, making her feel warm. And then his face came up before her, really close to her, and he was mounted on top of her, grunting like a stuck pig from the exertion. She had locked herself up in her bathroom after her ordeal and looked at her breasts in the bluish light. There were bite marks all over them as if she had been attacked by a pack of wild animals. She looked at the areola she had encircled fondly so many times earlier. It was now ruptured, caked with dried blood, looking ghastly in the blue light. She could not forget how she had scrubbed herself again and again and again till she had collapsed from the strain in the shower. But the blood flow never seemed to disappear from her legs and the floor was shiny with a mix of streaming blood and water.

She shook her head and forced herself to shut her mind's eye and look at her new surroundings.

The rhythmic chugging of a tractor filled her ears and her senses with words and noises she desperately wanted to forget. The grunts of different men exploded in her brain as they climbed on to her. The grunting overpowered her and in the background her father's voice sliced through it all: 'She will have to leave, she will have to leave.' And then she heard the most terrifying sound, which actually could not be heard, coming from her mother, forming at her lips. 'My daughter is a witch . . . She ate her brother, she had it coming . . .'

A tear rolled down her cheek and she understood that the real ordeal of being raped actually truly began only with the passage of time. She looked at her aunt, Kulwinder Sondhi, sitting next to her. Her husband, Harbaksh Sondhi, sitting ramrod straight next to her, eyed the driver cautiously. Harbaksh's white beard was plastered well with a favourite fixing agent from the sixties called Simco. He wore his best coat and tie from his regimental days for the occasion. In an age of hyper information dissemination, he had turned up in his best. Who knew if somebody might report him back to the Bangas? He was very clear that the hands that fed him and their family should always be kept in good humour. A worrying thought crossed his mind. He looked at the driver closely. Had the man got a whiff of the scandal plaguing the family?

The car turned into the dusty village and negotiated an unpaved, broken road. It skirted a pond coated with a cover of green slime. Buffaloes wallowed in its waters under the watchful eyes of a young boy brandishing a cane. The boy wielded the cane well but was unable to control the snot oozing from his nose. The broken road gave way to streets cobbled together with brickwork. There were two- and three-storey houses on both sides, in a kind of windless interconnected passageway. Drains flowed on either side and a jumble of dish antennae dotted the roof tops. All the rooftops were so incestuously conjoined that a person, instead of walking through the brick-layered streets, could very easily take a stroll upstairs on the rooftops.

The car pulled up in front of a largish two-storey house with a room on the top. It had a central courtyard and an engraved front door cut out from a log of pure Burma wood. Nearby, a couple of derelicts warmed themselves in front of a fire which crackled from a supply of dry, broken twigs and wood shavings.

Simran was led into the house and Harbaksh introduced his niece to her two cousins who stood in attendance.

'Happy and Dolly, this is Simran. Simran, these two are . . .'

Harbaksh stopped himself from completing his absurdity. It dawned on everyone in the room that all of them were jumpy. Simran's descent into infamy was known to all of them. No one quite knew how exactly to deal with the situation. It was a unique and repulsive situation for the Sondhis.

Harbaksh dismissed the siblings and asked Simran to follow him to the room on the top. Simran picked up her bag and trailed behind Harbaksh and her aunt, up the stairs. She remembered her mother furtively packing her bags and issuing instructions: 'Be soft-spoken, girl, or try not to speak at all. Otherwise there will be questions. We've kept what happened to you a secret and it should remain one . . .'

Once in the room, Harbaksh asked his wife to close the door. He coughed a little self-consciously and invited Simran to take a seat. She looked around. It was a bare-bones kind of a room, a kind of room that baked in the summers and froze in the winters. Kulwinder rummaged under the bed and brought out a coil heater and plugged it in.

'We have thought of everything,' she launched into self-explanation. 'You will be warm and secure in here and really there is nothing to be afraid of. You relax here. No one will disturb you. Everything will be all right . . .'

Harbaksh coughed again, this time more forcefully, signalling his wife to shut up. A tense silence filled the room. Harbaksh rose to speak as if he was addressing cadets at a military parade. 'Simran beta, the very worst has happened to you. It would be inconceivable to think that there can be anything worse beyond this point but let me tell you, beta, that more dishonour could follow if we are not careful. You see, beta, if word of what has happened to you gets out, then our family name will be blackened forever. I have promised Nirmal and Balwinder that such a thing will never happen and we will cover the tracks. I am a man of honour and I will keep my word. But I will need your help in this. You must keep a very low profile during your stay here. Avoid mixing with the locals and keep to yourself. You have your own room here. You can use your time to reflect and build your resolution. You could study further; for instance, you could take up a course at the local polytechnic. The director of that institute is a friend of mine.'

Harbaksh coughed once again a little self-consciously. She stared vacuously at him.

'As you can see, Simran, Dolly and Happy are at a very impressionable age. Especially Dolly—you know how these things are with girls in our society. I would suggest that you keep to yourself and leave those two alone. We have made arrangements for your meals to be sent up to your room. As I explained in the beginning, you will be quite comfortable here. With the passage of time and as things settle down, who knows, there might a suitable boy for you . . .'

There was a flicker of shock in Simran's eyes.

Harbaksh Sondhi coughed once again and looked helplessly at his wife. She nodded her approval. He asked her, 'Kulwinder, is there anything more you would like to add to what I have said?'

'No, you said it all quite well, ji,' she concurred. Both left and a servant came up shortly with Simran's meal. Then she too left. Simran sat in a chair staring at a point on the wall for an inordinate length of time.

The meal remained untouched. Then she got up and looked out of a window in the room. She saw the upturned soil and the furrow marks in the field where a tractor had been at work earlier in the day.

Beyond the field she saw a vista of the countryside in the grip of a severe winter. She heard the rhythmic running of a motor nearby and saw a channel of water snake its way from the motor shed to the fields. She looked closely and saw a disused spring-tooth harrow kept near the shed. It was an outdated piece of farm equipment and it showed. It was completely rusted, its red paint peeling off and its claws, used for tilling, had turned to junk. She thought about what she had seen. It was another piece of machinery that had run its course and had been abandoned. The retch came up in her strongly and she puked out of the window. Her stomach began to hurt and some of the vomit was smeared on her sweater. But she stood there and looked out of the window till it was night-time.

The next day she stayed in the room and lay on the bed the entire afternoon. At dusk she looked up at the ceiling and saw a lizard dart up to an insect near the fluorescent white tube and devour it. She began to shiver as the cage reappeared and the walls began to close in. She shook uncontrollably, her teeth clattered and frenziedly she made preparations to prevent the walls from crushing her from all sides. She balled up like a string of cotton and lay still, waiting in complete terror for a touch that would eventually break through her defences. She could smell something dying and that rotting smell seemed to have settled within her permanently. Late in the night she felt she could no longer breathe normally. She rushed to the window and drew in a lungful of the cold air outside.

The next day she stood at the window and watched a farmer till his land. She sat by the window through the day, looking out. Early evening, she fell asleep near the window. It rained the whole night and the spray came in through the window but she was lost to the world.

She woke up at daybreak and the rotting smell pervading her nostrils and senses was gone. Light was breaking out in the sky and she smelt the fresh earth after a night of intermittent showers. It was a smell like no other. She opened the door to her room and raced down to the courtyard and opened the door leading out of it. She ran to the fields and the smell of fresh earth filled her senses. She danced like a madwoman in the middle of the fields and then she sank into the soft soil and grabbed fistfuls of it and rubbed her face, her arms, her hair and her breasts with it. She began to laugh and then she remembered all that had happened to her and she screamed her guts out at the world awakening around her and her body convulsed with deep sobs. She cried till she could cry no more and the words tumbled out of her in a scream: 'Damn you, damn you all! They tore my insides out, they shoved their filth deep into me, they filled my nose, my ear and my mouth with their dirt and not a word of empathy from any one of you! Damn you, my mother—I came from your loins; damn you, my father—I am your flesh and bone; and damn you, my lover, for filling my ear with lies and more lies!

'Damnation to all of you and may your heads be filled with ash and one day may you all be buried in that heap of ash!'

And then she became completely still. She slowly got up and walked back to the kothi, to live her life.

12

The next day Simran walked downstairs to the
dining room where the Sondhi family had gathered
for breakfast. Harbaksh with great relish had begun
to attack his regimental-style double-egg cheese-and-
spinach omelette when he saw the girl sweetly banished
from the house standing at the door. He frowned and
left the omelette unattended. The others looked with
gaping mouths at the unwelcome presence. Harbaksh
wiped his curling moustache with a napkin and got up.

'Is something the matter, girl? Has the servant
forgotten to serve you? You need not have come
down . . .'

Simran cut him mid-sentence: 'I came down to
tell you that I will not follow your diktat. If you have
anything sensible to say I will listen to you, but don't
take that as a promise. I know you will spy on me and
report my activities back to my parents but I don't
care. Don't ever forward their calls to me. I am not

stupid and I understand that this relationship is based on a monetary transaction. I believe my father will be paying you every month for my upkeep. So here's what I need. I need money and also some kind of transport to move in the village. Have I made myself clear to you?'

Harbaksh looked quizzically at his wife. She was at a loss for an answer.

He said, 'What do you need the money for? We'll take care of all your needs. Also, I had explained to you some time back that it is not yet advisable for you to be seen moving around . . .'

'So you want me locked up in that dingy room like a criminal. You want me holed up in that hideous room as if all this was my fault? I am not asking you for a favour, Uncle!' Simran's voice had risen by a minor decibel but it was enough to send a chill through everyone present at the dining table.

Harbaksh quickly pushed the chair back and fumbled with his wallet, a little desperate to avoid more humiliation in front of his children. He took out a couple of hundred-rupee notes and thrust them into Simran's hands. He guided her by the elbow out of the room into the courtyard.

'There was no need for you to talk in this manner in front of the children. We have been so considerate to you. I am like your father.'

He paused and stepped back, a little startled, when

he looked at Simran's taut face with the repressed fury bobbing somewhere below the surface.

'Don't talk to me about fathers and grandfathers, ever again,' she said with her mouth full of spit. She paused, leveraging the little scene with her uncle to her advantage. 'I asked you for a ride. Is there one in this house?'

Harbaksh quickly gave in. 'There is an old cycle in the shed at the back. You will have to get it fixed.'

Simran turned her back to him and left the courtyard. She located the cycle which apart from a puncture and the inevitable rusting was still in good shape. She wheeled it out of the shed and began to walk away from the kothi. Her breathing normalized and her body shook as she recaptured her first-ever act of defiance in her mind.

She walked across the village with the cycle and came up to a community health centre that stood out with its yellow distemper paint coat. Traces of the early-morning fog still hung about the main village square. Shutters were half down in some of the adjoining shops as if people could not make up their minds whether to go to work. From the corner of her eye she could make out that a man behind the counter in the grocery shop was looking at her closely. The tailor cranking up an old Singer machine paused on the foot pedal. Upstairs in the community centre a doctor wearing a white coat leaned out from the balcony to take a close look at her. Another local, face wrapped in a wool muffler, joined him. Even the boy whose job it was to tend to the buffaloes, unmindful of his runny nose, stopped in the village square to look at her. Just about everyone in the village square was staring at her.

It was then that she knew that this was not the rude scrutiny of a people assessing the newly arrived amidst them. This was the voyeuristic stare of a people who knew that the victim of a gang rape was in their community. And who else but her aunt or some Sondhi family member could have leaked the news, perhaps, even before she had set foot in the village?

Her hands were tingling and her breath was a little short as she slowly and defiantly wheeled the cycle to a puncture repair shed down the line of shops. A man with a gaunt face was holding a tube in a basin of water. He looked up at Simran and a light shone in his eyes.

'You must be the new girl,' he said. 'So what have we here, ah, Harbaksh's old cycle? Let me take a look at it.'

He took possession of the cycle and removed the tube and sealed the punctured area. He busied himself with the spokes and fixed the bent ones and finally refitted the tyre. It spun well after he gave it a push.

'Good as new,' he said, pleased with his own effort. His gaunt face showed excitement. Simran held out a currency note but he licked his lips and smiled obscenely. Simran then closely noticed his eyes. They looked glazed.

'No, I can't take this. You are a guest. You have come from London, right? They say there are white women there who marry you for a sum and then give you a divorce after you have got an immigration card. Now you wouldn't know about such a person, would you?'

The gaunt man's reptilian fingers extended towards Simran. She shrank back and threw the currency note at him and mounted the cycle. She furiously pedalled her way out of the square and the man's jabbering receded behind her. From behind her she heard the collective cries of a gang of schoolchildren who gave chase to her bike. She stepped up the pedalling and shot past high-school girls all dressed in the trademark blue-and-white salwar-kameez with chunnis draping their shoulders. She disappeared into a lane lined with houses on both sides and panic seized her and she had a sense that she was hurtling down through her hole once again.

A group of women draped in shawls, gossiping about the day's events, came up and all of them turned their heads at the same time to look at her. She felt like ramming her speeding bike into them, to tear the shawls from their heads and stomp on their faces, to make them cry out in pain. Her body was twitching involuntarily with anger and fear as the cycle rattled on the brick-layered lanes and she felt that she was losing her mind and the entire village was giving chase to her.

And then in an instant she was out of the maze of interconnected streets and soon she was cycling past the lush crop that stretched interminably as far as the eye could see. The village was disappearing behind her and to her right, the main gurdwara, built in the village outskirts, came up. A small group of people had gathered near the Nishan Sahib flagpole. The gurdwara *granthi*, head priest, Tarlochan Singh, was shouting at a man who sat on the ground, in front of the flagpole. He looked around at everyone in a dazed state. His turban had come off and his hands were folded.

Simran on an impulse braked the cycle and got off it. The granthi noticed her and his anger and the invective went up.

'This is the last time I am tolerating this breach, Hardev! If you try and sneak into the gurdwara ever again then I will have your legs broken. Learn to stay within your limits. Understand this—the Mazhabis are not allowed in this gurdwara!'

Hardev gathered his turban and slowly and

painfully got up. He draped the turban around his head and with folded hands turned away, muttering to himself, 'But the Gurus opened the doors for everyone.'

The granthi heard that and he once again showered the devotee with abuse. Then he chided the assembled crowd and told them to disperse. He noticed Simran and called out to her.

'Child, I need to have a word with you. Wait for me.'

The granthi descended the steps of the gurdwara and came up to Simran. He put his hand on the cycle's steering.

'I know all about you, child. It is a very sad story. Why don't you come in and sip some amrit? There are ways and means by which you can purify yourself.'

Simran looked beyond the granthi at the majestic dome of the gurdwara and the saffron flag of the Khalsa panth, fluttering in the gusty wind, atop a spire. She removed the granthi's hand from the steering with some force. The granthi looked at her in shocked surprise but she had a determined look on her face. Without saying a word she got on the cycle and cycled past the furious granthi and disappeared in the fog that had come up swirling from nowhere across the fields.

She rode blindly in the fog and when she came

out of it she noticed that the lay of the land had changed. The fertile land teeming with crop was a mere speck in the background. The fields in these parts were overgrown with nettle and clumped bushes and littered with small rocks. The soil appeared loamy and the trees growing along it were stunted. A roughly hewn path cut through this wilderness. She paced her cycling and followed the path and it led to a small log cottage. Smoke was coming out from a chimney in the cottage. The sun had completely disappeared and gusts of the fog were still coming in. She saw a woman working inside a fenced field on what appeared to be citrus crop. The woman was wearing gloves and her back was turned to Simran as she came up on her cycle.

Simran slowed down her cycle and the woman turned to look at her. Their eyes met and Simran was struck by the presence of the woman living at the edge of the village, close to wilderness. She was in her early fifties, quite tall, and her angular face and sharp cheekbones, coal-black eyes and wind-lashed hair highlighted her fading beauty. But it was the intensity in her eyes that drew Simran to the doorstep of the mysterious stranger.

'I was looking for the polytechnic. Is it nearby?' asked Simran.

'No, it's on the other side,' she replied. 'You

must have lost your way in the fog. This is private property—my property.'

'I am so sorry.'

'Don't be,' said the enigmatic woman and she turned her back to Simran and went back to tending the citrus plants on her property.

13

The government polytechnic was a well-funded three-storey building set on a sprawling campus, off the village limits. Simran finally got her bearings right about the location of the institute. She reached the place and parked her cycle at a bicycle stand. A peon led her to the director's office on the first floor. Dr Bagga warmly welcomed her and patted her head as he had been expecting her. He insisted on speaking in English and on showing her around the campus. She followed him to all the three floors and looked in at the students in their classes. They were enrolled in courses ranging from working on lathes to beekeeping. Dr Bagga twirled his moustache with pride and told her she could pick any one course.

'Simran, you are an honoured guest in our village. And Harbaksh is an old friend. This is the least I can do for you. You let me know what you have decided. You can pick and choose any course you like. Usually there is a waiting list for these courses. But you know in India nothing works if you don't have connections. And you are fortunate that you know me . . . Well, in an indirect way.'

He smiled and his seventy-year-old craggy face lit up. His turban covered his entire forehead, coming almost to his eyes which were red-rimmed and Simran with suddenness had a sense that he was a heavy drinker, very much like her father. She could smell a noxious smell of alcohol and cheap cologne on his breath. Maybe he had put it on to conceal the alcoholic stink or, worse, to impress her. She suddenly wanted to get away from this place.

'I will let you know, Dr Bagga, what I have decided. I should get going. The fog is coming in.'

Dr Bagga smiled again and deftly took her by the elbow and guided her through a narrow passage from the back to his office on the first floor.

'Of course you have to get back, my dear girl. But what would Harbaksh say if I did not offer you a cup of tea? It's a cold and foggy day. I have some fine Darjeeling tea in my office. I will make it personally for you. Then you can be on your way.'

She found herself being led by him and climbing up the narrow passage up the stairs; he missed a step and fell back behind her. His hands brushed against her buttocks.

'So sorry,' he apologized, 'that was clumsy of me.'

Her mouth became dry and she felt hemmed into the tight passage and she wanted to break free and run away from the polytechnic. But he was persistent and he guided her to his office, into a chair. He began to hum a low tune as he took out teabags and boiled water in a percolator. He opened a cookie jar and lined up the cookies on a plate.

Simran could feel the terror coming back as the seventy-year-old man busied himself with tea preparation. He offered her a cup, which she left untouched, and he sipped from his cup and she looked at him unsure, waiting for his inevitable next move. She controlled her panic because this time she had foreknowledge and she wanted to see how it would play out. She almost felt as if she was saddled with a kind of perversion but she wanted more than anything else to see how he would make his move in real time. She did not have to wait long.

'My dear girl,' said the geriatric. 'You have all your life lived in the West and we are still a very rustic society. But I am different from the rest out here. I have always espoused Western values.'

'Really?' she found herself saying sardonically. 'And what kind of values might these be?' she asked, her head cocked to one side, looking pointedly at him.

The old man flashed a craggy smile. 'You know,

dear girl, we are unfortunately a very repressed lot. Unlike your society, out here girls and boys seldom mix with each other. Whether it be classes or the playground or recreational facilities, they always hang out with their own. Now I have tried to change all this. You know, I am a bit of a revolutionary in the sense that I encourage my students to mingle with each other, share physical intimacy. That is the law of nature but we go on pretending otherwise.'

Dr Bagga leaned forward. Simran saw a wolfish smile on his face; it was the same smile she had seen earlier on the faces of men.

'Simran beta, I understand how lonely it can be,' he said speaking in hushed tones. 'You must be feeling like an exile, in this godforsaken village. Away from the fun, the touching and the bedding that is so common in your society over there. If you must know, I am also so lonely. My wife does not care for me any longer . . .'

It then happened too fast for Simran to even react. Dr Bagga pushed his face into Simran's breasts and with his gnarled hands he grabbed her left hand and forced it to rub his fly. Simran's right hand shot out and grabbed Dr Bagga's throat in a vice-like grip. The old man began to choke and Simran did not scream or shout but held him as long as possible till his bloodshot eyes were almost popping out and he was close to asphyxiation. Then she let go and kicked the chair he sat on; semi-conscious, he tumbled on to the floor.

She bent down to him and slapped him hard. 'Look at me, Dr Bagga. If you must know why some people are lonely and confined, it is because predators like you roam freely, choosing their victims.'

She slapped him once again and then calmly walked out of the room, went downstairs and opened the padlock on her cycle. She cycled out of the polytechnic and took the road to the village. The shock hit her on the way back and the cycle wavered under her grip. Her eyes stung with tears but she forced herself to ignore them. The fog was clearing in the wilderness but it still hung about the undergrowth. She quickened her pedalling because it was late afternoon and the light would soon start fading away. A weak sun briefly emerged from a sky that looked like a cataract eye in dire need of some clarity. The dirt track ahead of her was completely fogged up and she never saw the boulder in her way and the cycle steering flew from her hands and she flipped over the handlebars and rolled down into a ditch.

She got up and saw that clusters of trees ringed the ground. She picked her cycle up and dusted herself. It was then that she noticed something shine in the fast-fading light. She hesitated but then decided to explore. She crossed the thick eucalyptus tree cover and noticed the shine was reflecting off of some object in a derelict-looking U-shaped brick wall. She approached the wall from the open end and a strong, addictive smell assaulted her nostrils. She immediately knew what it was that had attracted her attention. She had seen and smelt enough of that stuff around Southall and the adjoining areas.

Inside the brick wall, four youngsters were injecting and rolling drugs of every shape and variety. The ground was a mess of crinkly, shiny or blackened strips of foil, which had caught her attention. The enclosure was a graveyard of empty cough-syrup bottles, strong-smelling black balls of opium and even syringes and injections dipped in tainted blood. A couple of the youngsters were consuming *bhukki*—a local poppy extract—and a third one was injecting his vein with great concentration. The fourth boy was staring into space, listening to a musical jingle on his mobile.

She shrank back as she looked at the wasted youth with sunken eyes and cheeks—all dressed incongruously in trendy denim and Nike shoes. They saw her staring at them from outside the enclosure. The one who a moment ago had injected his vein with a needle got up unmindful of the fact that his syringe had drawn blood and was still stuck in the vein. He walked up to Simran. There was a desperate edge to his voice.

'Sister, would you be having some money on you? Help a brother. I am in real trouble.'

Simran stifled a scream and started to run away from the enclosure. The four youngsters with surprising alacrity jumped the enclosure wall and gave chase. Simran ran through the trees and the boys swiftly gained ground on her and all the while the light was fading away fast. She looked around in complete terror and the world had closed in on her like a trap made up of dense tree cover, rolling fog and weak light. One of the boys launched himself mid-air and brought her down on the ground. Then all of them were on top of her like scavenging dogs. They brutally beat her and searched her for currency. Having drawn a blank, their anger and frustration peaked and one of the boys sat on her throat and picked up a large rock to smash her face with.

A shot rang out. The rock fell from the boy's hands. He looked around in complete terror. The tall woman emerged from the tree cover holding a sawed-off shotgun, aimed at the boy. She walked towards the boy and fired another shot that missed his ear by a whisker. He screamed and crawled away and all four ran back into the tree cover.

The woman expertly reloaded and brought down the shotgun and gave a hand to Simran to help her stand up.

'You are in shock,' she said. 'And that is not good. Come with me to my cottage. You can wash up and sip some water and once you recover, you can be on your way.'

The light had gone by then but she could still make out the profile of the intense woman standing in front of her like a guardian angel. Simran gratefully took the proffered hand and rose unsteadily to her feet.

'Thanks, you saved my life.'

'That's okay,' replied the woman. 'Try not to think about what happened here. But we should hurry. It will be dark pretty soon.'

14

The winter of 1983, Amritsar

It was not even five in the evening and the shutters were being pulled down by the shopkeepers in the Katra Jamail Singh Bazar. Aranjit felt refreshed after a darshan at the Golden Temple. She walked the length of the bazar, observing the Hindu shopkeepers shut up shop. Ever since the assassination of Lala Jagat Narain two years back, the traditional easy equilibrium between the two major communities in the state had been disrupted. The camaraderie and brotherly affection had been replaced by fear and suspicion on both sides. Gangs of All India Sikh Students Federation (AISSF) youth patrolled the back lanes of the bazar and other places of commerce on their motorcycles. A young man on a mission, driving a motorcycle, had become the leitmotif of the times. Death usually came fast and quick from the snout of a .38 bore revolver carried by a man riding pillion on a motorcycle.

The real terror was not in the actual killing itself but in the sound of a motorcycle engine being revved up by someone round the corner.

At the end of the *katra*, Aranjit heard the ubiquitous sound of a motorcycle being primed up. She noticed the panic-stricken looks of the shopkeepers to her right. She smiled when she heard the sound. A motorcycle leapt across the by-lane, which in an instant became deserted. The rider of the motorcycle came up near Aranjit, smartly traced a figure of eight on the ground with the bike and then charged up the bike till the spot became a mess of exhaust fumes and deafening sounds.

Sukkhi always had a flair for the dramatic, thought Aranjit, as she straddled the bike from the back and held him firmly.

He shouted over the din, 'They are shitting bricks, you know!'

She shouted back, 'Wouldn't you also if you were in their place? But they will live today.'

Sukkhi then revved up the engine to the maximum and shouted, 'Yeah, they will. But for how long?'

He said that and the bike like a tracer shot forward and it was gone from the congested katra.

Sukkhi dropped Aranjit near her two-bedroom first-floor apartment in Gumtala Colony. She got off the bike and Sukkhi held her hand.

'Will my entire life be spent in giving you pillion rides? Just tell me once that there is some hope for me.'

Aranjit snatched her hand away and tilting her head with an amused look on her face she spoke in matching hyperbole, 'Of course there is hope for you, Sukkhi. I could slip off my Amritsari jutti right now and give you a tight whack on the head with it or else I could fetch my high heels from upstairs. What would you prefer?'

In response, Sukki, in good-natured humour, closed his eyes, kept his right hand on his heart and blew her a kiss. With his eyes closed, he spoke, '*Jo soni oh Sikhni . . .*' (A Sikh girl is always beautiful.)

Aranjit began to laugh. 'You want me to complete the proverb, you moron?'

Sukkhi replied, '*Asi te thaude pyar wich kad de jhalle ban gaye hah!*' (It's been quite a while since I have become an idiot in your love.)

'Keep dreaming, you moron!' she shouted at him as he revved up the engine. 'And don't drive with your eyes closed. If you die on the road there will be no one left to give me rides.'

He saluted her and the motorcycle was off in a flash. She shouted at him as he shot out of the neighbourhood.

'I will see you in the evening at the meeting!'

She found herself humming as she climbed the stairs leading to her apartment. She opened the door to her apartment. Her father, Gurmukh Singh, stood in front of the old black-and-white TV set, fiddling with the switches. She went up to her father and affectionately kissed him on the head. He was full of complaints.

'What's wrong with this TV set? I can't get to watch my favourite programme, *Krishi Darshan.*'

Aranjit gently guided her father to the easy chair in the room. 'Let me get you something to eat, Pitaji. You must be hungry. You didn't eat anything in the afternoon.'

'But what about my programme?'

'It comes late in the evenings, Pitaji. I promise you that I will switch it on at six thirty,' she responded and turned to go. 'I will be in the kitchen.'

Aranjit went into the kitchen and turned on the gas. She emerged a short while later and sat next to her father and fed him a meal of roti, mashed spinach and a whole onion.

'Saag—it's your favourite, isn't it?'

Gurmukh Singh nodded as Aranjit fed him. His rheumy eyes lit up at the mention of saag.

'Yesterday they said on the programme that a new variety of fertilizer has been developed that is twice as effective as the old lot. We must get sackfuls of it.

It will be good for the land.'

Aranjit kept quiet and wiped her father's mouth with a hand towel.

'Are you listening to me, Harmit? That land is all that we have. For a farmer his land is like his child. He has to take good care of it, nourish it with his affection.'

Aranjit spoke quietly, 'You don't remember, Pitaji, but we sold off the land two years back. It was a small holding and we could not sustain it. We were neck-deep in debt. We sold it to the village landlord, Pyara Singh. From whatever money that was left, we bought this place.'

Gurmukh Singh eyes had a vacant look. Then he said, 'Is that so? How sad. How sad. But what do I have to worry about? My daughter is a PhD, a molecular biologist. We are blessed by Wahe Guruji.'

Aranjit fed her father the last bit of the roti and she tidied up the dining table and took the plate to the kitchen. She murmured under her breath in desperation, 'And what good does that PhD do for me, Pitaji? I can't even get a job as a biology teacher in a school.'

She rinsed the plate in the sink and wiped the stone ledge clean and took a roti from the hamper, put an onion on it, garnished it with pickle and salt and chewed on it.

From behind her, she heard her father call again.

'Navjot, what is wrong with this TV set? I can't watch my favourite programme. Navjot, are you listening to me?'

A tear rolled down Aranjit's eye and she replied, 'Coming, Pitaji . . .'

Late in the evening, after Aranjit had settled her father and put on his favourite TV programme, she left for the secret rendezvous. She took a cycle rickshaw and walked the rest of the way, skipping lanes and covering her tracks, just in case some Punjab Police sleuth was following her. She reached what looked like a large but relatively nondescript house; it belonged to a prosperous Amritsar businessman on Ranjit Avenue. She spoke the password given to her to a man at the gate. She was let in. In the large drawing room some of the rank and file of the AISSF had already gathered. She saw Sukkhi in a corner, chatting with an acquaintance.

She did not notice it then but she was the lone woman in the room. Unlike the previous meetings, there was a newfound energy in the gathering. Everyone knew that the meeting had been called to introduce them to the new area commander of the Amritsar district. Everyone also knew what it really meant. This would be the man who would take charge of the Golden Temple during the final showdown. The man was presumably the most trusted aide of the other man who had unfurled the flag of rebellion and insurrection—Sant Jarnail Singh Bhindranwale.

A hush fell in the room as the evening's speaker walked in with the benefactor businessman. If the assembled lot were surprised to see the man, they did not show it. Unlike the tall, strapping AISSF students, the area commander was a diminutive, slender-looking man. There was nothing of note that one could say about his physical appearance, except the eyes. The eyes were an intense window to the man which instantly conveyed fierceness, shrewdness and, above all, the capability to strike fear in others. He could do all that at the same time. The man was dressed in beige battle fatigues. The students recovered and raised full-throated slogans of 'Khalistan zindabad!'

The commander held out a cautionary hand. He spoke slowly, a little haltingly. There was a smirk on his face.

'If only wars and insurrections could be won by shouting slogans. Remember, if you shout at the top of your voices, the CID will descend on this house and it will be all over, even before you get started.'

The mild rebuke silenced everyone. The commander's eyes glittered as he raised his fist and whispered, 'Khalistan zindabad! Sant Jarnail Singh Bhindranwale zindabad!'

After receiving the cue from their commander, the

others followed. Then the commander spoke to them in a low, halting voice.

'I am not an orator. I am a man of very few words. I know that I don't look and sound inspirational but I actually am. And I will tell you why. I am the man who fashioned the Indian Army's most spectacular victories during the liberation of Bangladesh in 1971. My men and I broke the siege in Dacca and liberated it from the Pakistanis. Twelve years later, do I think it was worth it? I don't think so. Later, I was court-martialled by the same army on flimsy grounds. I never rose to a senior position. My batchmates, who had built a career pushing paper and had forgotten what a weapon looked like, rose to be senior generals in the army.'

The speaker kept quiet and his face looked grim.

'Each and every one of you in this room is a victim of state repression and discrimination. I know that. I have read your files. So we share something in common. What we don't share in common is our preferred method to go about achieving our objective. You are young and impetuous and I am middle-aged and cautious. We have to find a way to marry the opposites. Here is what I have in mind.'

The speaker sat in a chair and crossed his legs. The intensity in his eyes was undiminished.

'We take over the state by a mixture of pinpointed

killings and stealth. We take over our shrines and spread our message. We radicalize the countryside. The Jat farmer will come to us once he feels his back is against the wall. We encourage a migration of populations.'

He leaned forward and looked at them closely. 'And above all, we give no room to breathe to the people— especially our opponents. Let them live in constant fear of where the next bullet will come from.'

And then the speaker was spent and he leaned back in the chair, lost in thought. One of the students reluctantly put up his hand.

'You have a question?' asked the commander.

'And what about the Golden Temple? There are rumours that you have plans for that as well.'

The speaker once again smirked as he got up. 'Our young friend here wants to read the last chapter even before he has read the book. Impetuosity, impetuosity, I say . . .'

Some in the audience laughed. The speaker faced them and spoke slowly and with great emphasis.

'Yes, I am in charge of the Golden Temple. That is all you need to know, as of now. And if you are a true Sikh and are prepared to bear the pain then you will not squeal this fact to the police if you are captured by them.'

Everyone in the room was silent. This was the real thing, they all knew. And the day was not far when the denouement would be played out.

The speaker spoke again. 'I have drawn up a list. Some of you are being sent to the countryside. A select few will spearhead the operations in the cities. If this lot falls or is captured, the others will step in.'

The commander read out a few names. He paused at the last name and asked, 'Kaur . . . Your full name is?'

Aranjit had never before been so struck by a man in her life. It took her a moment to comprehend that the commander was addressing her. She blurted, 'The name is Harmit . . . Harmit Kaur.'

The commander smiled. 'I have been told you have the heart and the tenacity of a tigress.'

'I do hope so too,' she replied with brightness.

'If that is the case then join us in the next room.'

The handpicked front-line squad was led into the next room. Sukkhi was not among them. Aranjit had a feeling that with this one step she was leaving a life behind. Something completely new was beckoning her. The commander closed the door to the room and signalled to an aide. The aide brought out a crowbar and opened a crate with Pakistani military markings. Then he tore open the oilskin wrapping.

Stockpiles of the AK series assault rifles gleamed in the yellow-bulb-lit room.

15

Present day

Aranjit cleaned Simran's face with a hand towel soaked in warm water and then she applied antiseptic to the nicks and minor cuts on her elbow and face. The antiseptic burned her but she had never felt better. She felt that after a long time someone was not pretending to look after her. She looked around at the spartan setting inside the log cabin. There were functional pieces of furniture in the room which catered to the needs of its single owner. There was an Internet connection and a desktop computer in a corner. A bookcase was crammed with books on Sikh political and military history and papers. An inexpensive rug covered the wooden floorboards. There was a portrait of Guru Gobind Singh on one of the walls. Next to the portrait, two crossed swords, with a small shield wedged in between, adorned the wall. Below the mantelpiece there was a genuine fireplace. Logwood ready for use was kept near it.

Aranjit capped the antiseptic bottle and closed the first-aid box.

She then spoke as she tidied up the table in front of Simran, 'Old saying—don't step out when it is foggy. You could lose your way. You not only lost your way but also came close to losing your life. You were cycling like someone possessed in that fog. It was your good fortune that I spotted you.'

She flashed a smile at Simran. 'Trouble follows you or you seek it?'

'What do you mean?' asked Simran.

'Well, did someone not tell you that after dark it is not safe in these woods? All the druggies gather there. Half the youngsters in the village are addicted. They could slice your throat for as little as a fifty-rupee note. I am surprised Harbaksh did not warn you of the lay of the land. Not your fault. How is a girl from Southall supposed to know what goes on in this forgotten village?'

'So you know,' spoke Simran, the disappointment creeping into her voice. 'You know about me.'

'Yes, I do. Not that Harbaksh or anyone else from the village told me. Why would they confide to the village pariah? But I do have my sources. And pray, what is so secretive about you, eh? That you were gang-raped and packed off to the last place on earth? Ha! Big deal! Girl, you and I—we both have holes and men have lusted for them for centuries. They have always wanted to explore them. Some take the so-called decent way, through marriage, and others take the way of the beast. You were unlucky that the beast knocked on your door. Don't let an activist tell you otherwise. It's that one chase men, all men, are never going to give up.'

Simran looked disgusted. 'So are you saying that we should spread our legs at the first signs when they come hunting?'

Aranjit did not reply. She disappeared into the cottage with the first-aid box. When she emerged a short while later, she was holding a syringe. She noticed a worry line crease Simran's face.

'What's that for?' asked Simran.

'It's a tetanus shot. It will take care of the infection.' Aranjit pulled up Simran's shirtsleeve. 'I have a degree for this if you really must know.'

Aranjit felt the nub around Simran's forearm; she found the vein and then tied the forearm with a rubber tube. She injected her and said, 'It takes some guts to trust a strange woman with unorthodox views and a needle. You have what it takes.'

'Is that supposed to make me feel better?' groaned Simran as the antibiotic shot through her system.

Aranjit broke the needle in a crusher and sat next to Simran. 'I will tell you what will make you feel better. I did not answer your question earlier because I am sick and tired of women who choose to become victims. Maybe you can't stop it but you damn well can do something about it. If somebody splits open your skull, will you stay at home for fear of public exposure? Won't you rush to the hospital to get it stitched up? It is the same or should be the same with the cunt. But what do we do? We will use all the damn pathos, psychology, sociology and the victim's grief–pleasure syndrome to analyse the issue and parade the cunt for somebody's postdoctoral thesis.'

Aranjit stood up and frenetically paced the room. Then she exploded, 'For fuck's sake, analyse it! Look at all those shitters, those holy cows, the women activists, talking on TV about rape and especially those so-called empathetic men! They are probably lusting for a hole even as they speak a different language.'

Aranjit then became completely quiet. She faced Simran. Simran was undecided whether the passion in the woman facing her had subsided. Or was it burning at its most dangerous level?

Aranjit came up to her and put a finger to Simran's forehead. She spoke in a measured, soft voice, 'I will tell you how I would deal with rape or any other kind of injustice. I would stop talking about it and start doing something about it. Personally, I keep a shotgun with me. That is my weapon of choice—you decide what will be yours. That's all to it. We are all caught in the great hunt. Some time, some day, we will be brought down. But then again, maybe one day, we will get a clean shot at the perpetrator.'

The two women stood quietly facing and examining each other with intensity. Then the older woman held out her hand.

'Aranjit Kaur,' she said.

Simran nodded and took the hand.

'Simran Kaur Banga, but you already know that.'

'Yes,' said the older woman. 'And my doors are always open for you. Come any time. I sense we might have something in common.'

It was late at night when Aranjit escorted Simran to Harbaksh's residence. Surprisingly there were no questioning family members waiting for her. The front door was ajar and her room at the top had been cleaned and kept ready for her arrival. She closed the door to the room and slept peacefully after a really long time.

She woke up late, next morning, to the sounds of someone persistently knocking on the door. She opened the door and her aunt, Kulwinder, came in and patted her on the head. She was smiling with some warmth.

'You are blessed, Simran, the Sache Padshe has listened to our prayers. Wait till you hear the news!'

Simran braced herself for some more duplicity from her aunt.

'We had thought it would take months to find a suitable boy for you. But your uncle was on the job and he had mentioned to an old friend of his to help us find a suitable match for you.'

Simran rolled her eyes. But Kulwinder was persistent. 'And guess what? The friend called up last night and told your uncle that his son Kuljit might be interested.' Her voice dropped a bit. 'We even told them of what had happened to you. But the Bhattis are a very forward-looking family. They accepted all that. They are well off and let me say it is a match made in heaven. Kuljit is coming to meet you in an hour's time.'

Kulwinder stopped speaking expecting a gesture of appreciation or maybe some kind of a thank-you note. Simran stared at her, stone-faced. Kulwinder picked up her spiel.

'Shy, aren't we? That's perfectly understandable. So why don't you get ready? We will make the arrangements downstairs.'

Simran sat down heavily on the bed. She wondered about the outrage Aranjit had spoken about that comes after being subjected to pain. But she could feel nothing. The anger had still not touched her where it really mattered. Maybe it was slowly building up in her into something cataclysmic. She shuddered when she thought about it. In her present state she only felt deeply humiliated.

Kuljit was a six-foot, strapping Jat boy, dressed in a Calvin Klein T-shirt and matching jeans and Gucci shoes. He came to see the girl alone, without the family. His beard was closely trimmed and when Simran saw him she suspected that he did not keep the obligatory long hair, under the turban. He kept his eyes glued to the floor and answered in monosyllables. Harbaksh for Simran's benefit kept on repeating that the boy was an engineering graduate. It was a dialogue of the deaf and the dumb. Harbaksh became a little exasperated that the boy and the girl were not communicating with each other. He finally suggested they spend some time alone to talk things out.

The elders left the room and Kuljit finally looked at Simran. She looked at his face, his eyes and she knew. She found herself speaking a language she had never spoken before.

'You are an addict. Your eyes tell a story. What stuff do you chase?'

He did not look shocked. He was beyond that.

He replied to her question, 'Anything I can get hold of. But it's been ages since I got hold of some cocaine . . . the real stuff. You wouldn't be carrying some on you, would you?'

She realized at that instant there were people worse off than her in the world. Aranjit had been right—one could not deal with one's pain and grief by being a victim all the time. She steadily looked at him with curiosity.

'No, I don't do it—period. But that is not why your parents sent you to meet me. Tell me the real reason.'

He looked at her pathetically. Finally, he said it: 'I . . . well . . . they . . . sorry, all of us . . . thought if we could get married, for say a year, it would serve everyone's interest. You would have a cover story when you go back to Southall. The story could run along these lines: we got married in Punjab but because of the cultural clash the marriage did not work out. Our marriage would give you protection from people questioning your past, if there are any. In return you could help me get a permanent immigration status in the UK. After about a year when we are divorced no one will care to question you about your past. Both of us will move on, going our separate ways. That simply is the deal.'

He said that and he stared at the floor again.

She looked at him expressionlessly and then she whispered, 'Get out now and don't come back anywhere near me ever again.'

He got up quietly and left the room. She did not bother to tell her relatives the outcome of the meeting. She strode out into the courtyard, wheeled out the bike and cycled all the way to Aranjit's cottage.

It was a clear winter day and a sea of yellow mustard danced in the brilliant sunshine. She took the pebbled road to the cottage and saw Aranjit working on her farm with the shotgun slung across her back. The older woman without a greeting opened the wicker gate to let her come in. Aranjit wiped her sweat-drenched face with a scarf and beckoned Simran to follow her. They went uphill on the farmland till they came to a tool room which also housed the main pump.

'I was just about to let the water flow into the crop furrows,' Aranjit told Simran. 'It is a sight to watch. Come sit with me.'

Both women sat next to each other on the incline and Aranjit switched on the motor. Water surged in from the feeder canal and jets of water flowed into the channels from all sides, licking and satiating the parched earth and the crop. Simran dreamily looked at the water flow soaking the blistering earth. She dropped her head on Aranjit's shoulder and the older woman caressed her forehead with calming strokes. Simran felt as if she had pulled away from the world to some peaceful place somewhere else, for the first time in her life.

16

October 1983, road to Katra

The commander wiped the sweat beads gathering across Aranjit's forehead which helped her to focus. He took out his handkerchief and rolled it and dipped it in his water canteen and pressed the soaked cloth to Aranjit's dry, cracked lips.

'Do you need a drink?' he asked.

'No,' she responded.

'Is the finger getting numb?' he asked

'Not really,' she replied.

'What do you see?'

'I see light traffic on the road, mostly pilgrims, coming down after the darshan.'

'Good,' he said with finality. 'Stay focused.'

Aranjit's eye did not waver for even a second from the scope fitted on a bolt-action rifle. Aranjit had taken her position with her rifle on a steep, rocky overhang overlooking the road below meandering its way to the plains. The cross hairs of her rifle were locked on a spot on the road where it curved sharply in almost a U-turn. From that turn the road fell dramatically into a steep descent. It was a treacherous bend and that was the reason that spot had been chosen. It was late afternoon and the pilgrim traffic coming down from above the sacred Mata Vaishno Devi shrine had thinned down. Occasionally a truck or a bus crammed with devotees shouting 'Mata Rani ki Jai!' would pass by. All the trucks, buses and cars were fitted with the *dhwaja* (a red-coloured flag), fluttering in the light breeze.

Almost two hours ago the commander's team had infiltrated the area. The commander had personally supervised the operation. He left nothing to chance in Aranjit's first major operation. He had helped her to professionally assemble the various detachable, components of the rifle and begin the stake-out well in advance. They had selected an ideal location completely concealed from the road below. Aranjit held the rifle steadily in her grip; she had completely immobilized herself, save the rush of blood coursing through her trigger finger. Nothing else existed for her except for the bend in the road.

Even the most disciplined soldiers break routine, once in a while, to refocus on the task ahead. After lying completely immobilized for nearly two hours on the hilltop, Aranjit could feel that her body was cramping badly. The target area was still in sight but her mind had begun to wander. Why had they set up shop in a civilian area so early on? Was it really a high-value target? What really was going on?

All she knew was that the commander was not in the habit of sharing operational details. He would only confide on a need-to-know basis. She had her doubts whether anyone really was privy to what this man thought about or planned. His whisper broke through her reverie.

'What do you see?' he asked, perhaps for the millionth time since the stake-out had begun.

'Light pilgrim traffic . . . no, even that has died down,' she answered tiredly.

'Good, keep looking,' he said. 'Do you need a drink?' he asked as an afterthought. She did not respond. He knew she was at the end of her tether. She had been moonstruck with him. Now she was coming to grips with what life really was like with him in the raw. And he was nothing if not a field man. The commander did not ask her again if she was thirsty. He took initiative and inserted a straw into his water canteen. Without taking her permission he forced the straw between her parched lips.

'Take slow sips. The cramping will go away after a while.'

Half an hour later he asked again, 'What do you
see?'

'An empty road . . . nothing else.'

'Keep focusing,' he warned. 'Don't let your
emotions overwhelm you.'

Then as was his habit he asked, 'Do you want
something?'

She was quiet for a moment and then she said, 'I
made a mistake when we set out. I did not pee. My
bladder is full now. It is on the point of bursting. If
you permit me, I would like to pee in my pants.'

'No, that will not make you feel good about
yourself. You are so close to completing your mission.
If it's okay with you, I will help you with that.'

'Okay,' she said without hesitation.

He rummaged through his bag and brought out
a tin cup. He unbuckled her belt and slid down her
olive-grey trousers. Then he pulled down her panties
and stuck the tin cup near her slit. She gratefully
discharged her load. He pulled her pants up and
threw the urine behind a boulder. Then he came and
lay next to her.

'They are coming,' he whispered.

She saw through her scope a blue Matador van
come down the road. The dhwaja fluttered in the
breeze. A chill ran down her spine. It was not a high-
value target. She could see through the windscreen

of the Matador that the seats in the van were taken up by an ordinary family. There was an overweight husband and his wife who was presumably singing Mata bhajans joyously after a successful darshan. The front seats of the van were occupied by the aged parents of the couple, sleeping peacefully. The rear had been taken up by four young children, aged around ten to twelve years she guessed, all jumping up and down in a mock fight. Her blood ran cold when she saw all of them. The van was less than a hundred metres away from the target spot.

'I can't do this,' she whispered fiercely. 'These are innocents, children . . .'

'Yes, you will,' he said in a voice that demanded complete obedience. 'This is your test. Don't take your eye off the target.'

A scream was building up inside her and her forehead was drenched in sweat. The sweat began to trickle down to her eye, locked on the scope. It partly blurred her vision but this time the commander made no attempt to wipe the sweat drops. In less than a full second the moment when her life would change for ever came up in front of her. Her vision was blurry but her trigger finger was rock-steady. She had to decide and decide fast and she took a decision based on pure reflex. There was no time left to listen closely to the rebellion raging in her mind. She slowly applied pressure on the trigger, her eye not leaving the target spot even for a millisecond.

A shot rang out from above and suddenly the speeding Matador's front tyre ripped open and the driver, unable to control the van, crashed into the bend against the mountain face. Two men emerged from nowhere and began to rake the van with machine-gun fire—from the windscreen end and through the windows. It was all over for the family of eight and the driver in a matter of seconds. The mountain road resounded with slogans of 'Khalistan zindabad!' The doors of the van had caved in from the impact of the crash. The bodies were still huddled in the van, only the blood had seeped out and had begun to spread as a dark patch in the middle of the mountain road.

The two assailants disappeared into the mountain passes after throwing Khalistan leaflets across the road. Mission complete, the commander helped Aranjit to her feet and told her to look him in the eye. He held a moving finger before her eyes and told her to follow it. He then snapped his fingers and told her, 'You are getting your orientation back from an intense experience. You know parts of this road are sanitized with security personnel. We have less than one minute to make our getaway. Get moving.'

Aranjit, without a fumble, detached parts of the rifle and put them in a duffel bag. The commander in the meantime sanitized the spot of any clues pointing to them. They parted ways and took different routes to go down to Jammu and then board separate buses to Chandigarh. They had decided to spend the night in Chandigarh in a motel just in case the heat had been turned up in Amritsar.

Both checked into the motel as a couple, using aliases. As the commander completed the formalities downstairs, Aranjit left the reception and jabbed the elevator buttons to the second floor. She opened the door to their modest room and took off all her clothes in the middle of the room and rushed to the shower. She turned on the shower full blast and like a maddened woman she began to scrub herself violently with a bar of soap till the welts showed. Her body shuddered with deep cries and wailing and finally, completely exhausted, she sank in the middle of the shower, letting the water cascade drench her.

The commander then came up to the room and politely knocked a few times but Aranjit would not come out of the bathroom. He heard the sound of the shower and finally, he forcibly opened the door and despite her weak protests, he wrapped her in a towel and dragged her out. For the first time since she had known him he stood unsure in the middle of the room. Finally he picked up her clothes and put them on a chair. He selected another chair for himself at the far end of the room. He sat on it, crossed his legs and waited for her.

She wiped her face with her hands; the towel slid down and she lay completely naked on the bed. She did not care. She sat up on the bed and looked at him, her eyes swollen, her face seething.

'You are such a bastard! You made me butcher ten-year-olds today. You made sure that I would never again sleep peacefully in my bed for the rest of my life. I had not signed up for this, you coward! I had believed in our cause, which is a just cause. But cowards like you have . . .'

She began to choke on her words. She recovered and was full of spit again.

'Answer me! You made me do that entire song-and-dance routine for three hours as if I was going to shoot down a top general or a minister. All that for an ordinary family . . . for those young kids . . . Why are you silent, you coward? Speak up!'

The commander took his time to reply. Finally he got up and took off his turban and put it on the bedside table. Then he sat at the foot of the bed, close to her. She was horrified to see his scalp. It had very little hair on it but what stood exposed in the dim light of the room was a long scar running across the centre of his head. He looked at her as perhaps a Buddhist monk would look at a young disciple who questions the order. He answered her accusations with whatever little patience and energy he was left with.

'I am an ugly-looking man, a diminutive man.' He spoke as if talking to a child. 'Some say small men are devious—there could be truth in that. I wouldn't know. People like you will be the judge. Now, let us for a moment look at someone like you sitting naked on this bed. You are tall and lissom and beautiful. You are a truly desirable woman. So we are two physically very different people, bound by a common cause in the theatre of conflict.'

The commander, as was his habit, crossed his legs as he sat at the foot of the bed.

'Now let us, Harmit, look at another theatre of conflict. It is December 1971 and I am moving with my detachment through the streets and houses of Dacca. We have to win each and every street and each and every block in the city, infested with Pakistani soldiers. We do that mostly through hand-to-hand combat. But to gain an upper hand over the Pakistanis, I have requested both artillery and aircraft support. That is a standard tactic in street fighting. Our shelling and bombardment flatten out the Pakistani defences and it becomes easier to move in.'

The commander took a deep breath. Aranjit could not take her eyes off him. He betrayed very briefly the slightest of emotions.

'We swoop in on the Pakistanis along with the Mukti Bahini and we decimate them completely. We force the others to surrender. But another event has occurred before this happy turn of events. You see, Harmit, scores of innocents Bangladeshi men, women and little children have died in the shelling. We bring out their bodies from the bombed-out houses and they pile up to become a huge mound.'

The commander now leaned forward, looking at her intently. 'Harmit, a tank or an artillery shell does not discriminate between nationalities, soldiers and civilians. Whoever comes in the path dies or is maimed. That is what we mean by collateral damage. As soon as we cleared Dacca, I received a message from General Aurora congratulating me and my men. Do you believe that he was not aware that innocents had perished along with the Pakistanis? That is the price of war or for that matter of any conflict and I was being rewarded for it.

'But wait, there's more. I got my reward on my last day in that war theatre. A Bangladeshi woman crept up behind me undetected and stuck a knife in the centre of my head. I survived the attack. It was not a Pakistani who did it. It was a Bangladeshi woman—the same people we had set out to liberate. Later I learnt that woman's son lay in that mound in the city centre. He had been killed accidentally by artillery fire from our side.'

The commander lay down on the bed, completely spent. He looked up at the ceiling.

'Why have I told you all this? Wars, conflicts and freedom struggles are dirty business. They are not for the faint-hearted because they are carried out with cruel irony. There are no clear lines of morality in a conflict. You kill a child and a civilian along with many soldiers in a conflict and you get a medal. You kill a child and a civilian in peacetime, they will hang you. The biggest casualty in a war is our sense and proportion of justice. Some say the only thing that works in a conflict is getting the job done by whatever means.

'If you had any doubts about your role then you need to re-educate yourself. You are not an agitator. You are not a back-room girl, printing propaganda material. You are essentially a front-line natural-born killing machine. The only challenge for you lies not in your competence but in the acknowledgement that you are such a person. You see, Harmit, the thing with us humans is that we hate to acknowledge to ourselves who we really are. It is an old trick of the human mind. Keep pretending to be what you are not.

'And finally, why did I make you lie there for over three hours in wait for an ordinary target? Harmit, I deliberately chose an ordinary family as your first target because the emotions they would stir in you would not be ordinary. I made you lie there for three hours because your next test will not be on the road to Katra. It will probably be in a farmhouse or in a house in the city where you are surrounded by close to a hundred police and paramilitary forces. When that happens you will remember this day and event. Your eye and your trigger finger will never waver, even if the siege extends for days. You will then mercilessly eliminate your opponents.

'And now you are free to decide whether you want to continue with us or you want out. You are perhaps the only person I am prepared to give that option to.'

The commander stopped speaking and lay completely drained next to her.

In response, Aranjit got up and threw the bath towel on the floor. She came up to the foot of the bed and straddled the commander and unzipped his battle fatigues.

'You talk too much,' she whispered. 'Hold me and show me what you can do.'

17

Present day

Hardev's face was pressed against the wall in the position of a supplicant as he looked up at a portrait of Guru Nanak pinned on the wall. Tears were streaming down Hardev's face and he held his turban in his hands, which were folded. The devotee kept on repeating and crying, 'Sache Padshe! Why do they tear me away from you? I want to be so much with you. I want to serve you, do *kar seva* at the gurdwara, run the smallest and biggest of tasks in your honour and glory. Oh! My Sache Padsha, show me the light, create a way for me so that I can come in your service, that I can sit in the cool comfort of the gurdwara and listen to *shabad* kirtan and that I get immersed and swept away in your remembrance. Oh! My Lord! My sweet Lord, I want so much to be with you . . . so much to be with you . . . please make it happen . . .'

Hardev cried his heart out and at the entrance of his humble abode, his childhood friend Mangat Ram watched him, not interrupting his painful communion with his maker. After a while Hardev was spent and he turned away from the portrait, his mind and soul still searching for answers. He saw his friend near the door and he asked him to come in.

Mangat came in and put an affectionate arm around his friend.

'I feel for you, my friend. You are a pure soul. I see you in torment all the time. You are a man who works hard all day in the fields. When you come back there is nothing you would like better than to sit in the gurdwara and listen to shabad kirtan which cleanses the soul. I understand that but I also understand that those doors have been closed to our lot.'

'Don't say that, Mangat. How can the doors of Guru Nanak be closed to us? Such a thought is blasphemous.'

Mangat spoke, 'Guru Nanak was the most enlightened person of the millennium. He opened his arms to everyone; he showed the light to both Hindus and Muslims. He was a great pacifist and he preached tolerance and brotherly love. It is the greatest irony and cruelty that today we are denied the right to celebrate his teachings in the gurdwaras. Who are these pretenders who have appropriated their hold over the shrines and gurdwaras? They are people who have always trodden over the lower castes. They forget the secular and casteless message of Guru Nanak and discriminate in the very same gurdwaras that hundreds of years back had ushered in social and religious change.

'My friend, we cannot face up to them. Well, not as yet. We don't have their strength. Maybe one day we will. So why torture ourselves with what is not within our reach? I say we move on. We look for new gurus, new gods and new messiahs that are responsive to our needs and our aspirations. And there is one right next door. You must have heard of Baba Santokh Singh and his *dera*?'

Hardev wiped his tears away. 'Don't mislead me, Mangat. The man is a charlatan, are you comparing him with . . . ?'

'Says who?' questioned Mangat. 'My friend, lakhs from our caste have already joined him. His following swells every day. His message is simple and effective. He understands our needs; he knows where we come from. To join him, to follow his teachings, to bow before him, to give an offering in his durbar are acts of piety. He has words that will slake the aspirations of the parched soul. Give him a try. Save yourself the misery.'

'I don't know, Mangat. There are things I have heard about him that are deeply offensive.'

Mangat tightened his arm around his friend. 'My friend, we have one life to live. We did not choose the caste we were born in. But we are free to choose the God or man we want to worship. You are an important leader of people from your caste. Come with me to his darbar. You will be lionized by him. Trust me on this.'

18

Simran selected the lounge music section from a world music site on the desktop computer and put on an uninterrupted feed. Soft, lilting music filled the room and she hurried to the kitchen as the roast was almost done. She tested the golden-brown skin of the chicken with a knife and garnished it with spices, homemade butter and baby potatoes. She heard Aranjit come in through the back door, all sweaty from working in the fields.

'I'm going in for a bath,' she called out from the drawing room. 'There's a bottle of local wine in the drawer near the sink. I got it from the *theka* a long time back. It would go very well with your roast.'

'Yes, ma'am,' agreed Simran as she spiced up the cooked chicken with garnishing sauce. She took out the cutlery and began to stack up the plates and the quarter plates. She remembered the wine bottle and looked for it in the drawer below. Simran was not sure whether she should open it for a casual evening dinner. She took the wine bottle and went looking for Aranjit in her room. The latter had stepped into her bathroom for a shower. The door to her room and the bathroom were open. She saw Aranjit, completely naked in the shower. The shower faucet was an antiquated piece and many of the pores were choked with rust but the water flow was strong, courtesy of the pump that drove water into the fields. She was struck by the elder woman's well-toned body. Her body had the burnished, muscular tonality of someone used to working in the fields. The breasts were small but still firm and the nipples were hard and protruding. Her salt-and-pepper hair reached up to the small of her back. She had propped her right leg up against the sink. She was soaping the inside of her leg vigorously and her pubic hair glistened in a mask of soap and water beads.

Simran had a feeling that she was watching poetry in motion. She could have sat for hours and watched her bathe. Aranjit's face was like that of an ardent student—perhaps an older student with a weather-beaten face and fine, craggy lines, but nevertheless an intense student. It was the face of someone who had still not had its fill from the pool of knowledge and discovery.

Aranjit noticed her staring at her from the door and she smiled.

'Don't just stare, give me a helping hand,' she said. 'I can't reach the small of my back. Soap me up there, will you?'

Simran kept the wine bottle on the table and went into the bathroom and took the proffered soap bar. She gently soaped Aranjit's back and her eyes could not help but look at her crack, vanishing below, and the legs, which were bent just a little. There were no sounds in the bathroom save the occasional dripping of moisture from Aranjit's body on to the floor. Perhaps the quietness of the bathroom made her realize the absurdity of the situation. She hardly knew this woman. She found it remarkable that she had travelled such a long journey in such a short period of time. Aranjit thanked her and stood under the shower and opened it. A strong cascade of water descended and Aranjit vigorously rubbed off the soap and dirt from the fields.

Simran stood staring at her, her hands soaped up. She suddenly realized with a sense of shock that ever since she received her letter of appointment at the post office her life had changed completely. She had once resigned herself to leading the life of a recluse, comfortable in her introverted universe with maybe some poetry thrown in to colour her colourless existence.

But she was being led on by one shocking event after another. Like the explorers of the New World, she had a sense that she was standing outside the gateway to a new land, a new life, a new way of thinking. The thought of stepping into this new world terrified her. But she had made up her mind. After what had happened to her she was prepared to risk everything. From somewhere deep within her she sensed an utter wildness and ferocity that was straining at the leash to get out. She had made up her mind to listen to that voice.

Later both women ate the roast and drank the wine. Aranjit remarked, 'Best meal I have had in a long time. I could get used to this, you know.'

Simran murmured happily. She helped Aranjit clear the dishes and wash them in the sink. After they had tidied up the kitchen, the older woman invited her to lounge on the sofa with her. They lay on the two ends of the sofa and Aranjit pressed Simran's feet. The girl from Southall remarked, 'You could get used to my meals and I could get used to this kind of pampering. Ah! The press of your strong hands on my feet! It feels really good!' Both lay on the sofa, each content in their different ways, responding to each other, exploring the beginnings of a relationship that was uncertain, mysterious but full of possibilities. Simran, in a mood of languor, asked Aranjit, 'Tell me about yourself. You are such a mystery. I sometimes wish I was you. I feel like drawing from your strength.'

'You should choose your wishes carefully, young lady,' said the older woman without humour. There was a bit of an awkward silence after that. Then Aranjit explained, 'I have been on my own for a long time. I till the land, make a living from it. I could have been a research scientist but I ended up being a farmer. I was married for a short time and the only good that came out of that short-lived affair was that the man left me with some kind of an income. I built this place from that. I like living alone. I can only share my space with someone to a certain extent. Beyond a limit, I feel suffocated. I believe in the right to bear arms. I do believe we live in a very violent world. I don't trust any other man or woman to protect me. I take care of my own self. In my spare time I read a lot. I have no patience to watch television. That's it, then . . . that's me. As I was trying to tell you, there is nothing remarkable about me.'

Both women again drifted off into worlds they had created for themselves. Something bothered Simran. She questioned Aranjit, 'Where do I fit into all this?'

Aranjit held Simran's hand. She told her, 'I see a bit of me in you. Frankly, only for you, house rules don't apply. You can come and go whenever you feel like it.

You can come and stay as much as you like. There is always someone in life for whom we break the rules.'

*

Not far away from Aranjit's cottage, another man had thrown away his old rule book in the search for something new. Hardev looked around him in complete fascination, like a kid who walks into a candy store for the first time. He was in the centre of Baba Santokh Singh's realm in the nearby village of Pind Jhalan. Everything around him was bigger, bolder and hugely imposing. The Baba's estate was a sprawling six-storey building made of white marble; it stretched for acres on rural farmland. The dome and latticed windows and huge ornate doors were an eclectic mix of the finest of Sikh and Persian architecture, amalgamated with pleasing lines and contours. The sprawling estate was called 'Baba Niwas' and it was designed as a half pentagon; the centre was taken up by huge estate grounds that could take tens of thousands of the faithful for the Baba's darshan. The grounds were lined on both sides with giant screens which disseminated the Baba's message. At any given point in time there was provision for water tankers and a community kitchen to feed and slake the thirst of the thousands that came in for darshan.

It was close to five in the evening and the faithful had started to stream in for the evening darshan. Hardev watched in fascination as hundreds came on foot, on tractor trolleys, cycles, cars, scooters, even bullock carts. Everyone was dressed in white—a symbol of purity. The grounds were abuzz with excitement and a strange kind of fervour had gripped the masses. The giant screens flickered to life and the cameras panned across the stage as the Baba walked in. A deafening roar went up in the crowd.

The Baba wore a long tunic and an expensive satin cape. He wore various necklaces embellished with pure diamonds and rubies. He had a flowing salt-and-pepper beard and sported a peacock-feathered silk turban, bedecked with emeralds and pearls. As Baba strode to the centre of the stage and held his hands up in the posture of a rock star, the crowds went delirious.

Chants of 'Baba! Baba! Baba!' rose in the sky. Someone passed a mike to the Baba and the Baba, to Hardev's complete surprise, began his address with greetings in Punjabi, Hindi and English and then he began to croon a song!

Hardev was stunned. The Baba sang a catchy tune addressed to the youth. The song was a Punjabi–Hindi mix based on an old seventies' pop song. The crowds danced and joined in, with the Baba belting out his unique message of didacticism and entertainment.

And then came the moment that Hardev would never forget for the rest of his life. The song was over, the cheering and whistling had subsided and Hardev could not believe his eyes when he saw his face being shown on the giant screens. He shivered and looked around and noticed that everyone was staring at him. His friend Mangat Ram had also stepped away from him and was smiling as if he had been privy to a great secret. Then the Baba's voice came through, clear and strong.

'My brothers and sisters, today we welcome amidst us a brother who took his time in coming to us but now has joined us with full fervour and dedication. He is a man who is hard-working, an honest farmer with a pure soul. He is also a great leader of all men and women of his caste in the village of Kasba Chardi Kala. They all look up to him for guidance and direction. Dear brothers and sisters, it gives me great pleasure to welcome into our fold Hardev, who along with his followers is joining us today. Brothers and sisters, I give you Hardev!'

Hardev never knew when hundreds rushed towards him and lifted him up and carried him through a sea of screaming and cheering faces to the stage in the welcoming arms of Baba Santokh Singh. The giant screens then flickered with shots of hundreds dancing in ecstasy and the Baba embracing a bewildered Hardev on stage.

19

Both women lay on a charpoy under the midday sun, dupattas draped over their heads. They sipped *kanji*, a fermented drink made from black carrots. A cold wind had blown across the field till almost noontime but now all was still and the temperatures were steadily rising. Aranjit's dupatta half covered her face and also her constant companion—her sawed-off shotgun. Simran finished her drink and snuggled up to Aranjit. The older woman stroked her forehead but a part of her vision was glued to the wicker gate leading into her cultivated fields. Simran opened her eyes under the vast blue canvas that stretched interminably above and said to Aranjit, 'My life had taken a strange turn, Anu. I was lost to this world. It held no interest for me. But here, thousands of miles away from home, my wounded soul has begun to heal again. I feel so cut off from the life I have led so far. Tell me, will this last or is it my soul clutching at straws?'

Aranjit did not reply at first. She lifted her shotgun and trained the weapon at the wicker gate and searched for any intrusion from outside.

Then she put it down and spoke, 'Simran, even in this dusty, forgotten Xanadu, real mortal danger exists. The mind always seeks conclaves of exclusion and peace. But the real world cannot be denied. It is closer than we think and it is always deadly and violent. The answer to your question is that you can enjoy these moments of bliss. But they are interruptions rather than a continuation of life's violent script.'

'So I will never be allowed to forget the violence heaped on me?'

'And why would you want to forget it? Do you want to accept your gang rape and move on? Forgive, forget your perpetrators? Seek excuses for them? Your personal outrage should be like a hot ember, always sizzling in the deepest recesses of your mind. When your spirits start flagging and your will is lost, the memory of that outrage will help you pull back. It will give you a reason to exist.'

Simran shivered in the hot sun.

'Sometimes I feel,' she said, 'that I don't really know you. But then I can't hold back from meeting you.'

'The truth shall set all of us free, Simran,' replied Aranjit, 'but unfortunately the truth takes a long time coming out.' She then playfully smacked Simran on her buttocks. 'But till the time that great event happens, your education continues. Enough wallowing under the sun like buffaloes! Grab a change. We are going to the next village.'

'For what?' asked Simran in genuine surprise.

'To see what Baba Santokh Singh is up to! Something is in the air. It's time you knew what goes on in utopia!'

The two women, dressed in pastel and off-white kurtis and churidars, wearing Ray-Bans, headed for Pind Jhalan on an Enfield motorcycle. Crowds were already thronging the estate grounds. A black rain-filled cloud had come up from nowhere and it covered the sky end to end. Lightning rumbled across the sky but it did not affect the enthusiasm of the streaming crowds. The entire area had become a confused sea of impatient disciples and honking vehicles with headlights switched on in the gloom. The Baba's volunteers grappled with the crowds till they finally persuaded everyone to sit on the estate grounds. Ever since that morning, rumours that the Baba would make a momentous announcement in today's meet were doing the rounds. The mood of the assembled crowd was sombre: it was in sharp contrast to the upsurge of gaiety that had prevailed over the estate grounds a couple of days ago. More lightning rumbled across the sky. In the distance a dust storm slowly picked up speed, funnelling up in a frenzy. But the crowds squatting on the estate grounds were oblivious to what was coming their way.

The crowds tensed up as the Baba walked on to the stage. His walk was purposeful and the levity of the previous days was missing. The diamonds and rubies had also disappeared and his rustic tunic conveyed the impression that he was in mourning. Armed sentries flanked him on the stage. Everyone knew that today's address would be significant. Complete silence pervaded the estate grounds. For a moment it seemed as if even the approaching dust storm had paused in its path. The air was shot with expectation. The Baba slowly and with the appearance of great sorrow climbed the podium and tinkered with the array of mikes placed before him. He then looked at his flock intently and began his address slowly but forcefully.

'My dear brothers and sisters, I speak today in front of you but my heart is full. Deep sadness fills me. I will tell you what disturbs me no end. But first I seek your permission to make a slight departure from the evening routine. We always begin the evening address with a thanksgiving prayer to the Almighty. But today I have kept our daily prayer to him on hold. We will pay homage to him at the end of my speech when hopefully all of you and I are in a better state of mind.

'No, no, my brothers and sisters . . . I am not angry with him, I have not lost faith in him, I am not in a sulk against him. After all, how can I turn my back on him? I am his chosen one, he has entrusted me with the task of showing you the light, and he has vested his wisdom and faith in me.

'Ever since the day he came in my dreams and entrusted me with the responsibility of leading the poor, the down-trodden, the oppressed castes, I, my dear brothers and sisters, have been on the job. I abjured the fruits and joys of married life, embraced *brahmacharya* and plunged headlong into the task of bringing hope and succour to the oppressed. It has been an eventful journey. We have together covered a great deal of distance, even walked the extra mile. And the results have been there for all to see. I have banded together the oppressed castes, given them a voice. I have given you an identity, I have made you believe in your own selves. Today, all of you have come closer to the seat of power and glory than at any other point in your lives. I have, my brothers and sisters, closed the gap of inequality and deprivation that had plagued us for centuries in a remarkably short time.'

The Baba paused and sipped some water. He then spoke and changed course dramatically. He now thundered like a demagogue. 'But dear brothers and sisters, there are forces out there who have not accepted the great change that has come in your lives! They sneer at us, they vilify us, they use the media packed with upper castes to run us down, they mock us! They threaten me with lawsuits, they accuse me of imaginary financial and personal crimes, they send emissaries to me, warning me to downscale this vast movement or else that they will throw me in jail! Not a day passes when they do not threaten me, not a day passes when my peace is not shattered and not a day passes when I am not made to feel that a violent death lurks somewhere around me.

'Brothers and sisters, do we suffer all this because we were not born of a high caste? Do we suffer all this because they cannot tolerate the huge progress we have made in our social and economic well-being in such a short time? Do we suffer all this because we have thrown off the yoke of the upper castes and chosen to elect our own leaders and take our own decisions?

'Tell me, brothers and sisters, is this fair? Is this just? Do we have to take this lying down?'

A roar of disapproval swept through the crowd. Chants of 'No! No! No!' built up to a deafening roar and in matching response, Baba Santokh Singh's voice rose, challenging and provoking his followers.

'Brothers and sisters, you have given me the answer to the questions that haunt me. Your support raises my spirits and gives me the will to wage this war to the very bitter end. And make no mistake about it, brothers, this a bitter battle to the very end. This morning I received reports that our dera in Fardikot was burned down by the upper castes and two of our *sevaks* perished in the fire. But you will be more shocked to know that the state government has dismissed our accusations as absurd! They say the fire was the result of an electrical malfunction. The deaths of our brothers there have been dismissed as a "freak accident".'

Howls of disapproval swept through the crowd. A large number of women began to wail at the announcement. Cries of 'Shame! Shame! Shame!' broke out and the younger lot shouted slogans against the chief minister of the state. The charged emotions of the crowd built up to a frenzy and then Baba Santokh Singh plucked a mike from the row in front of him and jumped down from the podium. There was a spring and purpose in his step as he strode to the centre of the stage. The crowd rose to their feet in anticipation of the dramatic announcement. Baba Santokh Singh looked charged, intense and, in the position of a rock star, he began to goad his flock.

'Are you with me? Are you prepared to go to battle? Are you ready to sacrifice? Are you ready to stand up to your oppressors?!'

The crowd went wild with the challenge and now

cries of 'Yes! Yes! Yes! Baba!' built up to a crescendo. Everyone joined hands and a Mexican wave surged through the crowds with a united roar of 'Yes Baba!'

And then in another dramatic flourish, Baba Santokh Singh asked the crowd to be still, keep quiet and listen carefully. The Baba now looked like an intoxicated rock star on stage. His hands were raised to the heavens. A security guard held a mike close to him for the dramatic announcement. From behind him the banshee noise of an approaching dust storm grew in intensity. The sky had blackened completely and the Baba looked unreal against the powerful halogen lights that lit up the stage.

The Baba spoke, 'There is no justice for us in this state. We know it! We know it! We have known it for a long time! They do not want us, they oppress us and they deny us! If we stay like this we will always be on the margins, cut off from the mainstream. The world as we know it has changed. The forces of oppression are being swept away before the politics of identity. We also have an identity. We also seek our own oasis of peace. The way forward has already been shown to us by our brothers in Telangana. Why should we be denied? It is time to leave the old and step into the new. From this stage I give the call today, my brothers and sisters, that we will create a separate *suba*, a state within this state, for only the lower castes. That is our right and we will not be denied. If necessary we will fight to the end . . .'

The vicious dust storm struck the Baba Niwas and the estate grounds with horrific intensity at that precise moment.

20

The path of the dust storm covered the entire estate grounds but its core spun around the scaffolding near the stage. It tore into the scaffolding's steel grid, a shower of sparks erupted and a column came crashing down. There was a loud noise and all the lights went out. The emergency lights came on but not before the speed of the dust storm ripped apart the tungsten lights from the scaffolding. The sheer power of the tempest flung the lights around like misdirected missiles. There were screams all around as the lights crashed on to the stage and careened into the panic-stricken crowds. The sharp-edged fresnels covering the lights came off and flew like lethal blades in all directions. Several people were wounded; there was guttural screaming all around. The Baba was saved by his posse of security guards who formed a wall around him and dragged him to safety below the erected stage.

Choking dust swirled and filled the estate grounds. This was followed by a sharp crack in the sky and the rain began to come down in sheets. People scrambled for safety and the grounds soon became a mess of fleeing people, empty mineral water bottles and discarded footwear. Most of the people ran for safety towards the sprawling community kitchen complex built adjacent to the Baba Niwas.

The arc of the dust storm spared Simran and Aranjit as both women fled towards the rear side of the dera, to the settlement which lay at the opposite end of the community kitchen. Not many dared to come to this end because the area was out of bounds for everyone. It was ringed with a barbed-wire fence and armed sentries constantly guarded it.

Both women flung themselves into a kind of enclave covered with a giant awning. The wind speed was incredible and the fury of the storm was uprooting and destroying everything that came in its path. The fence had been uprooted and flung a mile away and the guards had disappeared. The ends of the awning drooped to the ground in an inverted V and the two women scrambled to the deepest corners of the enclosure to escape the battering of the storm.

They held each other for comfort and from a distance they saw people fleeing for their lives. The storm triggered off a memory in Simran. She was once again caught in a vortex of fury which had risen from nowhere. In a flash she understood what Aranjit had told her some time back. Her personal ordeal could never really slip out of her consciousness. It had become a part of her being; she could not run or hide from it. She could, however, harness its violent energy to shape a future for her own self and in that moment she decided to do so.

Aranjit, on the other hand, had more practical things on her mind. From her secure corner she saw a man come out of the odd-looking tower built between the rear end and the building facade. She saw the man run desperately towards the tree cover next to the uprooted fence. Aranjit smiled at the opportunity that had presented itself before her. She knew the man had abandoned his post on the sixth floor of the tower because the fury of the storm would have been at its worst at that height. She turned to Simran, her face flushed with excitement.

'A man has left his watch in the tower. I need to go up there right now.'

'Why? What's so important about the place? Should we be risking our lives for that?'

'The tower is like the head of this animal spread out all around you. It houses the master control room for all audio–visual activity in the dera. It's like an all-powerful eye that looks into each and every activity on the dera premises.'

'How do you know that?'

'I have my sources, Simran. There's a lot you don't know about me.'

'What do you hope to find there?'

'I can't say but I have my suspicion about what I will find there. You don't have to come with me and take this risk. I will meet you here again in a short time.'

'That is simply out of the question.'

Both women emerged from their hiding place and made a run for the tower. The wind shear cut into them like a knife but the arc of the storm had moved away and they only suffered the casualty of being drenched by the downpour by the time they reached the tower.

The elevator would only function with an elevator key and fortunately for them the lone technician who had fled in panic had forgotten the key in the console slot. Aranjit jabbed at the elevator button and the doors slid open.

'Our lucky day!' said Aranjit and they stepped in; she turned the elevator key and the elevator shot up. The doors opened to the sixth floor and they walked to an empty glass cabin smashed to smithereens. Chairs and furniture were upturned and some more hardware damage in the form of splintered computer screens lay scattered about the room. But almost miraculously the control board of the master control room (MCR) and the embedded screens looking into the facilities within the dera had survived the dust storm.

Aranjit knew what she was looking for. She held the toggle switch and pressed a number of switches that operated the robotic cameras installed in each and every room below in the basement. The screens flickered with life and when the first images flashed on the screens Aranjit raised her fist in the air and exclaimed, 'Yes, I knew it! I knew that he was a bastard! Look at this, Simran! This is what I had come looking for!'

The embedded screens showed naked women, mostly white women, walking, sitting in their rooms with terrified expressions on their faces. Most of the girls were quite young and there were even some underage children sitting in the corners, looking completely lost. Aranjit looked closely at their eyes. They were all red-rimmed. Their mouths were open with surprise, their cavity-filled teeth clearly visible. Aranjit saw the needle marks on their skinny forearms. Many stood huddled, shivering in corners.

Aranjit took her cell phone and took rapid snaps. Simran stood watching in shock at the scenes in front of her so when Aranjit said, 'Let's go!' she didn't move. Aranjit quickly closed the system and pushed Simran out of the room. She jabbed at the elevator buttons and the doors opened for them. They stepped into the elevator would take them down.

'I found what I was looking for,' she told Simran. 'Keep your mouth shut about what you have seen here today. These are very dangerous people. They will not hesitate to eliminate anyone who gets in their way. I will find a way to deal with all this.' Simran nodded mechanically.

The intensity of the storm had died down when they came out of the tower. Near the uprooted fence they ran into a familiar face.

'Hardev!' Aranjit could not hide the surprise in her voice. 'What are you doing here?'

The usually self-deprecating Hardev looked at her calmly.

'That's a question I should be asking you, Aranjit. I am with my own out here. You are not. What are you doing here?'

Aranjit through the corner of her eye noticed some movement. The dust storm had flattened out by then and even the freak thunder shower that had followed it had weakened to a drizzle. People had started to come out from the community kitchen, hopeful that the worst was over. Time was running out for her and Simran. Anything could happen to them if they were caught near the tower area. She made a last-ditch effort with Hardev. She caught him by the wrist.

'It does not matter whether I belong here or not. You are a good person, Hardev. This place is a den of sin. It will suck you in. Come with us back to the village. You might not have seen the things I have seen here today. You belong with us in the village. Don't let anyone else tell you otherwise.'

There was complete contempt on Hardev's face. He shrugged off her appeals.

'That same village of yours has shown me my place. I respect you, Aranjit—you are a hard-working woman and you live by your own rules. But at the end of the day you are a Jat—you are one of them. There is a divide staring us in the face. We cannot run away from it. I have only chosen to go to the side I should have crossed to long ago. The village granthi and the elders in your village cured me of my delusions. Goodbye, Aranjit. I will see you on the other side.'

And having said what he wanted to say, Hardev ran away to join the stream of people coming out of the community kitchen. For a moment, Aranjit was struck with what Hardev had told her. She was transported back in time. She had heard the same arguments a long time ago. Even at that time a cleavage had split the two major communities in the state. The decimation of identity and the contradictions within had not stopped after rivers of blood had run their course through the state. The insidious process of splintering was still continuing. Only the identities and the aspirations had changed.

Aranjit shook the thought out of her head. She caught hold of Simran's hand and they ran past the uprooted fence, through the tree cover to the parking lot. A lot of smashed transport lay strewn around. They eventually found the Royal Enfield—the headlight was broken but it looked good for the road. Aranjit kick-started the bike and Simran rode pillion and soon the Enfield streaked across the rubble and destruction and to the open fields.

Simran held Aranjit from behind and as soon as they hit the open road she questioned her strange friend.

She shouted over the deep roar of the Enfield engine to make herself heard: 'We took a big risk going up the tower. I can understand that there is something really evil going on in the dera. But I don't understand your role in all this. Forget your role in all this, I don't think I have even got your measure. I feel so connected to you and yet there are times when you scare me because you are such a mystery.'

Aranjit responded with complete silence. Simran debated whether she should let it pass. But her complete unease with her older friend was beginning to peak. She shouted some more over the din of the running engine, 'Don't pretend you can't hear me. I asked you a question but it seems you don't want to answer me. This really troubles me, Aranjit.'

Aranjit then responded to her charge, 'Do you know yourself?'

'I am trying to'

'If that's good enough for you then understand that there is a part of me I don't want to talk about. Sometimes I don't even admit that part to myself.'

'Is that supposed to satisfy me?'

Aranjit kept quiet. Then she said as she took the motorcycle deep through a path in the fields known only to her, 'Simran, you are the only person in the world I would even care to give an explanation to. That should tell you a story. My past is irrelevant and what I might do tomorrow should not prejudice what we share in the present. What you see of this day is what you get.'

Aranjit drove the motorcycle with one hand and stretched her other hand in the air.

'Hold my hand,' she said. 'Tell me you feel for me. That is the only truth I really care for.'

Simran breathed deep and unevenly. She looked at the hand held in the air waiting for her touch, for a sign. She felt a deep sadness engulf her. She thought of the pain of utter loneliness that struck people when they least expect it. A lifetime spent waiting without hope for someone to love you. She then knew that there were worse things in life than the violence inflicted by nature and man. She reached for Aranjit's outstretched hand, held it and lightly kissed it. They rode across the fields, connected and yet severed from each other.

21

Aranjit came home one winter night from an AISSF meeting to find her father sprawled on the floor. The stuff of her nightmares had finally come true and she was seeing it. She knelt down, controlling her panic, and rested her father's head in her lap. She felt his weak pulse. She stroked his forehead. Maybe there was a chance.

The commander was conducting an operation deep in the interiors and she could not bring herself to ask him or anyone else for help. The discipline the commander had inculcated in her tested her now. She controlled her tears and made her father as comfortable as she could and ran downstairs. She hailed an autorickshaw and the driver and she together lifted Gurmukh Singh and carried him downstairs. They sped through the crowded streets and she fought the slow-growing realization that soon she could be left completely alone.

They arrived at the ICU of the government hospital and she ran inside and spoke to the duty doctor. The bored-looking doctor counting the last few minutes of his shift told her that the rooms were full and a doctor would attend to her father in the next shift—which was early next morning.

'But he won't survive till then!' she exploded between sobs and anger. 'Get someone to look at him, please?'

The doctor shrugged his shoulders. 'Look, I want to help. But the ward is crawling with patients. All the senior doctors have gone home. What can I do? My help would be like giving aspirin to a dying man. Is that what you want for your father?' The doctor shook his head and proceeded to tick some entries in a ledger.

Aranjit felt her mouth go dry with helplessness and despair. She could not allow her father to go in such a way. Not like this. She felt at that moment the complete impotence of her radical ideology. It could kill hundreds of innocents but it could not save a life. She knew she was failing completely and it was not some state conspiracy that was bringing her down. It was the lethal power of ordinary day-to-day situations that had exposed her powerlessness. She began to sob and looked wildly around her in complete panic. The doctors, nurses, ward boys, all of them moved up and down, completely ignorant of the girl who was close to losing her father.

The autorickshaw driver had collected his fare but on second thoughts he went back to her.

'Sister,' he said, 'I will look for a stretcher. There should one in the mortuary nearby. We could wheel your father in and maybe plead with some doctor to take a look at him.'

She could not find any words of gratitude to say to the driver. The driver delivered as promised and got her a stretcher on wheels. The stretcher was covered with a sheet stained with a patient's dried blood, someone who had perhaps died a couple of hours ago. She thanked the driver, who left after his timely intervention. She quickly wheeled the stretcher towards the cabin of a senior consulting doctor near the ward area. The room attendant tried to stop her but she brushed past him and crashed the stretcher into the cabin. The senior doctor with bags under his eyes shouted at her but she went down on her knees and implored him.

'Please doctor, just look at him. He's probably had a stroke. I have a PhD in molecular biology. Please, as a person of science to another, I beg you. Look at my father. Maybe he can be saved. I know I am out of turn.'

The call to a larger world of science did the trick because the senior doctor looked mollified.

'Okay,' he said wearily and got up. 'I will take a look. Wheel him into the room next to this cabin.' She wiped her tears and got up and it was then that he saw her clearly in the light. He looked at her and frowned. He stood for a moment, oddly staring at her.

He asked her, 'What's your name?'

She hesitated just a bit before she said, 'H . . . Harmit. Harmit Kaur . . .'

The doctor continued to stare at her, and then he recovered and seemed businesslike. He helped wheel her father into the next room and she gratefully thanked him. He nodded and told her, 'You stay right here. I will make some arrangements. We will get the situation under control, I promise you that. I am closing the door from outside. You know how it is in these hospitals. Other patients create a ruckus if someone jumps a queue. There's water next to the table. Calm down. I will join you shortly.'

She stood in the position of a supplicant as he left her and closed the door from outside. She moistened her dupatta with water drops and pressed it against her father's cracked lips and sweaty forehead. She stroked his white mane tied in a knot and anxiously looked at the door, waiting for the doctor to turn up.

'It will be all right, Pitaji. Hold the line for me. I will pull you out of this.'

She said that again and again, more to reassure herself. The minutes ticked past. She looked at the door. And then it struck her like a body blow. How could she have ignored it! The doctor had instantly recognized her from her sketch circulated by the police to all police stations and hospitals. Ever since the Katra incident the police had spread their dragnet far and wide looking for a highly motivated, tall, striking-looking female terrorist.

She thought about her situation. The bastard doctor had in all probability alerted the police by now. Her tears dried up. Her training took over. She quietly walked across to the door. It was locked from outside. She walked to the far end of the room. She lifted the slats and looked out. She was not wrong in her estimation. Police jeeps filled the compound outside. Outpatients and other hospital staff were being herded away quickly from the line of fire. She looked around the room for possible weapons. She opened a shelf and found the requisite tools for a surgery lying in an enamel box. She selected a scalpel. She remembered what the commander had told her once. Her next encounter would be in a place where she would be heavily outnumbered. That day had arrived. Her fear gave way to experiencing the thrill of the encounter facing her. All her training and skills would be put to the severest test today. In a strange way she welcomed it. She was ready for them.

She walked up to her father and allowed herself a brief final moment to look at him with wonder and pride. She had always been so proud of him. He had a leonine head and was staggeringly handsome. Ever since she was a child, when he would drop her daily to school, all the female teachers would devise some excuse or the other to talk to him. He was the kindest father one could have ever asked for in this world. He had given her the most precious gift that any young girl ever hoped to have—a free and happy childhood.

Now he was lying helpless in her arms and she marvelled at herself, at how she could prevent the tears from falling when she looked at him one last time. He looked so peaceful and handsome lying with his white mane on the stretcher. She knelt down and kissed him on the forehead one last time.

'I will always be your girl, Pitaji, always. And that is a promise.'

A single tear rolled down her eye.

'And now you need to sleep, Pitaji. Sleep away all your worries and cares.'

She brought up the pillow lying on the bed and she put it on his face. She closed her eyes and then strongly pressed the pillow down on his face. There was no struggle but when she opened her eyes she saw his hand tremble a last time and then it became still. She removed the pillow from his face. She could have sworn that he lay on the bed, eyes open, smiling peacefully.

Aranjit looked up and with a deep sigh she uttered, '*Sache Padshe, sarbat da bhala, shanti baksh! Shanti baksh!*' (Oh, my Lord! May peace descend on all of us, give us peace!)

There was a slight knock at the door. She knew what it meant. The expression on her face changed and then ossified. She wielded the scalpel in the subterfuge posture of a combatant. She opened the top two buttons of her kurta and crept near the door. It opened just a crack. She saw the shining, sweaty face of the senior doctor, smiling at her. He eyed her cleavage. He looked at it as he said, 'I have made all the arrangements. I am coming in.'

'Do please,' she murmured.

The crack opened some more and his face looked in. There was a flash before his eyes and he felt a slight prick against his throat. Aranjit moved swiftly and brilliantly and an entire army of police personnel, armed with assault weapons, were stunned when they saw the venerable doctor turn his terrified face towards them, a scalpel pressed against his throat, the state's most dreaded female terrorist holding it there from behind.

Aranjit murmured into the doctor's ear, 'Dear doctor, you should not have looked at my cleavage. It took your eyes away from the scalpel which at that moment pricked your jugular. You have begun to slowly bleed. If we do not hurry out of this compound you will die a very quick, painful death. You know the power of this scalpel. You cut human beings with it in your dissection class. I also cut my fair share of frogs. Get moving, dear doctor.'

She stepped out into the corridor with the doctor. The passage was choked with Punjab police commandos, all of whom had trained their assault weapons on her head. She balled up her left hand and slid it into the pocket of the doctor's white coat.

'So listen up, everyone,' she said with great emphasis, pushing the doctor ahead of her. 'I know you will not hesitate to shoot me and this doctor. If you do that I will pull the pin of the grenade I have in my left hand. I swear to you that I will take more than half of you down in the passage along with me.'

She stopped the intervention they had planned as she effectively planted the seed of doubt in their minds. Then she deliberately screamed at the top of her voice as she pressed at the advantage.

'You fuckers! I have just killed my father in that room to prevent him from being taken hostage. I know all about your brutal methods. But you know shit about me! If you don't fuck off from this passage now and give me safe passage, I will litter the walls with your brains and intestines! Don't push me to do that! Get the fuck out of my way!'

The young patka-wearing strike team leader lowered his weapon by an inch. He was not sure whether she was telling the truth. But her reputation preceded her. It was rumoured that she could blow a man's head off from an impossible distance. For her, anything was possible. He could not put his entire team in jeopardy.

He quietly instructed his team, 'Back away.'

The strike team broke up into two sections against the wall on both sides of the passage. She thumped the doctor swaying unsteadily on his feet and forced him out to the compound outside. A hundred policemen watched in complete frustration as she emerged and commandeered an empty police jeep, with the doctor in tow. The doctor was completely dizzy by now and as soon as she had taken control of the vehicle she let the scalpel do the talking. She sliced the doctor's throat clean and a blood shower erupted in front of the jeep. The sheer horror of the decapitation slowed the response of the strike team by a couple of seconds. That probably saved her. She turned the ignition and backed the jeep out of the compound at great speed before the team leader gave the order to rake the vehicle with machine-gun fire.

She swung the jeep in figures of eight as machine-gun fire peppered the jeep from the back. Entire belts of ammunition were emptied into the speeding jeep but she, for the moment, had escaped the dragnet spread outside the hospital. It was a different matter altogether whether she could remain on the run for long and survive the night of the long knives.

22

Present day, Goa

The locals had got used to him by now. One fine day, he had landed in their sleepy little village from nowhere. He had stayed on and had become a part of the swaying palms, the little whitewashed churches spread across the coastline, the sequestered backwaters, even the green chequered keelback snake found in the waterways. He would surface around noon and sightings of him could be made at the shack in Salegaon which went by the somewhat lyrical name of 'Cantare'. A careful observer could see him downing his toxicity for the morning and that would be four large vodka shots. Food is incidental with this kind of a diet but on the occasions he felt like eating he would order Bombil fried fish and clams.

An intake of vodka would set him in the mood and he would gun his battered motorcycle to speed across the old Airport road, next to the sea, and head for the domestic airport. It was rumoured that he would stand waiting outside the arrival lounge, sometimes for hours, for a passenger who had died in her sleep many months ago. He would return disappointed from the no-show and he would head back to his one-room apartment in Salegaon in Casa Medici, which he had bought from a local landlord some time back. The intriguing days spent by the man from nowhere were definitely of interest to some of the locals. They had come to know the man—that is, on the rare occasions that he chose to speak—as a kind-hearted and generous person. With their years of experience the locals knew that the stranger was well provided for. He was at a loose end but he was not a budget visitor like the many foreigners who thronged the picturesque village of Salegaon.

Besides the locals, the other non-resident locals, especially members of the Russian mafia and ex–Israeli armed forces personnel, also took an interest in the man. The non-residents had acquired property through an old organized racket in Goa in which a local fronted a company that was actually owned by these illegals. The company would give the non-residents an excuse to stay put in Goa and continue their drug trade. Some of these mafiosi had eyed the stranger warily. They did not want their operations disrupted due to any kind of threat. So they had decided to confront the stranger. They sent an Israeli hatchet man to look the stranger up at Cantare at a time in the afternoon when the stranger was downing his vodkas.

The Israeli selected a table next to where the stranger sat drinking. The Israeli leaned forward on his table in such a way that he crossed the stranger's line of sight. The stranger would have no choice but be obliged to look at him, especially at the shoulder strap under the off-white linen shirt housing a Jericho 941 semi-automatic pistol. If the weapon was meant to intimidate the stranger then the man's reaction reflected anything but intimidation. The stranger leisurely finished his fourth drink and leaned back on the chair and crossed his arms behind his head as if he was taking a siesta. The Israeli's blood ran cold when he looked closely at the lean, muscular crossed arms. The tattoo of the Indian Special Forces coat of arms, like that of an elite bloodline of a privileged class, was on display on the upper forearm of the stranger. It took no less than an ex-Isayeret officer to spot one of his own kind in a forgotten bar-cum-eatery in Goa. The Israeli got up quietly, paid his bill and walked out of the eatery.

The combined mafiosi got curious about the presence of an Indian Special Forces officer amongst them in Goa. They made discreet inquiries through their contacts in Delhi. Finally, when they received enough information to create a snapshot of the stranger, the effect on them was like that of a fearful man shaking in his boots. The stranger was none other than Suvir Suri, the most celebrated counter-insurgency officer in the annals of the Indian armed forces. The man, on at least two occasions, had saved the country from a nuclear attack, and had also prevented the destruction of large parts of Delhi in a major terrorist attack from elements embedded deep within the Pakistani civilian and military establishment.

Much of what they learned about Suvir Suri was in any case out in the public domain because the man had given up active duty a long time ago. It was rumoured that he had lost interest in everything around him because of a series of personal tragedies he had suffered over the years. Perhaps he was now part of a small band of individuals who turn up in Goa, seeking answers where none exist. Perhaps the man was a burnt-out case, seeking to escape his own legend, to a time and place where nothing else mattered. It was best to leave such men alone. The mafiosi decided to turn their gaze away from him.

Suvir Suri arrived later than usual in the evening to his pad, from his afternoon vigil at the airport. Night had fallen and the old magic of Goa had still not lost its shine. Anything and everything seemed to be within reach and attainable. It was just so humid that it could make a man thirsty for a drink. The backwaters looked settled and eternal, the shacks along the waterways were seductively lit with their strings of fairy lights and the night air was suffused with desire. The ghosts of girlfriends past were in communion with him this night and it awakened memory and longing. Somewhere in the distance a band struck up. His ears were tingling with the imaginary sounds of wine bottles and beer bottles being uncorked and opened. He could smell and hear the gush of spirits and froth escaping glass and after a long time it felt good to be alive. He looked at himself in the mirror under the yellow light. The soldier had disappeared and the mirror reflected a man struggling to find a reason to live and carry on. He now wore his hair long and the seven o'clock shadow on his lean, handsome face defined him as did the slow greying of the sideburns and the fine lines that were coming up near the eyes.

In another lifetime, he would have laughed it off and said that he was ageing gracefully. Now he did not care. He rubbed the bristles on his chin and on impulse he went to the washroom and began to shave. He was not sure if a new man or the old one had begun to emerge as the shave wiped off the shadow. He was in the mood to live it up that night.

He stepped out of his pad and walked the distance to the nightclub across the street. In a short time, Soul had earned a reputation as a classy place that encouraged unknown talent to come and perform, give it a try. Everyone from the ageing hippies of the seventies to the ex–City banker who had given it all up to pursue his passion accepted the invite. Every night, men and women from different generations, all united in their love for music, could be seen singing, crooning and belting classic pop numbers, or whatever, in the smoke-filled interiors and on the beer-stained wooden floors of Soul. When Suvir reached the nightclub, he heard a strange, eclectic medley of pop numbers with a Goan twist wafting through the air. He selected a table outside the rim of the main dance area where all the action was happening. He ordered a bottle of wine and looked at a girl of probable mixed parentage sing the next number, 'Are You Lonesome Tonight?'

Suvir could not help but appreciate the way she broke the traditional melody and the beat of the song to inject a Goan flavour into it. He sensed she was not an ordinary crooner. She had a natural tan that gave her an enticing allure and her eyes, liquid brown pools, reminded him of someone else from a long time ago. He replenished his glass with wine and walked to the edge of the rim, still outside the main dance area. He stood near the door leading into the main hall, appreciating her rendition. He sipped his wine and cheered for her, holding his glass to the light.

A sizeable crowd was packed in the middle, on the wooden floorboards, all dancing the night away and he was about to turn and walk away when he saw the girl look at him intently through the multitude of bobbing heads. He felt she was silently communicating with him to stay on. He hesitated and the look was there again and he went against his principle to walk away from all that was over and behind him, things that held no meaning for him.

He continued to sip his wine and after some time the girl completed her performance to the sounds of loud cheering. The girl then spoke complimentary words about her band and disappeared through the doors leading to the back. Suvir walked back to the table and poured the dregs of wine from the bottle into his glass, prepared to call it a night. He smelt an exotic perfume and looked up. The singer who had captivated the crowds some time back was standing before him. He could see that she had gone in for a hurried change of clothes. Her smouldering dress for the evening had been replaced by a sober beige top and black denim. But the clack of her high heels and a dash of flaming-red lipstick still indicated that this was the same girl who had put the crowds under a spell earlier in the evening.

'Is the chair next to you taken?' she asked playfully.

'No,' replied Suvir. 'It's always vacant. If the chair had a voice it would be singing "Are you lonesome tonight?"'

The girl laughed, sat down and extended her hand and Suvir shook it. There was mischief lurking in her brown eyes. 'Rosalina,' said the girl.

Suvir raised a toast to her and drank the remaining wine. 'This Suvir raises a toast to you, Rosalina, but you can only appreciate the rose with a fresh bottle of wine. What would you prefer—white wine or red? Actually, all kinds of flavours are bursting at the tip of my tongue after your performance.'

Rosalina gave a half-smile and raised her eyebrows. 'Hmmm. A ruggedly good-looking man who speaks in evocative symbols! Now how often does that happen? My lucky night! Darling, I think I would prefer a red. Now do they have a wine in the cooler whose bouquet will sit on my tongue with indeterminate taste for some time? And then perhaps it will burst at the right time with the passion of the night.'

Suvir dragged his chair close to her. 'Now that's a thought. I see no reason why such a wine cannot be managed.'

Suvir signalled to the waiter and, when he came up to the table, he whispered to him. The waiter nodded and disappeared and came back with the finest wine the club could offer. Suvir and Rosalina swirled wine in their glasses and Rosalina asked him, 'What are we drinking to?'

'To a night that comes along rarely—when you have wine, song and Rosalina all under a starlit sky.'

She smiled broadly at the tribute and both clinked their glasses. Suvir continued, 'I say, a charm has been at work this night. Your songs were like a suggestion. They touched a chord and brought forth memories in me. Talk to me, Rosalina. Is the singer more beautiful than the song? Or is the effect it casts so powerful that one cannot differentiate between the two?'

'I did not set out to do what you attribute to me. I am happy that I can give some joy to someone who listens to my songs. That is all that matters.'

Both sipped wine and kept quiet and let the night do the talking for them. A strange attraction pulled them to each other and both did not bother to talk trivia and weaken that pull.

Suvir felt as if he was holding her oval face in his hands, his finger tracing the cut of her chin, her nose and her lips ablaze with red lipstick. But it was the eyes, always the eyes, that he would dive into. He never knew when he spoke words of intimacy to her:

'You are a woman a man desires. Your music, your song and your beauty give me wings. Where did you come from?'

She looked at him, sensing the fatal sensitivity this man exuded like a powerful drug. You would want to consume it. You would want to touch his muscular leanness, feel the shadow of stubble growing on his face. You would want to look inside him to understand why he spoke in hyperbole; why he had the capacity to intrigue, perplex and perhaps even set on edge the woman who tried to get closer to him. He was there in front of her like low-hanging fruit. All she had to do was to reach out to him.

'So why not?' she thought and took a decision.

It was a starlit night, as he had said. It was humid and warm and the night belonged to those willing to set their foot outside. There was a stirring both felt intensely for each other.

They drank wine, lots of it, moved away from the dance floor to a corner that looked out to the backwaters encircling the club's fringes. It was alive with the sounds of crickets and other creatures of the night. They talked of themselves, of their longings and desires, of the lands they had visited, of what Goa meant to them, about the futility and the joyousness of life.

'My father is Goan and my mother is Spanish. I spend half my time in Barcelona.'

She wondered why she was telling him that. And then it struck her. The words she had spoken earlier had been so potently true. His wine, like a delayed reaction, had burst its flavours into her. All she wanted was for him to pick her up, tear off her top, take off her belt, and hold her at the door in a clinch. She felt like thrusting out to him, to look into his eyes—the eyes of an invader—as he worked his muscular frame to ravage her.

She could no longer bear it and she told him huskily, 'I have a room on the top floor of the club. Take me there. I want to feel you in me.'

The physicality of what they were trying to say to each other during the course of the night then took over. She took him into the elevator to go up to the second floor. She turned the key on the first floor and stalled the elevator and went down on her knees and pressed her face against his jeans. She felt his throbbing desire and she looked at his flushed face.

'I am not a whore. I have never done this before. You make me do it.'

They made love in the second-floor corridor, uncaring of public exposure, their passion uncontrollable, spilling over. They then burst into her room and they squeezed and thrust into each other, licked and caressed each other forcefully and slowly at the same time. They wanted their passion to rule the entire night. She found him like a coiled spring in a battery that slowly uncoils outwards, trembling for contact. She knew he had filled her with all he could offer but some last vestiges of his passion had survived, leaving him greatly troubled. He fully parted her legs and with great cruelty, he violently thrust himself into her one final time and a terrifying scream built up in him as he completely spent himself in her.

'Naazish, you make me do it! You make me do it! You always make me do it!'

Stunned, she collapsed on the bed and he fell on top of her after having lost out to the demons that always lay bundled deep inside him. She slowly removed his hands from her breasts and sat cross- legged on the bed, unable to move, undecided about the man. She sat like that and slept awhile and when she woke up the sun was streaming in through the windows and he had begun to stir to life. More shock awaited her. He opened his eyes and she was not sure this was the same man she had met last night. He was mumbling under his breath, unsure, close to panic, fearful of loss.

'Kalpana, I forgot the blanket. It was chilly outside. Hope you haven't caught a cold. Forgive me, forgive me . . .'

Both woke up to a morning devoid of passion and full of doubt. But she had travelled the world and seen things. She knew she did not want to take this further. They met politely at breakfast and she smiled at him. She sipped her coffee and spoke to him with a tinge of sadness, 'Knights in the night, with the world at our feet, we are ordinary men and women in the light of day. Men and women who carry scars, troubling memories, who seek to exorcize their past by whichever way. I had hoped, you know . . . well, never mind that. You are haunted by your past. And I am too much of a free spirit to share your burden. So it ends here. Those idiot critics have a name for it. It is called a one-night stand.'

'I am so sorry for all this, Rosalina. I have to say, I do not deserve someone like you.'

She suddenly smiled brightly. 'You know, if we could edit the passage of time I would still take the time when we were coming on to each other. It should have ended there, without the regret. But such is life.'

'I know,' he said wistfully. He held out his hand to her. 'We part as friends?'

'Of course,' she replied quickly and shook his hand.

He got up and hesitated but then he kissed her cheek. 'You are truly the name of the rose. What I said about you in both the edited and unedited versions was true. A man would find himself in real luck to deserve you. But I am not that man. Goodbye, Rosalina.'

She blinked in surprise but he was gone from the breakfast room and her life.

He descended the stairs to the lobby and an attendant came up to him.

'Sir, a man is waiting for you by the poolside. He has been waiting for you for a long time.'

He nodded and followed the attendant outside to the pool area. A man dressed in a tie and a suit, in the sweltering heat, waited for him outside. The man shook hands with him.

'Prasad,' said the man. 'That's my name. I work as a senior solicitor for the Jindal Group. It took me some time to find your present location. You see, I have an urgent matter to discuss with you.'

Suvir suddenly became alert. There was a history linking him to the Jindal Group. He had undertaken an operation for Mr Jindal to eliminate the killers of Mr Jindal's daughter, holed up across the border. It was a time when Kalpana was still in his life, even though she had slipped into a coma—life had seemed somewhat liveable then.

Prasad had large bony hands and he spread them out to explain the reason he had taken a flight to Goa in the morning.

'I was cleaning my desk some time back and going over papers stored for a long period of time. I came across this letter which had been written by your fiancée, Kalpana, almost seven years ago. The letter was given to a junior associate of mine who was careless with it and it was filed away inadvertently. I know that Kalpana worked as a senior accountant with the Jindal Group. You were engaged to her then; she never really recovered from a car accident on the eve of your marriage. I also know she died last year after being in a coma for a number of years. All this makes this mistake on our part truly unpardonable. I am truly sorry for that.

'I read through the contents of the letter. It was written by her around the time you were in training at the Special Forces facility at Variengte. She probably thought you had read through the letter and might not have mentioned it to you. You see, this letter is actually an affidavit. There is a specific request made to you in this affidavit. Here, read it yourself.'

There were two parts to the affidavit: a legal document that transferred a vast property she owned in rural Punjab to him, and a personal letter. The letter explained why she had transferred the property to him. His hands shook when he read it through:

. . . Suvir, you know how passionate I am about the health situation of young, adolescent girls. We are both Punjabis and we both know that a cancer epidemic is spreading across the state of Punjab, unchecked. The cancerous pesticides used extensively in the fields have gone deep down into the water table. People are falling sick and dying and now there are cancer trains transporting these sick people to neighbouring states for treatment. The situation is really bad in the villages and the young girls are the worst affected.

A couple of years back, my mother and a distant relative of hers, Kulwinder Aunty, jointly purchased a large tract of land in rural Punjab for investment purposes. Mum gave me the joint property papers a few months before she died. This is the only property I own. I have a simple request. If ever something were to happen to me, promise me you will negotiate with the joint owners of the property and free the land from them. The idea is to use the land or sell it to build clinics for the detection of cancer with free across-the-board treatment for young girls.

That is my dream. So, my darling, if ever I'm not there, I urge you to make my dream your own. If I'm not there, this property is yours and the fulfilment of its purpose also yours.

Love,
Kalpana

Suvir felt numb after he had read through the affidavit. Kalpana was speaking to him from beyond the grave a day after he had desecrated her memory by bedding a stranger. Earlier, too, he had betrayed her by falling in love with Naazish. He looked up at Prasad and asked him, 'What is this affidavit asking me to do?'

Prasad's large hands rested on the table as he spoke. 'Sir, this affidavit is asking you to go to the village of Kasba Chardi Kala near Amritsar. There you have to negotiate a deal with the other joint holders of the property so that this property is relinquished in your name. We have an obligation to fulfil Ms Kalpana's wishes as she was so close to the Jindals. If you are agreeable to fulfilling the terms of this affidavit then I can make all the arrangements for your travel.'

23

The violin is a difficult instrument to master but those who pass the test produce nothing less than the music of the gods. Simran, out of nowhere, had begun to feel the deeply satisfying strains of violin strings close to her ear. She knew her condition was brought upon by the sense of fulfilment she had begun to experience for the first time in her life. Aranjit had a role to play in that. Simran responded by spending more and more time at Aranjit's place. They would talk endlessly, work at the farm, read books, take hikes in the countryside and sometimes even let silence rule between them. The music of satisfaction filled them both.

It was on one such day, when Simran was spending the weekend at Aranjit's place, that the older woman suggested something that seemed out of character with her personality. She casually asked Simran, who was reading a book, comfortably ensconced in the sofa, 'I hear that well-known pop singer Breezy Singh will be performing outside the village. Do you think we should check him out? It could be fun?'

Simran cocked an eyebrow.

'Now that's a surprise.'

'Why? Do you think I am so old that I can't enjoy what your generation offers?'

Simran laughed and closed the book. 'I never said that. Well, sure. Let's do it. I have no idea who this character is but if he can promise us an evening of fun, why not? It would not be a bad idea to get the adrenaline pumping in this sleepy little village!'

An errand boy purchased tickets for them and Aranjit locked up her place and both headed for the outskirts of the village where the performance was set for the evening. The entire younger lot in the village and even youngsters from far and beyond had turned up for Breezy's performance. A vast stage was garishly lit up with psychedelic stage lights, and sponsored jingles, with their ear-splitting messages, blared uninterrupted. A sea of turbans filled the grounds and the primarily male audience was charged and excited. Slogans of '*Jo bole so nihal, Sat Sri Akal*' and 'Breezy, Breezy' rippled through the audience. Simran and Aranjit chose a spot a little away from the mad rush near the stage and waited with bated breath for the show to begin.

Fireworks popped in the sky and Breezy, mounted

on a white stallion, holding a sword, with scantily clad blonde and brunette girls holding garlands, made an appearance on the stage. The crowd went wild. Catcalls and unstoppable cheering surged through the crowd like a wave. An inebriated fan desperately tried to climb on to the stage to hug Breezy but security carted him away.

Breezy began to sing or lip-sync his own songs and dozens of people broke into impromptu bhangra among the frenzied crowds. The noise and the music became deafening and Breezy breezed through a string of his hits without pause.

Simran's mouth was wide open and she turned to look at Aranjit, who had a frown on her face. She shouted over the din to make Aranjit listen to her, 'I can't understand a word of what he is singing. It's too strong and rustic for me. Do they do it this way out here? Seems to be more of a carnival than a pop show!'

Aranjit shouted back, 'Yeah, his lyrics are what we call "*thait* Punjabi". It's the hard-core version; sometimes even I find it difficult to understand! But it's popular with the rural masses! Why don't we step back a bit? This noise is too much for me!'

'Great idea!'

Both women wormed their way back through the crowd and climbed a minor hillock that gave them a good view of the performance down below, sans the ear-splitting noise and the crowd frenzy.

They lay on the hillock and looked at the stage till Simran turned her head and asked Aranjit, 'Are you enjoying this?'

'Nope,' said Aranjit with finality. 'I think he's a crashing bore.'

They laughed and Simran perked up. 'And I don't like the way he dresses. He can't make up his mind if he is a religious preacher or a rock star. Such a character would be booed and booted out in England!'

'You said it, girl,' said Aranjit. 'Plus he's fat. I bet you he's wearing a belt under his jacket to push in the tummy!'

Peals of laughter broke out as both women bitched about and made fun of Breezy Singh. Aranjit suddenly sat up, energized.

'It's a beautiful night. We can't let this crashing bore ruin our evening. Let's make our own party here on this hillock. Why don't we sing our favourite songs to each other?'

Aranjit took out a half whisky bottle from under her belt and Simran rolled on the hillock with pleasant shock and laughter.

'Anu, you really surprise me! But hey, what an idea! Let's rock the evening!'

The two women started their own separate party. They took turns to drink the fiery spirit neat and then Aranjit lay back on the hill and looked up at the sky. She held Simran's hand and for both women the irreverent sounds and sight of Breezy began to fade away.

'Listen, girl,' said Aranjit, feeling the magic of the night inside her. 'It's going to be a Joan Baez night for me . . . her eternal music . . . the lyrics . . . her voice . . . the times . . . I have no idea if you have heard her but you should. So here goes . . . my song of tribute . . . "No Woman, No Cry" . . .'

Aranjit sang lustily, full-throated under the night sky and for both women Breezy Singh, the crowds and the noise ceased to exist and there were only the two of them left in the wide world. One sang her heart out and the other listened. Aranjit followed the song with 'Diamonds and Rust' and wound up with a rendition of 'Suzanne'.

She stopped to take a breather and it was only then that Simran once again heard the sounds of Breezy's performance somewhere in the distance.

She tightened her grip on Aranjit's hand and there were tears in her eyes.

'That was so beautiful,' she whispered. 'You touched my heartstrings with your voice and the feeling you put into it. I could sense it was so personal for you. As for me, I felt I belonged to another time, another place, a time of great belief. My generation knows of no such time. You surprise me every day. And I see you unpeeling before me into something new every day. I still feel I have not understood who you really are.'

Aranjit laughed and rolled from her position on the hill. She rested her head in Simran's lap who sat cross-legged, her back to the Breezy performance.

'It's okay, you know, those were the times. It wasn't my generation either but we idolized their idealism and passion. The thing was that we believed in something. Maybe that's why I appear so intense to you. But that's all past. And the night is still young. Sing something for me, Simran . . . anything. I want to know what you believe in. I want to hear you sing.'

'Anu, I have no talent for that. My brother did. He was a great singer. After he went away the music in my life died. In a sense, I have always listened and never sung. That, sadly, is me.'

'No, girl, you deny yourself. I might not have any other talent but I have a sense of people. At your core you are unusual, completely exceptional. All your life you have concealed it. But it will come out one day. Now don't make me beg. Sing for me. I am sure you can at the very least sing an ABBA song. Anyone can.'

Simran lustily drank from the bottle and told Aranjit, 'Yes, I will sing but not today. I am writing a song, a kind of song that I have always wanted to write. When I am finished with that you will be the first person I will sing for. That's a promise. Till then the night belongs to you.'

Aranjit sang some more, and both drank till the empty bottle rolled down the hillock. Completely smashed, they held each other and trudged down the hillock and took the road home. Aranjit sang more songs on the way and by the time they reached the cottage the whisky had completely claimed her. She was now on the downhill curve of her drinking spree and all she wanted to do was to roll on her bed. She had become quiet and decided to quickly make her bed before crashing on it. The whisky had affected her younger partner in a different way. Simran walked up and stood near her bedroom door and casually asked her as she made her bed, 'I know I sound like a broken record. But I still feel uncomfortable about what you were really trying to do at the dera. You have still not given me a satisfactory answer. Why are you holding back?'

Aranjit looked up sharply. 'You have asked that question before. Look, Simran, we had a good night. Let's just stay with that feeling. I am tired and I really need to catch up on my sleep. We will talk tomorrow. Tell your mind to take a break from all that and let things rest. Goodnight.'

'No,' said Simran with dogged insistence. 'You are

being evasive. Tell me what's really going on?'

Aranjit's back was turned as she finished making her bed. 'You make it sound like an inquisition. Let it go.'

'No, tell me.'

Aranjit turned and her eyes were blazing and her mouth had twisted into a snarl. 'Okay, Miss UK-returned, pokes-her-nose-where-she-shouldn't smarty pants! I went looking for evidence to nail that fucking bastard called Santokh Singh. Why would I want to do that? I want to do that because that man has become the single biggest threat to the Sikh identity. This man is weaning the Sikhs away from their faith with his ungodly deeds and actions. He has pitted caste against caste. He is a master of equivocation. His silken words and the promises he dangles before our youth have completely led them astray. Look at our current state of being. Every second youngster in the state has become a drug addict. Entire villages and small towns have been struck by this blight. Mothers have lost their sons; wives are left with husbands who have lost their will to work. The Green Revolution has turned to poison. The state is flooded with drugs. It's easier to get all kinds of drugs from the chemist than it is to get a toffee.

'Do you seriously think all this is a coincidence? There have been forces inimical to the Sikh identity even before Independence. Sant Jarnail Singh Bhindranwale recognized the threat in his lifetime! He took steps to turn the situation. But the same forces eliminated him so that the process of undermining the Sikh identity could continue uninterrupted. That is the real story.

'And now the same forces have propped up this man to completely marginalize us. And this man is succeeding! He has sapped the robust energies of our youth with drug abuse and with his promises of a false dawn. Every second, every day this man contrives and conspires to undermine our Sikh identity, weaken the Sikh cause and diminish the glory of the Khalsa panth! That's what is really going on!

'Is that the truth you have been trying to ferret out of me the last few days? Now you know! Ask me the next question. What will I do next after I have the evidence? Miss Banga, let me tell you. I will go after this man. I will make that my life's mission. I will utterly, completely destroy him. I will make an example of him so that no one dares to mess with our unique identity ever again. People will quake in their shoes, fearing that they will share his fate if they ever emulate the desecrating devil! I will be the avenging angel who will put him to the sword! Now do you understand me? Or am I still a romantic mystery to you?'

Simran stood wide-eyed and in complete shock when Aranjit finished her rant. She withdrew from the room and whispered, 'My God! You are a fanatic, a complete extremist. There is so much hate in you. Who are you really? Are you a woman who sings Joan Baez peace songs or an extremist who is looking for blood?'

Aranjit laughed and then she smirked. 'It's not really your fault, Simran. Your generation is to blame. You were never really taught to believe in anything. The only thing your generation seeks is where the next excitement comes from. You are all politically correct with the same demented responses to the environment, women rights, gays and all that blah-blah. You close your eyes to the real world. The real world is visceral, Simran. It always has been. It always was dog eat dog, man conspiring against man. Real battles are won not by being politically correct but by decapitating the opposition.

'But you, Simran, you of all people should have empathized with me instead of questioning me. You should have understood. You were flung into the middle of the storm. They parted your legs and took turns to rape you. Surely you should have known better.'

Simran then screamed at the top of her voice. She continued to scream till her lungs were close to bursting. She struck the equally volatile Aranjit to complete silence. Once her pent-up anger had come out she continued to tremble with uncontrollable fury for a long time. Then she turned and walked out of Aranjit's home in the middle of the night.

24

Both women regretted the parting of ways the next morning. A niggling doubt had rocked their relationship but they understood that the whisky had also contributed to the damage. The question now was how to repair the strings of the violin that had broken. Aranjit packed some essential items in a duffel bag and left the cottage to take the initiative with Simran. Simran also wheeled her cycle out of her uncle's courtyard and rode it aimlessly near the fields, secretly hoping that she would meet Aranjit on the way. Both women convinced themselves that last night's episode was an interruption rather than a break in their relationship.

Aranjit saw Simran sitting under the shade of a tree, looking vacantly at the sky. She approached her cautiously and put down her duffel bag. Simran looked up.

'Hi,' said Aranjit. 'How are we this morning? Are you still mad at me?'

Simran's eyes were a little puffed from uneven sleep. She considered Aranjit's question. Her voice was low but respectful. 'I don't deny that I am in a sulk against you. You hurt me pretty badly last night. I was shaken up by your ideology.'

Aranjit sat down next to Simran under the tree and plucked out a blade of grass and played with it.

'I meant all that in a relative sense. We can agree or differ in our personal and political convictions. But I would never dream of hurting you. I think the whisky took over after some time.'

Simran looked at Aranjit moodily.

'You talked of killing . . .'

'I would kill, girl, but only for you. Let's leave all that. Let's look at what all we feel for each other, what we have in common.'

Simran drew in a deep breath and put her head against Aranjit's shoulder.

'You are the only person I can relate to in this world. What we have between us is precious. I would never be able to get over it were we to lose it.'

Aranjit stroked her head.

'I would never let that happen, silly girl. I know you are hurting within. Let me make it up to you. I want to give you a gift.'

Simran smiled and looked at her older friend.

'I am curious. What is it?'

'You will have to wait for it. You will have to trust me and follow me deep into the forest for that. Are you ready for that?'

Simran's face was animated. 'Lead the way. I will leave the cycle behind,' she said.

Aranjit picked up the duffel bag and took Simran's hand and led her through a path known only to her. She led her through the ripening mustard fields till they arrived at the edge of the forest. Aranjit took out her shotgun from the duffel bag, cradled it in one hand and beckoned Simran to follow her. They walked through marshy land and then a dense field of elephant grass opened up before them. Ahead, they could see the outline of a eucalyptus tree forest. They walked deep into the forest and it was completely silent. They could only hear the sounds of their shoes crunch against a carpet of brownish-yellow dead leaves covering the entire forest.

Somewhere ahead of them, a furry creature emerged from a hole and ran in the opposite direction in desperation. Simran drew in her breath and held back.

'Don't be afraid,' said Aranjit. 'Rabbits, foxes, even snakes, they are all afraid of the creature with two legs. Just a little ahead is the place where we will take a break. Follow me.'

They walked some more and beyond the treetops

Simran saw birds circling in the sky. They came out of a thicket of trees and saw a large pool of water glistening deep amid the forest cover. The clear water of the pool and the play of light on it from the refraction took Simran's breath away.

'Where did this come from?' she asked in wonder.

Birds were diving into the pool of water to peck at the abundant aquatic life in it. Simran turned to look at Aranjit.

'It's beautiful. This is my gift, is it not?'

'No,' said Aranjit flatly. 'This is merely the location where you will master your gift.'

Aranjit rested the shotgun on the ground and opened her duffel bag. She took out a sleek-looking black handgun.

Simran's mouth became dry and she looked in fascination as Aranjit chambered an entire clip into the weapon. Aranjit turned the grip towards Simran and spoke quietly, 'Hold it. I am giving you the power to become fearless. This is my gift. If you develop the guts to pull the trigger then you develop the capacity to shoot down any kind of oppression you might ever face. That is not an ordinary event in anyone's life. Most people spend their lives withering away because their anger is blocked, finding no release. This weapon enables you to unblock the anger. The mind is the greater weapon because it controls this weapon. An idea can only become a reality if someone implements it. That is what a gun will do for you.'

Simran gripped the weapon and felt a surge of alien power shoot up through her. She understood what Aranjit was really getting at. She could see her helplessness, her hesitation and her great, deep pool of concealed anger, all of it, through the gunsight. Her finger shook as she caressed the trigger.

'Careful,' said Aranjit. 'The safety catch is off. When you take in a beast like the leopard as a pet then you have to make sure that it does not attack the master. You have to direct its energy elsewhere. This is a Glock 17 automatic. There are seventeen rounds in the clip. From today onwards I will train your eye, your finger and, above all, your brain to focus only on what really needs to be eliminated. You will learn that when you shoot, everything but the target should cease to exist for you. I will make a markswoman out of you, Simran, the best ever. When I am through with your training you should be able to take out a man's head from any distance.

'Now be completely still and slowly lift your weapon. Bring it up slowly. On my mark you will touch the trigger and not before that. When I say so, you will slowly squeeze the trigger. Look through your gunsight. Through it you should be able to see all the men who parted your legs.'

The forest reverberated with the crash of gunfire. The animals around the pool of water scrambled for safety. The birds wheeled away in panic. The bark of a tree opposite the pool of water was chipped away as the bullets crashed into it. There was deathly stillness around the pool of water after the first round of target firing was over. The animals crouched in the undergrowth, fearing for their safety. Only the sound of a fresh clip being chambered into the automatic could be heard. Then the crash of gunfire resumed. It went on for well over two hours before Aranjit called it a day. She took the automatic from Simran, took out the clip and packed it all up in the duffel bag. She looked at the younger woman.

Simran had become completely still and she was soaked in sweat. She stared wide-eyed into the distance beyond the pool of water. Only her lip trembled, as if of its own volition. She turned her head and then the tears claimed her. Her body shook from cries that came from a very deep well. She went down on her feet and buried her head into Aranjit's waist.

'Thank you, my friend, for releasing me. Today I am finally free. A shadow had come over me ever since the day they had taken turns to rape me. I could not speak about it to anyone, not even to you. The pain and the desolation kept on growing inside me—until today. You were right. It was not the weapon that released me. It was my mind that was unblocked today. Thank you, my friend.'

She got up and Aranjit inched closer to her protégé. Simran was trembling uncontrollably now and she was hot and flushed. Aranjit smiled, caressed her lips and then Simran could no longer see the refracted waters of the pool. Aranjit obstructed her view of the pool and kissed her on the lips. She embraced her and kissed her again and her tongue darted between her lips, seeking ingress. Simran pulled away.

'No, no, Anu, not this way. You are here inside me like no one else can ever be. But I don't want that to go away because of this. I am so sorry for this.'

Aranjit felt the shock and turned away to look at the pool of water. In that unique moment, Simran never knew the emotions that showed on Aranjit's face. The older woman took her time looking outwards at her life and then, a little more composed, she turned and met the younger woman's look with a wistful smile on her face.

'Sorry. I lost my head. You are right. This could destroy everything. There is so much we share, so much we can look forward to. I thank you for your discretion.'

'Don't say that, Anu. It sounds so clinical. It breaks my heart. All I know is that I am incapable of giving at this point in time.'

Both sat at the edge of the pool and Simran let her head rest against Aranjit's shoulder. They made their way back to the fields in the late afternoon and Simran wheeled her cycle away after they promised to meet each other the next day.

It had grown chilly as she cycled back and the sky was mottled with dust from the fields and smoke rising from kitchen fires in the hutments. There was no one around for miles and Simran felt she was cutting across a vast abandoned landscape. She thought of the eventful afternoon and the see-saw of emotions she had experienced a short while back. She stopped her cycle and it struck her that she had been completely obsessed with her own experiences and she might have neglected the rejection that Aranjit had to put up with. She resolved to articulate her feelings somewhat more clearly to her only friend in the world. She turned the bike and cycled back to the cottage.

The light had gone from the sky when she came up to the cottage. In the distance she could see that the wicker gate was open and a light shone in the cottage. She alighted from the bike some distance away. She had an odd feeling that someone else was in the cottage besides Aranjit. She wheeled the cycle into the shade of a nearby tree and looked in. The evening smog was getting worse and as she stood under the tree, she felt strange that she had not yet trooped in with a sense of entitlement as on earlier occasions. Something held her back. The front door to the cottage opened and Aranjit came out. There was someone else to her right, as Simran had suspected. The man was limping and she could not see his profile clearly. Aranjit stayed on the steps of the porch and the man came down the steps and suddenly turned and looked around him. Simran's blood ran cold. It was a face from the past, a face connected with her childhood. She could not be sure who it was but she felt certain she had seen the man somewhere. There was something about the man's face that made her shiver. He had coal-black eyes, and his white beard—or whatever was left of it—hung in patches from his face like dried straws. He tied his turban inelegantly, as if was permanently inebriated and sloppy. He had a deep furrow running from his forehead to his nose and that made him stand out. It gave him the look of a rat with bloodshot eyes, eating its way through a passage.

Simran suddenly felt scared and the feeling that she hardly knew Aranjit gripped her again. The light was fading fast and the man had disappeared in the smog. A short while later the light in the porch also went out. She had an overwhelming desire to confront Aranjit about this man but she held back. She would find out more about this man but not now. It suddenly occurred to her that she would have to be just a little bit more careful from now onwards and perhaps hold back things a little from her closest friend in the world. Her finger started to twitch and she knew that she had changed in the course of a single afternoon. She felt the overwhelming need to pack a weapon and feel its suppressed power next to her.

She rode back to her uncle's house; darkness had fallen. The lights were ablaze on the ground floor. Harbaksh and Kulwinder Sondhi sat sipping tea with a stranger in the main hall downstairs. Her uncle quickly came out when he heard Simran come in.

'Simran, come in and meet this gentleman,' he said, leading her in. The strange developments of the past hour had disturbed her immensely and, a little irritated, she went into the hall. A rugged-looking, very fit man rose politely to meet her. Harbaksh Sondhi made the introductions.

'Simran beta, meet Suvir Suri. He is a family friend. He's come all the way from Goa. And Suvir, meet Simran. She's come all the way from England, you know,' he said with some pride.

25

Something about Suvir disturbed Simran. He was like a speck that gets into your eye and then it becomes one big challenge to get it out. He would be constantly in and out of the house and Simran came to know that he was in active negotiations with her relatives about a large tract of land on the outskirts of the village. They would pass each other and nothing more than a perfunctory 'hello' would be exchanged. They inhabited different worlds and it was highly unlikely that their paths would ever cross. But Simran knew from experience that the unexpected had a way of creeping up in her life, unannounced.

The forest beyond the village limits would echo daily with the stutter of small-arms fire. Aranjit every day upped the degree of difficulty in the training module she had devised for Simran. She introduced a physical element to the training. She would make Simran do stomach crunches, push-ups and lifts till her back hurt and her arms and limbs were on fire. Simran struggled to cope with the new demands Aranjit was making on her mental and physical faculties. At the end of one such session she pulled a muscle. She had no choice but to cycle back to her uncle's house in great pain. Her back hurt, her insides ached and she was thirsty. She was quite irritated with everything around her. Some distance away from her uncle's bungalow, her cycle sustained a puncture.

'Shit! Shit! Shit!' she exploded as she dismounted from the bike. She kicked at the bike and in complete frustration she sat in the middle of a mustard field to catch her breath. A shadow fell across her. Suvir stood there, extending a hand.

'Looks like you need some help,' he offered.

She replied with dripping sarcasm, 'This is not a Bollywood shoot where the hero makes a timely entry, offering help. What is it that a man can do that I can't? Or are you a puncture-fixing expert?'

Suvir withdrew his hand and smiled slightly. 'Sorry, I must have phrased it inelegantly. I simply offered to help without the attendant terms and conditions. I am sure you can look after yourself.'

Suvir left her in the field and walked away to Harbaksh's house some distance away. Simran's breathing normalized and she regretted the manner in which she had spoken to Suvir. She got up and wheeled the cycle towards the repair shop. She decided to make up with Suvir the next day.

The next day, early morning, she came down from her room and almost walked into a heated argument taking place in the main hall downstairs. She decided to keep away from it and smiled and shook her head, thinking that after the initial pleasantries the stranger was finally getting to see the real face of her uncle. She wheeled her cycle out of the courtyard and waited outside the main door of the house. After a while, Suvir came out of the door looking flustered. Simran stood in the way.

'I guess today it's your turn to lose your shirt. In case you think rudeness runs in the family, let me put some distance between me and my uncle. I apologize for snapping at you yesterday. As for my uncle, let me just say that the shark circles in the water for a fair bit of time to measure up its kill. He must have gone for the kill today—your face shows it.'

Suvir let out a deep breath. 'Good to know that at least someone is sane in the family. If you must know, he quoted an impossible price for his share of the land. Pure blackmail—that's what he is doing. Whoever said that only the innocent reside in the villages?'

'Sounds like you could do with a cup of tea and someone to talk to, to let off steam. I could be that girl. We don't have a fancy Café Coffee Day out here but there is a decent tea shop just down the road.'

'That's the first nice thing I have heard since the morning. Sure, why not?'

'Great. So hopefully I won't be branded the feminist witch and your male ego won't be jolted if you ride pillion on my cycle?'

Suvir laughed and sat at the back of the cycle. 'I am basically a lazy bum. A back seat will suit me fine. Lead the way!'

The strange duo raised a few eyebrows and even a few titters as they rode into the village market to the tea shop near the fields. Simran ordered two cups of masala tea and insisted on paying for them. They took their tea and sat outside in the winter sun on a wooden plank, facing the mustard fields.

They sipped their tea and spoke little, soaking in the warmth of the mild sun. Suvir looked at her and said, 'You offered a shoulder to cry on?'

'It's there for the taking,' she said. 'So why are you so rattled about this piece of land?'

'Well, you could call it a soldier's honour. There was something I should have done for my fiancée a long time back but I could not, because of circumstances beyond my control. All I can tell you is that I want the land desperately. But your uncle is blocking the sale. He intends to make a windfall profit from it.'

'You can always call a bastard by his name.'

'How will that help me? My fiancée is gone and I am unable to realize her dream.'

'I have heard about your quest,' she said.

He kept quiet when she said that. He whispered, almost to himself, 'It's so difficult to keep things under wraps in a small village. I guess word gets around quickly.'

She looked quizzically at him. 'The cycle repair shop owner filled me in on you even though I did not want to listen. By the same token, they must have filled you in on me. Or rather the reputation I earned for myself in England.'

Suvir chose his words carefully. He looked at her in complete earnestness. 'I think you are too hard on yourself. My pain is nothing compared to yours— especially in one so young. Yes, they told me all about you, Simran, even though I did not want to hear about it. That is the truth.'

She looked at her empty tea glass. She thought of the incongruity of the phrase she had just invented for herself—emotions in a teacup. She looked at Suvir with a clear eye.

'You know, maybe we do have something in common. You are a war hero with a string of broken relationships and I am a woman raped and dumped at the far end of the world. Now what are the chances of two broken people, licking their wounds, meeting at the edge of the world in a forgotten, dusty village? I think I will drink another tea to that.'

He smiled and lifted his cup to cheer her.

'I like your play with words, especially in one so young.'

'Why do you keep saying that? You are not that old yourself?'

'No, I meant it in a relative sense.'

Suvir drank his tea and felt she was looking at him carefully.

'What? Okay, I see that look in your eyes. You are brimming with questions about me. So go ahead, ask me.'

Simran ordered another cup of tea and settled more comfortably on the plank.

'We are both looking for something. Maybe I can get a sense of what I am looking for from your experiences. What were you doing in Goa?'

'Running away,' he said matter-of-factly.

'From what?'

'From, I don't know . . . look, I landed there two years back to cut the cord that bound me to Naazish and Kalpana, the women I loved. They had gone away but their presence never left me. I had begun to grow delusional. I had to get away from it all. I trained my mind not to think of them. I let my senses and the needs of the body take over. What better place to do that in than Goa? It was as if for the last two years of my life I had been riding a giant wave which could find no shore where it could ebb and die down. But the sea did eventually throw me out. I accepted that I could never forget the two women.'

'So why Punjab after Goa?'

'I could break journey in Goa but it has to end in the land of my forefathers. Call it the circle of life. Call it my sense of honour to keep a promise. Call it anything. In the end we are left with so many questions and so few answers.'

'Aren't we?' she replied enigmatically.

She closed her eyes for a moment. She thought she had shut the door on a world of men. But she felt a stirring to open it just a bit to look at the man who stood on the other side. The man who stood there was lean, with greying sideburns, a man who was vulnerable and strong at the same time. He was a rare breed because he had eyes that showed he genuinely cared and he had hands that could rip off the throat of an adversary in the blink of an eye. She had known only a different breed of men. She felt a longing to reach out to him.

She looked at him and suddenly she felt happy, though there was no reason for it.

'Are you going back to Goa?' she asked.

'Yes and no. I am going back to wind up things

there. I will be consulting with my lawyers on how best to deal with your uncle and apply pressure on him. I should be back in a couple of weeks. I have a clinic to build.'

'So I can expect you back in these parts?'

'Yes, you can. And I look forward to spending time with you. So I will say goodbye for now, Simran. Stay safe.'

Suvir went away and Simran felt as though she had picked up the violin, rested it on her shoulder and was now fine-tuning the hair on the bow to strike the right notes. She could almost hear the music of ecstasy in the air around her.

26

The mentor marvelled at how still the protégé lay in the elephant grass, cradling the Winchester Model 70 sniper rifle. She had been lying in that posture on the road for well over an hour. The protégé was completely inert, not twitching a muscle, lost to the world, deep in concentration. The older woman could not help but wonder whether she had been as good in her time as this girl had proved to be under her tutelage. She knew that head-to-head, the younger girl was no match for her because she was still at the beginning of her learning curve. What really was remarkable was how quickly she had mastered all that she had been taught. It was almost as if she had discovered her real vocation in life the day she had handled a Glock for the first time.

Aranjit wiped the sweat beads off Simran's forehead and offered her a drink from the water canteen. Simran replied in the negative—not even for a moment would she take her eyes away from the target. Dr Bagga's official car stood outside the courtyard of the government polytechnic. The distance from the courtyard to the main road where the two women lay in the elephant grass was almost five hundred metres. The kill shot, if dispatched, would cover one of the longest distances any sniper had ever attempted. A light breeze fanned the landscape and the elephant grass danced in front of Simran, momentarily obscuring her line of sight. But she held her nerve. Aranjit shifted her binoculars as she noticed movement at the main gate of the polytechnic. Dr Bagga emerged out of the gate and a peon trailed behind, carrying his briefcase. It was a short walk to the waiting car and a limited window of opportunity had opened up.

Aranjit whispered to Simran, as she focused on the target with the binoculars, 'He's coming. Take the shot now.'

Simran lay still, unmoving.

Aranjit was full of tension during the moment of truth. The assassin remained eerily composed. Aranjit again instructed Simran, her voice rising, 'Do it now. The rifle is silenced. No one will know. You will be sending a message.'

The driver opened the door to the car and Dr Bagga got in. The peon respectfully put the briefcase in the front seat.

'Now!' Aranjit whispered fiercely. The driver got

into his seat, turned on the ignition and the car moved out of the courtyard, towards the main road. Near the outer gate, Simran once again trapped Dr Bagga in the crosshairs of her rifle. She had the man in sight and she let him go. The car turned away from the gate to take the highway route and Simran brought the logo of the Honda Civic in sight. Then, in a brilliant display of marksmanship, she emptied the five-round clip which took out the stainless-steel logo at the rear of the car in a flash. Dr Bagga never knew how close he had come to having his head blown off. Simran did not execute his death warrant but signed off in style, announcing her deadly arrival. Aranjit threw away the binoculars in disgust and buried her head in the grass.

Later in the day, unexpected winter rains lashed Amritsar and the surrounding parts. It was cold, wet and blustery and the weather showed no respite. Both women arrived at the cottage and Simran poured water into a glass from the filter and drank from it. She kept the empty glass near the sink; Aranjit spoke harshly to her, 'There are no servants in the house. A single woman runs it. When you drink from a glass, make sure you wash it.'

Simran silently washed the glass, dried it with a cloth napkin and kept it near the sink. The she went and stood near the large window in the living room and watched the rains come down in sheets to destroy the winter crops and spread the blight. After a while, a somewhat composed Aranjit came and stood behind her. The rain drummed on the frosted glass and the cold seeped in through the walls.

Without turning her head Simran said, 'I am done with your lies. Who are you? Tell me the truth.'

Aranjit replied unflinchingly, 'Why did you not take the shot? That was the man who tried to molest you.'

'Are the two questions related?' asked Simran.

'Yes, they are,' answered Aranjit. 'It was not a training exercise. I had told you that I was training you for a higher cause. I had not trained you to shoot innocent animals in the woods or hit dummy targets. The man does not deserve to live. Do you think you are the only one he has tried to molest? He must have tried that with hundreds of innocent girls in the polytechnic.'

'Maybe you are right,' countered Simran. 'But I changed my mind. I will not pull the trigger for what you think is right or wrong. That's my decision to make. So now answer my question. Who are you?'

'Look at me, Simran, when I answer that question.'

Simran turned and both women looked at each other, struggling to hold on to the love they felt for each other, burdened by the strain that was pulling them apart.

Aranjit had lost her usual equanimity and she

trembled slightly. She walked up to the younger woman and stroked her cheek.

'Simran, I was one of the most dreaded terrorists during the Khalistan movement in the late eighties. In the police files, I am presumed dead. My name is not Aranjit. My real name is Harmit Kaur. I survived Gill's witch-hunt after our movement collapsed. Aranjit is a fictional identity I took on when I moved to this village many years back. The village and the outside world know Aranjit as the abandoned, headstrong wife of a rich farmer.'

Simran felt as if she had been struck with something. She could hardly breathe. She walked across and sat heavily on a chair. Her lips trembled and she could not hold back her tears. She looked at her mentor and her voice was choked as she said, 'So it's all a lie. Your entire existence and what you stand for—all that is a lie. Aranjit, Harmit or whoever you are, you should have told me the truth. I came halfway around the world to escape from all the lies and the deceit that have always dogged me. I came here to escape my father who remains a closet Khalistani to date. I poured my heart out to you and for a while I truly believed that there was one person in the world who understood me, a person who loved me for who I am. But it is all a lie. You are a prisoner of an ideology that my generation does not identify with or care about. Killing comes so easy to you, does it not? Now that I know your secret, will you kill me too, Harmit?'

Aranjit rushed to Simran, went down on her knees, embraced her and smothered her with kisses.

'Oh! You dear, dear, stupid girl, how can you think like that? I am and always will be Aranjit to you. I told you the truth because I did not want any lies to come between us. You hold my life in your hands, not I. You can walk to the police station and report me. I get up in the morning thinking about you and about what we will do next. That is what keeps me going.'

Simran began to cry like a small child and Aranjit kissed her on the forehead.

'Look at me, child,' she said. 'Yes, I have a past. And I think you suspected that. But you have to understand those times, Simran. You have no idea what we were up against. There were no jobs, they introduced policies that destroyed our land holdings, there were forces out there actively conniving to destroy our identity and there was a government at the centre that subtly encouraged discrimination against us. During the 1982 Asian Games, the Haryana police stopped innocent Sikhs from entering Delhi, fearing we might disturb the games. They insulted our athletes. The actions of the central government turned an entire generation of Sikhs against it. A cry for freedom and against the yoke of the government's oppression went up. I never knew when and why I became a terrorist. We were all swept away in a tidal wave of protest.'

'I want to empathize with you, Aranjit, but I can't.'

'I don't blame you, dear girl. You have lived in a country that takes every instance of discrimination very seriously. You have not known this state of affairs.'

Aranjit held Simran's hand and implored her, 'Yes, we have our differences and I respect that. But there is one thing I have learnt over the years, Simran. At the end of the day what the world holds for us or withholds from us is irrelevant. It is the personal space that really matters. You are the only person I really care about. I have travelled a long distance over the years. I have no regrets about what I did in the past. But there will be regret if you choose to go out of my life.'

Both women fell silent. Aranjit rested her head against the chair but clasped Simran's hand. Simran asked her, 'Who was that man with a deep furrow on his face whom I saw the other day in your house? It is a familiar face.'

Aranjit hesitated and then replied, 'There are a lot of burnt-out cases like me still floating around. It is no one you need to fear.'

Simran squeezed Aranjit's hand. 'Much like you, I also cannot hold back my love for you. But I cannot support what you did in the past. That is my moral dilemma and I will deal with it. I will continue to see you. But I have a question that dogs me. I want a truthful answer. Nothing less than that will be acceptable.'

'Ask me,' replied Aranjit, knowing where Simran was headed.

'Why did you train me? What did you hope to achieve?'

Aranjit closed her eyes, which had watered. She breathed deeply.

'Simran, what does a father hope for when he sees his son growing up? He hopes that one day his son will embellish his legacy. That the son's life will be a spitting image, or perhaps a better version, of the life the father has led. The desire for legacy is a deeply primeval one. All I wanted was to teach you whatever I have learnt over the years, before my time is up. I want you to be more skilled than me in the trade I had mastered a long time ago. After that I leave it to you to either wrestle with your moral dilemma or reconcile with it to bring real change in the lives of people.'

27

March 1984, a farmhouse near Tarn Taran

Fear was strung across the highway and the roads leading in and out of Tarn Taran. Police jeeps patrolled the roads daily, searching for improvised explosive devices. Police pickets had come up every hundred metres and units trained for interdiction were raiding farmlands around the Tarn Taran area daily. The traditional trust between people of different communities had completely broken down. Many extremists sought sanctuary in the farmlands and the local gurdwaras and not a day passed without a firefight or an encounter in the villages. Tarn Taran had become the nerve centre for the Khalistan movement; seen in that light, it was nothing less than audacity that the commander's followers decided that they had to get their commander married to his lady-love in the wee hours of the morning.

The commander and his band of followers were holed up in a farmhouse and the terrorized landlord was given the task of fetching the local granthi to perform the marriage rites. The commander and even Aranjit had no use for such a social sanction but the boys insisted that the two shining stars of their movement enter into formal wedlock. The commander and Aranjit reluctantly agreed to the proposal to inspire the boys and give them something to look forward to. They were all stretched to breaking point, days and nights on the run, the torture in the police stations, the unexpected rattle of gunfire and the whine and scream of police jeeps encircling their hideouts. All that and more tested their ideology and resilience. A marriage in a season of bloody violence could only give them hope.

At *amrit vela* (auspicious time), the harassed landlord and three of the boys were seen by some early risers in the village, rushing to the local gurdwara. Then after some time the four men came out of the gurdwara carrying the Guru Granth Sahib with the utmost respect and the granthi quietly followed behind. The landlord instructed his wife to prepare the traditional karah-prashad to mark the joyousness of the occasion. The granthi tied the knot between the commander and Aranjit in the dim light of a paraffin lamp. He began to recite passages from the Guru

Granth Sahib. The *anand karaj* ceremony, a marriage ritual, began and culminated with the *laavas* that solemnized the marriage between the commander and Aranjit. The granthi then offered a final *ardas* (prayer) before the Guru Granth Sahib in which he praised the sacrifices of the Sikh community and the Gurus; he prayed for matrimonial bliss between the newly-weds and hoped that the dream for Khalistan would become a reality.

The boys impatiently waited for the ceremonies to be complete and they all gathered around their commander and Aranjit and raised full-throated slogans of *'Jo bole so nihal, Sat Sri Akal! Wahi Guruji ka Khalsa! Wahi Guruji ki Fateh!'*

Then the boys embraced their leader and offered greetings to Aranjit. An impromptu bhangra broke out and Aranjit joined the boys who all danced with great energy and verve. Smiles and sparkling laughter broke out in the room, bawdy marriage jokes were exchanged and for some time they all forgot the fragility of their situation. It was almost as if they had left their troubles behind and stepped into the brave new world their leaders, heroes and the martyrs to their cause had promised them. A feeling of complete liberation gripped them and their spirits soared. The landlord's wife walked in with a steaming bowl of the freshly prepared karah-prashad and the granthi invited the commander to stand next to him.

'Commanderji,' he said. 'Tradition says that the head priest slices the karah-prashad with the kirpan to distribute it evenly in the community. But we are in a unique situation here. We have one of the most daring commanders in Sikh history in the same room with us. It would only be in the fitness of things that Commanderji distribute the karah-prashad to everyone. And perhaps say a few words to inspire us,' he said as an afterthought.

Someone offered the commander a kirpan and he examined it in the weak light.

'The hilt and the cutting edge,' he said enigmatically. He smiled and looked at Aranjit and she understood. He spoke slowly, haltingly, a man of few words, as he cut the karah-prashad and distributed it.

'Why do we keep the kirpan by our side? Do we really need it in peacetime? All these are pertinent questions. My young brothers, we keep it with us in peace and war to constantly remind us of where we come from. We have a unique identity. Some understand that but many don't. Our backs will always be against the wall. That is our fate. There will be inevitable cycles in our history when our land will be soaked in blood. We are going through one such cycle. I can't even promise you that our movement will be successful. But we will be sending a message to the ruling dispensation and even to future rulers. Don't ever mess around with the self-respect of the Sikhs. There will be hell to pay.'

The commander looked tired after the short speech and Aranjit took over and led him away to a connected room. She closed the door and embraced him. She put her head against his chest, trying to feel his rhythm, excited that she could finally claim an indivisible part of him which she would not have to share with anyone else. She could own it uniquely now. She felt passion surge through her.

She undid his shirt buttons and he feebly protested, 'No, no, not now. I am not up to it. And it is nearly morning.'

She lightly kissed him and looked into his eyes. 'You always inspire the boys. Now it is my turn and I am standing in the queue. Remember, the cutting edge cannot function without the hilt. We are a team. Come to bed.'

She helped him undress and then she quickly stripped—her body hot and flushed, craving for communion. She kissed him behind the ear, stroked his nipple and directed his penis and bid him enter her. He felt her passion but could not respond and he broke out in a sweat and fumbled and looked out of sorts, unlike the masterful way he had inspired his men a short while ago. She kept coaxing him to come near her but it was of no use. He collapsed by her side and looked up at the ceiling. She also became still and looked at the uncertainty that stood before her like an elephant in the room. He got up, sat at the side of the bed and addressed it, 'We tried it in Jammu and it did not work even then. I had given you hints about all this. But you were adamant. What happened today was not a great idea. It will stress us further. There is already a lot we have to deal with.'

She swiftly moved to his side and embraced him from the back.

'Don't say that. I understand what you have to deal with. It can't be easy carrying the weight of the entire insurrection on your shoulders. We will take this bit a little easy and then slowly build on it. I will help you with that. The feelings and passion will take their course with time.'

He got up and cut her short, 'That will never happen. I just don't have it in me. I don't want you to live under any illusions.'

She began to cry and held his hand. 'Please don't say that. Give me some hope.'

He shook her hand away and moved to the centre of the room. 'No, I cannot do it. You have to accept that. Harmit, even today, after so many years, I see bodies piled up in a mound outside the gates of Dacca. Women and children thrown like meat into a huge pile.

Most of the women were stripped of their sarees, their legs opened up after they had been raped repeatedly. You went in closer and you could see their faces and especially their stomachs bloated from putrefaction and gangrene. And the little children . . . for some reason, they would always stare at you, even in death pointing an accusing finger at you. The horror of it all.'

She ran to him and flung herself at his waist.

'Give me a sign. Give me something to hold on to. At the very least, make it happen once so that I can carry your legacy in me and teach him when he grows up.'

'No Harmit,' he replied flatly. 'That is never going to happen. I only live for the next encounter, the next engagement with those who oppose us. That is all. But I understand that you have needs. I also know you were good friends with Sukkhi before you met me. I would look the other way if you were to carry on a liaison with Sukkhi.'

She cried in despair. 'How can you say such a thing? What do you take me for? Do you think I am some kind of an alley cat moving from block to block? I came to you because you inspired me. Why are you going to such great lengths to disillusion me? At least give me a thread of hope.'

The commander roughly pulled her up and looked at her fiercely. 'Harmit, I have spent my entire adult life waiting for a bullet to pierce through my brain. I have known of no other life. What do you expect of me? That I will give you my seed and we will settle into domestic bliss? This is the life we chose. If you cannot fulfil the requirements of the job, you deserve to remain unemployed. I hate people who do not let me do my job.'

He pushed her away and her tears dried up. She spoke in whispers, 'Forgive me for my momentary lapse. You are right. We all have a job to do. I have to learn to wall up my feelings and dam them for ever. I am sorry that I have not experienced the trauma of watching dead bodies piled up in a mound. But I have experienced something even more terrible. I have seen the breath of all my hopes and feelings being taken away in an instant. This experience will be my guiding light. I promise you that you will not be disappointed in me.'

28

It was damp and bitterly cold on the upper reaches of the mountain and a forest of hardwood trees, mountain holly, rhododendron and cranberry stretched for miles around. Two Chrysler jeeps snaked up the mountain road and finally stopped near a signboard where the road ended and the forest took over completely. The hunting party, cradling .22 Caliber rifles, got off the jeeps and the local spotter led them through a known trail deep into the mountain forest. The five-man group entered the reserve area and the lush green cover stood in sharp contrast to their orange hunting jackets. The air was still and wet and the spotter led them through oak and hickory trees till they reached a mountain pass where the forest plunged steeply downhill.

The spotter held up his hand and cautioned the hunting party to stand still and maintain complete silence. They all stood nervously behind the spotter, fidgeting with their rifles and shotguns, the fear of the unexpected and the excitement of the hunt charging them up like nothing before.

Ralph Ramsey Jr sneaked a look at the special invitee standing to his right and spoke in whispers to him, 'Chief Minister, do you feel the rush of the hunt especially when you are so close to taking a life?'

Gunvir Randhawa moved on his feet a little uneasily. He had travelled all the way from Punjab for this experience. Earlier, he had, in a sense, been indirectly involved when lives had been lost, especially those of his political rivals. But he was now living through a reality which would see him take the life of another through the physicality of his action. The unique sensation of the moment was overpowering and somewhat humbling.

He was quick to reply: 'Yes, I do, Ralph. I sense it. But are we well protected? This rifle seems a little underpowered.'

'Dead right, my friend,' said the host, smiling slyly. 'The boar is a large beast and dangerous and you need a headshot or a bullet between its eyes to take it down with a .22.'

Randhawa felt a quiver of fear run through him. 'Then why are we using an underpowered rifle?'

'Don't worry, Minister. You shall see soon why

the spotter recommended a weapon of this calibre.'

The spotter suddenly held up his finger and whispered, 'Load, everyone.'

They all tensed up and the metallic sounds of rounds being chambered into rifles pierced the still air. Then everything was still again. Nothing moved in the lush undergrowth and then out of nowhere a large shaggy boar emerged from a cluster of trees and stood not more than twenty feet away from them, looking at the hunting group in confusion.

'Take aim,' suggested the spotter. All five men aimed their rifles at the boar. The hunters and their prey looked at each other in complete stillness. The boar suddenly understood it was trapped and in the line of fire. It charged to its right and a volley of gunfire rang out and followed it. They all heard the sounds of the boar crashing into the undergrowth. Then after some time the hunting party heard deep and painful grunts in the foliage. The bloodied, bullet-ridden boar suddenly emerged and charged towards the hunting party but another volley stopped it in its tracks. The giant pig began to grunt in great pain but with great tenacity it got up again and tried to scramble away from the line of fire in a confused manner, having lost its sensory abilities. The spotter held up his finger and then brought it down; he said clearly, 'Fire at will.'

The five men surrounded the crippled boar and they

all reloaded and fired, their rounds ripping through the head, the intestines and the eyes of the boar, killing it instantly, small geysers of blood erupting all around the kill zone.

A loud cheer went up in the hunting party; Ramsey put his arm around Randhawa's shoulder and smiled.

'My friend, I see that one eye is still left intact. You want to perform the coup de grâce?'

'Why not?' replied the guest, now fully into the act, savouring the animal joys of the hunt. Randhawa stared into the boar's remaining eye, widened more than usual from the advent of rigor mortis. A loud cheer for his name went up and he blasted the remaining eye, almost vivisecting the animal's head.

The spotter and a help then completely gutted the boar and buried its parts and they all made their way back to the waiting jeeps. Ralph was in great spirits and he animatedly struck up a conversation with his guest.

'So Minister, to answer your earlier question, we deliberately used underpowered rifles to enhance the thrill of the hunt. Would it have been the same if we had killed the beast with a single shot from an appropriate rifle?'

Randhawa understood and laughed raucously; Ralph joined in. Ralph whispered conspiratorially in his guest's ear as they sat in the jeep and turned away from the dead-end mountain road: 'My friend, the good life is all about the thrill of the hunt. It's all illegal, of course, what we did out there but the thrill combined with the relish of breaking the law makes it more exciting. I think there is a life lesson here that we have learned.'

Ralph Ramsey Jr winked and both men laughed. The American host continued with his philosophical interludes.

'Sometimes I wish I was born in medieval times. The men then knew a thing or two about how to squeeze the maximum out of life. They were not bound, like us, by circumscribing laws, rules and fucking regulations. *Ultra vires*, that is, beyond powers—that should be the name of the game, be it in our personal lives or in our businesses. Let no man or government come between my intent and my enjoyment of its realization.'

The two men cracked up at the thought and talked excitedly as the jeeps descended the mountaintop to a log cabin below, nestled deep within the woods.

Later in the evening they sat next to a crackling log fire and Ramsey fixed single malts of rare vintage for his guest. Both men clinked glasses to the good life and Ramsey let his guest savour the delicate vintage before he came down to business. On his nod a help came in and put down a polished silver tray on the teak table between the two men. A blade of wheat was kept on the polished tray. Ralph Ramsey Jr picked it up and examined the blade in the light of the crackling fire. His face shone with an animal magnetism as he looked at his special guest from India.

He took a sip of his malt and said, 'Chief Minister, I give you the R480 strain of wheat. I give you the power to revolutionize the farming culture in your state and usher in the second Green Revolution in your state and the country.'

Gunvir Randhawa took the proffered blade of grass and looked at it thoughtfully.

'I wish it was that simple to bring this revolution in, as you say. This strain of wheat developed in your labs has caused more trouble for me than even the fiercest opposition in my state.'

'Change, my dear friend, is always frightening. And the R480 is all about change. The R480 strain will completely change the way people farm in your state. This strain is almost bacteria resistant. It does not need chemicals and fertilizers to nurture it. This is the change that people are opposing because there are vested interests in your pesticide and fertilizer industry that are dead against the import of this strain. They have paid off many environmentalists and political leaders who are leading the charge against what we have to offer. Look Randhawa—my company, Grain Next, is not a fly-by-night operating company. We are a multibillion-dollar transnational company. We have been an industry leader in the field of genetically modified crops for decades. Change is good, my friend.'

Randhawa swallowed his whisky from the cut glass and poured himself another stiff one. He smirked as he responded to Ramsey: 'Yeah, change is good, my friend, but I wonder what good it did for the thousands of farmers and consumers in Mexico and Colombia, where your strain of wheat was introduced. After the end of field trials and a close look at consumption patterns, many of these farmers and a lot of the guinea-pig consumers had developed different forms of cancer.'

Ralph Ramsey Jr's good mood suddenly vanished. He snapped, 'All field studies were inconclusive in that the wheat strain had anything to do with that. It was probably coincidence or a faulty aggregation of data and field studies.'

'Ralph, tell this to the sceptics in my country who accuse your company of desperately trying to get permission to move in and use India as a dumping ground for dangerous and untested technology. A kind of a technology that could cause unimaginable environmental and human disaster, the likes of which has never been seen before.'

Ralph Ramsey Jr's face hardened. He spoke with

pursed lips, 'Okay Randhawa, let's play the game your way. You have catalogued my weak areas, which we both know are for real. Now let me tell you why you have come all the way to the US at a time when tensions are running high in your state. The thing is, your idiot son has emptied all the coffers of your state. You are broke. State elections are approaching and you need massive funding. You need me to bail you out. If we are clear on this, then let us cut out this morality crap and negotiate. Are you willing to deal?'

A tense silence ensued between the two men. Finally Randhawa spoke up, 'My cut will be a 40 per cent take on the initial investment you put in. I know you won't stop with this only. You would want to set up a distribution network also. Plus, cold-storage supply chains and introduction of several other secondary products and services. I assume you would also want me to recommend you to the neighbouring state of Haryana and other wheat-growing states that are prepared to listen to me. For all the other deals, my cut will be 30 per cent on the value of each and every deal negotiated. That is my offer to you.'

Ralph Ramsey Jr began to laugh and replied with a sneer, 'Why don't I say fucking good night to you? I don't run a mission of charitable sisters here. I run a business. The malt was supposed to make you feel good, not crazy.'

Both men then got down to hard bargaining till they finally settled the deal: Randhawa would get a 25 per cent cut for the initial investment and a further 15 per cent cut for all other subsidiary deals.

Both men shook hands and Ralph liberally poured the malt into their glasses.

'Here's to getting drunk tonight and making a billion bucks tomorrow morning,' said Ralph. Both drank the malt neat and settled in the leather sofas. Ralph looked at Randhawa's pensive face. He then addressed the last issue on the agenda:

'Okay, my friend, I will address the elephant in the room. We are cheering to empty promises. The fact is that your central government refuses to let my company enter your country. They have been stalling us for two years now. More specifically, your prime minister is dead against giving us permissions. I want you to tell me today what's with the man. I am given to understand you were close buddies at some point in time and then you fell out. What happened?'

Gunvir Randhawa finished his malt and then drank straight from the bottle. He looked at his American host, eyes red-rimmed.

'So this is what really happened, Ralph. Yes, we were great friends but after some time I realized that because of his honesty, he would never be up on the bidding block for sale, and he discovered that at the end of the day I was basically a crook at heart.'

Randhawa got up, took a huge swig from the bottle and moodily looked at the fireplace.

'Avatar Sidhu, at fifty-four, is a young, dynamic prime minister who has endeared himself to the people. He is the only minority politician who has made it to the top job. In a sense, it shows how much the country has changed. I should be proud that a fellow Sikh has become the prime minister but I hate him from the core of my heart. He is honest, honourable and an idealist, and I am all but that. We started our careers together as Jat boys from farming backgrounds, with so many dreams and so much energy. Our families knew each other. Some cousins are also married into each other's family. There was a time when we used to till the land together and during nights drink country liquor and dream big. We both joined the same political party, hoping to bring real change in the lives of people. As we progressed in our political journeys, he discovered his passion for the truth and I transformed into a realist. I knew then that truth and honesty are the first ideals that one has to discard in a political career. We were bound to split and that happened sooner than later. He joined the opposition party and quickly moved out of the state to a larger role in national politics. So you see, my friend, therein lies the problem for us. Avatar knows me really well. He is not opposing granting a licence for your company because of some environmentalists and the other hysteria-mongers. He is, in essence, opposing me. He knows I have a vested interest in your company. He has sworn to oppose me every step of the way. That is the reason your company cannot get a passage into India.'

Ralph Ramsey Jr got up and as was his habit put his arm around Randhawa's shoulders. He spoke with quiet consideration: 'Do you feel regret, my friend, for what has happened? I am sure it must pain you that you are completely opposed to your friend, a fellow Sikh, a man who has made your community proud all over the world.'

There was some malt left in the bottle and Randhawa offered it to Ralph.

'My friend, I think you need a drink more than me. I am dead sober now—let me tell you a truth about my community. In all the troubles my community has faced, more Sikh blood has been shed than that of the adversary. During the Khalistan movement, many more Sikhs were killed than the members of any other community. We are a strong, industrious community which loves the good things in life. But we also hate with an equal passion, especially all those from amongst us who oppose us. It does not take a Machiavelli to turn a Sikh against a Sikh. It comes with our territory. And the answer to your question is, I have no regrets breaking away from Avatar. This is the life I chose, the life I wanted.'

Ralph Ramsey Jr withdrew and turned his back to the fire. He spoke next and his words chilled Randhawa, who thought he had seen everything in his life.

'So if what you say is true, my friend, then let me suggest to you a way out of this logjam. The purpose of the morning hunt, besides the pleasure it gave us, was also to instruct. Do you know that there is something called a feral hog which roams through the Virginia countryside causing immense ecological damage, a risk to human and animal lives? There are orders in the state to shoot it at sight. The feral hog is also a big pig. The point I am making, Randhawa, is that when an animal breaks away from the herd and roams free, spreading disease, then it has to be put down. Brilliant individuals provide breakthroughs but it is only the herd mentality that ensures mankind's progress. When a man breaks ranks and upsets the apple cart then he upsets the chain of command. Such men can cause incalculable damage. They have to be removed from the picture.'

Randhawa sharply looked at Ramsey. He looked stunned.

'Have you lost your head, Ralph? This is the prime minister we are talking about.'

Ramsey turned and faced Randhawa squarely. He shook his head and laughed.

'Don't be an innocent in this matter, Randhawa. Are you seriously telling me the thought has not crossed your mind? People change regimes and vote them out of power. But there are men who replace the men who lead these regimes. It happens all the time.'

Gunvir Randhawa was at a complete loss for words. His hands shook as he put down the bottle on the table. Ralph Ramsey Jr knew that he had made a connection with his guest. He spoke softly, with some endearment: 'Take your time, Randhawa, to wrestle with your conscience if you have any left. But don't take too long. Our eye is on India but we can't wait indefinitely. There are other underdeveloped countries waiting to welcome us with open arms. In the meantime, to help you relax and think straight I have arranged a night of pleasure for you.'

Ralph clapped his hands and a tall, blonde girl wearing a silken robe walked into the room and smiled at the two men.

'Cheryl, my dear,' said Ralph, 'take my good friend to the next room and tell me tomorrow morning if he was really "randy" Randhawa during the night. You know what you have to do.'

29

The unseasonal winter rains in the village of Kasba Chardi Kala were not just confined to scattered parts in and around the district. They spread all over the state and destroyed the standing rabi crop. The state, already reeling from empty coffers, broken infrastructure and out-of-control debt, moved closer to a complete collapse. The farmer worked tirelessly in the rains lashing his fields to extract whatever he could of the crop but it was of no use. The entire crop had been struck with blight. Whatever he had invested in his crop had gone down the tube. The turn of events affected both the big farmer, the tenant and the marginal farmer. A textbook economic nightmare situation of debt, scarcity, falling demand and high prices besieged the state. The trains bringing in hands for hire from the eastern part of the country steamed in the stations with empty carriages. The bad news from the farmlands affected industrial output, and high inflation, combined with stagnation, ruled over the state.

An ill wind began to sweep across the barren fields of the state and the resulting human toll began to mount. People began to flock to dubious preachers and gurus for solace; many more took refuge in the haze of drugs. Traditional religious and spiritual outlets no longer quelled the rising anxiety of the people. An age of uncertainty had dawned, everyone was on a short fuse and violence lurked in the behaviour, the thinking and interaction of men and women. It was almost as if an unknown rash had covered the state and even a slight, pressured nudge on the skin would start the bleeding.

The stage was set for a confrontation and it began in the village of Kasba Chardi Kala one Sunday morning. Tarlochan Singh was a prosperous farmer in the village and every season the Mazhabis and hired hands from outside would work on his farmlands for wages. Tarlochan lived in a three-storey brick house in the village and owned a Mercedes-Benz which he was not shy of displaying. After the blight had ruined the crops the dust gathered on his car because there was no petrol to run it. The threshers stood idle and a lot of farm equipment lay scattered and unused around the godown. His house and his fields were a picture of despair.

Sunday morning, his wife informed him that at least a dozen labourers from the farm were outside the door, demanding wages for the work they had put in over the last three months. Tarlochan reluctantly got up, tied his turban and met his workers outside the house. He talked to them reasonably, explaining his problems. He was short of cash but full of promises for the future. He told the workers that he would pay their dues with interest after three months. Perhaps in another time, the workers would have been prepared to listen to him. But the general mood had turned ugly and no one was prepared to give the other person a second chance. The workers began to protest and then a young farmhand completely lost it and roundly abused Tarlochan Singh, accusing him of being a cheat.

The normally unflappable Tarlochan rushed into the house in a fit and emerged with a 12-bore and began to fire wildly in the air. The farmhands ran away and word soon spread among the tenant farmers that the landlords were either deferring payments or simply refusing to pay. A wave of anger swept through their lot and scores gathered and marched to Tarlochan Singh's house. Tarlochan was dragged out of his house and badly beaten up and both he and his wife along with the servants were locked up in a room. The enraged farmers ransacked the house and set his Mercedes-Benz on fire. Raising slogans, they marched all the way to the dera of Baba Santokh Singh, seeking words of comfort from him.

The incident, serious as it was, took on monstrous proportions as all kinds of vested interests spread exaggerated versions throughout the state. The Jats began to believe wildly circulating rumours that Tarlochan's wife had been raped and that the landlord was lying in a coma in the government hospital nearby. Reports also began to circulate that Baba Santokh Singh had honoured the perpetrators of the outrage with *saropas* (cloth of honour).

The divide partitioning the Jat from the Mazhabi deepened further and the gurdwaras were full of angry men exhorting people to stockpile arms and take revenge for the outrage. Gunvir Randhawa received reports of the growing tension in the state and he could not help but wonder at how after his talk with Ralph Ramsey Jr all the dominoes were falling down, clearing the path for him. A grand strategy that would enable him to seize the day began to form in his mind.

In the midst of the growing tension, Suvir quietly entered the village and resumed negotiations with Harbaksh Sondhi. Suvir sensed that something good could still emerge from the desperate situation prevailing all around. Land prices had crashed and Suvir knew that Harbaksh, for all his bluster, would not be able to hold on to his share of the land much longer. Suvir proposed a fair compensation to Harbaksh.

Simran would meet up with Suvir as the negotiations for the land deal entered the final phase. Both would drift off in the evenings to the tea stall for endless rounds of the hot brew and a free exchange of views and opinions. Both sensed in each other a sentient being, someone with whom they could share their deepest secrets.

One such day, late afternoon, Suvir met up with Simran at the tea stall. Simran could see that his usual brooding intensity had vanished. He looked genuinely happy.

'What is it?' she asked. 'You look different, happier. Something is in the air?'

Suvir showed her a sheaf of documents and ordered a round of the hot brew.

'You read me well, Simran. It's a good day. Your uncle finally signed on the dotted line. We have a deal. I am free to use the land to realize my dream.'

Simran embraced him and he with some hesitation patted her on the back.

'Congratulations are in order. I know how much this means to you. Finally, you can realize Kalpana's dream.'

'Yes, that's true. And I have taken another decision. I am going to stop running. I have been wandering like a lost soul in different parts of the country. This is my land and these are my people. I think I have made peace with myself.'

Simran remarked, 'You have chosen a hell of a time to do that. I sense the state will go up in flames very soon.'

'I know what you say is not exaggerated. But conflict has always been the cornerstone of my life. I think I have begun to enjoy my state of being. I could not get the answers I have always looked for in an idyllic place like Goa. Maybe I will get my peace in the land of my ancestors. I think the circle of life teaches you that you can finally rest and put your feet up in the place where you began.'

Simran finished her tea and held his hand.

'Come with me to the gurdwara. It is a joyous occasion. We can sanctify what you have achieved today by listening to shabad-kirtan.'

'But I am an atheist,' he protested.

She smiled and responded, 'Even an atheist seeks succour for the mind. There is nothing more peaceful than sitting in a quiet gurdwara in the afternoon, listening to kirtan. You convert only to a spiritual state of being. You don't have to be religious to be spiritual.' He reluctantly followed her and they went to the gurdwara built at the edge of the village. It was quiet inside as Simran had promised and a young duo of brothers trained in Indian classical music sang mellifluous shabad-kirtan to a few devotees inside the gurdwara. Their spiritual rendition touched different instincts in Simran and Suvir. Simran felt a sense of elevation to a different spatial realm, away from a brutal, ugly world. Suvir's eyes watered as he remembered the purity of the love he had shared with Kalpana and Naazish. It had never occurred to him before but it struck him then that his love for the two women must have been intensely spiritual. He could not overlook the irony of the moment that he, a lifelong atheist, had stumbled upon the true nature of his love for the two women in a religious place. He looked at Simran, his expression grateful, thanking her for putting him in touch with an emotion he never knew existed in him. For a quiet hour, they floated in different dimensions and it must have been a day for miracles because both felt that the wounds they had carried in them for long had magically healed.

And then in the next instant the spell broke.

The ugliness of the world they had left outside the gurdwara forced itself in. A group of village elders and the landlords from the nearby area trooped in. Anger and hate was writ on their faces. They signalled to the brothers to stop singing the shabad. The young singers quickly packed up their harmonium and tabla; a village elder, after paying obeisance to the Guru

Granth Sahib, turned to his assembled audience, who were all too eager to hear words of retaliation and revenge.

The hate-filled speeches against the dera and its head resonated inside the gurdwara and Suvir shook his head and looked at Simran. He whispered, 'Do you want to sit through this?'

'No,' she replied firmly. 'I see it happening all around me each and every day. Let us be grateful for what we experienced before all this. I still think it was worth it.'

'Yes, it was,' he agreed.

They walked out of the gurdwara and Simran felt suffused with dread and hope. She had experienced something similar when Ash Kool had reached out to her. It had all turned to dust after that. She shrank with horror at the thought that she was habituated to making poor decisions. She felt her inadequacy in completing the loop of relationships with the men who had come into her life. There was a vital piece of learning that completely escaped her. She struggled desperately, looking for the missing piece. She knew that when she found it she would be magically transformed, for better or worse. Maybe the man quietly walking next to her could take her hand and help her cross the bridge. His quiet intensity separated him from the usual breed of men. But then she had trusted a man before and had plunged into the abyss.

'It's late,' he said as they reached his parked motorcycle. 'Let me drop you home.'

'No, it's okay,' she responded. 'I will make my way home a little later. I have to meet Aranjit. I haven't met her this entire week.'

He looked away as if he was holding something back. Then he faced her and said with some urgency, 'It's none of my business but I wanted to speak to you about this woman. I have heard things about her. She could be bad news for you. You are still hurting and raw. I would not like anything to upset you further.'

She did not immediately respond and his fingers, as if by their own volition, touched her hand. She trembled at his touch and waited for more. He frowned and mumbled a half apology and then he put the key in the ignition and mounted his motorcycle.

'Thanks again for the afternoon,' he said. 'The shabad-kirtan sparked something good inside me. I haven't felt this way in a long time. I felt I made a connection.'

He was about to kick-start the motorcycle when she kept her hand on his, which was resting on the motorcycle handlebar. 'I am touched by your concern, Suvir,' she said. 'It means a lot to me. But let me say that Aranjit is like us. She is also broken within. It can't be a coincidence that three people struggling with their demons have been thrown in together in the same place. I do not know what will come out of it but I do know that all three of us in our different ways are honourable men and women. And that is enough for me. No, Suvir, I cannot abandon her.'

He smiled at her. 'Okay, have it your way. I will see you tomorrow.' He kick-started the motorcycle and disappeared in a cloud of dust. Her breath came in easier when he had left. She knew something had changed during the course of the afternoon. She felt sure of it. *Could she dare to hope again?* But Suvir had also shot off a warning about Aranjit and she knew that his instinct could be right. But all she knew at the moment was that she needed to go on. She hurried to Aranjit's place.

Dusk had fallen as she knocked on Aranjit's door. She was shocked to see Aranjit when she opened the door. She looked frail and gaunt, as if she had fallen ill. There were circles under her eyes. She looked around furtively, the arrogant yet empathetic glow of her eyes a thing of the past. Simran embraced her and took her face in her hands. She then noticed what she had been unable to see clearly from the step outside the door. The older woman looked exhausted, almost drained of life.

Simran's breath came in quickly. 'What is the matter? Are you ill?'

Aranjit shook her head and smiled weakly. 'It is nothing. I have not been sleeping well of late. It will pass. You are a rare visitor now. I hear you have made new friends in the village.'

Simran frowned, unconvinced by her mentor's reply. 'Is that what the issue is, Aranjit? Yes, I have been caught up in the village and yes, I have a new friend. His name is Suvir. But I guess you already know that. I did not visit you but you also have my number. You could have called. I am not ungrateful, Aranjit. I will never abandon you. How can I? You made me believe in a part of myself I never knew existed before. My love for you is unshakeable, eternal.'

Aranjit kept quiet and sat on a chair with a sigh. She looked distracted, unconnected to what Simran had just told her. Simran's heart sank. She was now convinced it was a day of great change. Something completely new had wormed its way into her and had begun to grow. In a strange way, her mentor also appeared to have changed. She looked as if she was exhausted of the joy of living. And worse, she did not care about it.

'Tell me the truth,' pleaded Simran. 'What's eating you up? Are you mad at me because I stopped coming for shooting practice in the afternoons? Does Suvir bother you? Let me in, Aranjit.'

Aranjit shook her head. She stroked Simran's

cheek. She spoke as if from afar, 'Silly girl, you have said your piece, now listen to me. You are free to choose. I chose to be your mentor to give you options, not close them. We have not practised for a week and I have not called on you because I have nothing more to offer to you. I have taught you the basics; life will teach you the rest. I am not that kind of a mentor who exults in and then feeds into the success and glory of the disciple. I have taught you and it is time for me to move on. If you stop by to wonder at the craft you have taught the other, you destroy the sanctity of the mentor–protégé relationship. That is all.'

'Is it?' asked Simran, her eyes watering.

'Yes, there is no more to it, Simran. In the end there is only the functionality of living and nothing else.' Then she suddenly changed her tone. 'Look, I have to go somewhere for a while. I want you to have a spare key of the cottage. If for some reason I am delayed, will you check on the cottage for me?' Simran nodded.

Aranjit handed her a key. She then told her, 'Now go, my young friend. You do what you have to do with your life. Remember, you are not bound to anyone, least of all to me. Set yourself free. I would want to hear of your exploits in the world. It would make me proud.'

Aranjit shook hands with Simran and walked her to the wicker gate of the cottage on the way out. Simran held herself together but when she had cycled far away from the cottage she let her emotions overtake her. She stopped under a tree and wept till she could cry no more. She knew then that Aranjit had gone away from her life for ever. Her world had seemed so bountiful a couple of hours ago. Now she had been left to face the unbearable pain of great loss.

It was dark by the time she reached Harbaksh Sondhi's residence. A stiff wind had started to blow and the patter of the dreaded winter rains had begun all over again. Simran rushed to the residence but the rain beat her to it. She was soaked to the skin when she knocked on the main gate. There was no response but after repeated knocking, someone opened the door from inside. Harbaksh Sondhi stood on the other side with eyes blazing. He gave no chance to Simran to understand the shocking change in her situation. He threw out a suitcase in the pelting winter rain.

'All your belongings are in the suitcase!' he thundered. 'Get out of my house and don't show me your face ever again. You are dead to me. I tolerated your disrespect for a while but you have crossed all limits. The entire village is talking of your affair with that *mona*! I should have known better than to let a debauched woman like you into my house. You have brought infamy to my name. I don't care whether your parents pay me or not. They, like you, can also go to hell. And leave my cycle outside before you go!'

Harbaksh Sondhi slammed the door on Simran's face. She stood shivering in the winter rain; the fury in her uncoiled and broke free and she shouted at the top of her voice, 'Why should you care, Harbaksh Sondhi? Really, what is the need for you to care? You were paid off by Suvir in the afternoon, were you not? There is money in your pocket tonight. It was time for the beast that has always lurked within you to come out! You sick bastard! If you have the guts, come outside and face me!'

There was complete silence at the other end and she finally turned away from the door and walked away, undecided where to go next. Then she took out her cell phone and called Suvir.

'Suvir,' she spoke, a little out of breath. 'I have been thrown out by my uncle. Is there a place where I can spend the night?'

Suvir responded quickly, 'You stay right there, Simran. I am coming for you. I will take care of the rest.'

That same night, in another part of the world, Gunvir Randhawa received a call on his cell phone from an old friend turned foe.

'Prime Minister, now this is a real surprise!' said Randhawa, taking the call.

'Gunvir, I believe you are holidaying in the United

States while your state is burning.' Avatar Sidhu, all his life, had shown no patience for small talk and pleasantries. He was always quick to come to the point, as he had just done. He spoke with tough-minded directness: 'The Intelligence Bureau is telling me that there is a possibility of large-scale caste clashes breaking out all over your state. We cannot allow such a nightmare scenario to unfold in a sensitive border state. I need you to come back and take charge. I am ready to assist your police with central forces.'

Randhawa cut his old friend short: 'Prime Minister, if you do that you would be exceeding your brief. I need not remind you that law and order is a state subject. We are perfectly capable of taking care of any disturbance. Unless, of course, you want to use the ruse of sending central forces to impose president's rule. Is that what this phone call is about, my old friend?'

30

Later, when Suvir would look back at the calamitous
turn of events that changed the destiny of a state
and the country, he would be in agreement with the
time-tested logic: great change usually follows a series
of events, much of them minor and perhaps even
innocuous. The night Simran was thrown out of the
Sondhi residence the clockwork of disparate and yet
interlinked events moved swiftly to the final hours.

It was a strange night in more ways than one. The
intensity of the winter rain was almost animalistic:
unbound fury that scavenged whatever little remained
of the crops. The tube wells overflowed with water
and the small check dams were full to the brim. The
village teetered to the edge with the threat of flash
floods. Suvir came for Simran, the headlight of his
motorcycle illuminating her as she stood outside the
Sondhi residence.

He kept the motorcycle running and shouted over

the din of the falling rain. 'Hop on at the back. I have told the hotel owner where I am staying to organize another room for you. You have nothing to worry about.'

'Thanks!' she shouted and straddled the motorcycle, holding him from the back. 'I wouldn't know where to go on a night like this.'

He nodded and turned the motorcycle away from the row of houses and sped across the unpaved road near the fields. It was pitch-dark and the rain drummed a ferocious beat—the motorcycle beam cut across the broken road and the fields. Suvir kept his head low in the driving rain and shouted, 'I feel responsible in a way for what your uncle did. I gave him a big, fat cheque today. Maybe that's what emboldened him. I can put a stop payment order on the cheque first thing in the morning and renege on the deal.'

'Don't do that!' she shouted to make herself heard from her pillion position on the speeding motorcycle. 'I always knew he was a snake. He chose to shed his skin today. It's okay. I know this deal means a lot to you. You own the land now. And that makes me happy. I will figure out something for myself.'

The wavering beam of the motorcycle lit the fields ahead. Suvir thought he saw a white blur the size of a corporal body flash past him. He looked to his right and he couldn't be sure if he had imagined it or had seen some stray animal from the nearby woods streak across the fields. He debated whether to stop and examine the occurrence or to continue. It was then that he heard the sound of a powerful vehicle closing in behind him. A big Ford SUV with a powerful beam came dangerously close to the motorcycle and almost drove it into the fields. The SUV screeched to a halt further ahead, blocking the narrow mud road going into the village. Suvir had no option but to stop the speeding bike.

Men armed with automatic weapons, self-loading rifles and old army-issue Sten guns got out of the SUV.

'This looks like trouble. Hold tight,' Suvir whispered to Simran. 'Let me handle this.'

The search party flashed powerful torches in Suvir's direction and walked to him with slow, deliberate steps. A powerfully built man with a thick beard, spiky hair and close-set, beady eyes came up to Suvir. The other men flashed the torchlight at Simran, examining her closely.

'What is the matter?' asked Suvir.

The man with the thick beard held up a finger and spoke in a low voice: 'We ask the questions here. Who are you and what are you doing on the road at this time of the night?'

Suvir spun a story that they were staying at the nearby district hotel and had lost their way in the rain.

The heavily built man looked unconvinced and flashed the torchlight in Suvir's face. Then he asked him casually, 'Have you seen a girl go past? She is a foreigner and mentally unstable.'

'No,' replied Suvir. The heavy-set man continued to examine Suvir and then he signalled to his accomplices. They all turned and began to walk away. The heavy-set man stopped, turned and rudely trained the torchlight beam on Suvir's face.

'My name is Rana. I hope for your and this girl's sake that you are not lying. Otherwise it will go very badly for both of you.'

Suvir waited for the men to get into the SUV. He kick-started the motorcycle and drove it cautiously behind the SUV. He knew the men in the SUV were tracking his moves. He maintained his distance from the SUV and once the men in the truck were satisfied about Suvir's motives, they sped away at great speed. Suvir swerved the motorcycle and sped back on the mud road to the spot where he had seen the blur.

'We have to rescue the girl, Simran!' Suvir shouted. 'I have an idea where she could be hiding.'

The rain had eased up a bit as Suvir stopped the motorcycle near a field of elephant grass. Both got off and Simran looked in the dark across the field, waved her arms and shouted, 'It's okay, you can come out now! All those men looking for you have gone away. We are friends! Believe in us. We will help you!'

There was no response from the fields. Both continued to shout and finally Suvir shook his head and told Simran it was time to go. He turned the ignition key of the bike and pushed his foot down on the pedal. Barely a metre ahead of them, a girl with dishevelled hair came out of the fields and ran in front of them. The motorcycle headlight picked up a girl stripped of all clothes with deep, lacerations all over her body. She stood crouched, shaking uncontrollably as if in convulsion. Suvir killed the engine of the bike and Simran ran to the girl and hugged her. They opened Simran's suitcase and Simran helped the girl wear a set of clothes. Then they all sped away to the district hotel.

Some time later, Simran settled the girl in the additional room they had rented. She took blankets and hot tea with her and closed the door from within to confabulate with the girl. Suvir paced outside the closed door. He lost track of time as he paced outside the door and finally after a long wait, Simran came out alone, looking badly shaken up.

'Tell me what's going on?' Suvir asked her.

Simran looked at him, her eyes flashing in anger.

'I am not the enemy,' spoke Suvir quietly. 'I understand your anger. It does not require great imagination to see that perhaps those men in the truck and maybe even others have abused the girl.'

Simran breathed deeply and sat on a chair outside the room.

'The girl has not been hurt,' she replied, struggling with the outrage claiming her. 'She's been brutalized. Understand this, Suvir, my story is not half as sinister as what this girl has suffered.'

Suvir dragged a chair next to Simran and sat beside her. Her hands had balled into fists, her knuckles white. Her teeth were clenched and low, moaning noises of pain escaped them. Suvir with great patience opened her fists, the fingers one by one, and rubbed her hands.

'Don't shut me off, Simran. I am not one of them. You have to see clearly. I know the girl has touched something very deep and raw inside you. But if you close up, I won't be able to help her or reach out to you.'

Simran's face twisted with agony, her eyes stinging with tears. She snatched her hands away.

'That's all your sex can do, is it not? Either rape us or descend like guardian angels to help us? As if all of us are either saints or whores? There is no space in between for a woman, is there, Suvir?'

Her words like a tolling bell clanged a note of dissonance inside Suvir. He mumbled an apology, withdrew and sat next to her quietly, waiting for her emotions to settle down. After a while Simran said to him, 'The girl in the room is Greta Braun. She is a German national, a single parent. She is an architect and after her marriage collapsed she moved out with her daughter. Mother and daughter got along fine but the emptiness and the loneliness would often claim her. She searched the Internet for solace and stumbled across Baba Santokh Singh's videos on YouTube. With each passing day, she grew more fascinated with the man. She read all the literature available on him and avidly followed developments connected with him. Three months back she sold off all her worldly possessions and took a flight from Stuttgart and came to the dera for good, along with her eleven-year-old daughter. She was welcomed with open arms and paraded in meetings and public discourses by the Baba. He used her to send the message that his appeal had spread far and wide. She served the purpose of being great propaganda material for him. The subtext of his message was that even professional classes in western Europe were taking him seriously. During the initial months, every day, every event was rose-tinted for Greta. She met some of the most powerful people in the Indian social network—senior journalists, Bollywood stars, judges, politicians, religious leaders, yoga gurus, senior civil servants. She would constantly be by the Baba's side. She was introduced as his 'young sister from the West'. Greta felt grateful that she had made the correct choice in life. She surrendered herself completely to her new way of life.

'Slowly the freshness associated with the new arrival began to wear off. And along with that, the mask came off and the real face of the dera and its chief emerged. There was a life above the surface and one below it—quite literally. A subterranean world of sexual slavery, daily beatings and paedophilia existed below the dera in the cellars. The place was out of bounds but due to the access Greta enjoyed on account of her public appearances she penetrated the secretive cellars below the dera. She was shocked when she discovered that there were others like her from the West and other parts of the world, caged in the cellars like exotic animals. There were even ill-fed, scantily clothed children running around in the cellars. In her naivety she at first thought that rogue elements in the dera must be misusing the Baba's name and fame to carry on nefarious activities. She confided in the Baba. He told her not to worry about it and that he would take care of it. She kept quiet for a few days but she had a sense that nothing had changed. It was getting worse. At nights she could hear the sounds of muffled screams and manic laughter from below. She began to fear for her and her child's life. She had an opportunity to escape and forget about the entire episode, to write it off as a nightmare. But she had invested an important period of her life in being devoted to the Baba and her conscience drove her to seek answers from him. She sought time with him and in that meeting she again confronted him and demanded answers as to what was going on in the cellars.

The man who had inspired her dropped his mask during the meeting. He did not say much as he listened to her. But his eyes shone with manic light and she knew then that she had made a terrible mistake. All along, she had been living in the lair of the beast and had been completely unaware of it. She resolved to leave the dera in the morning. That very night her life changed for ever. Well into the night, armed sentries entered her room and dragged her out of it; they then marched her below to the underground cellars. She was locked up in a cell. Her daughter was taken away someplace else.

She was given the bare minimum to eat and when she protested they chained her ankle to a string bed in the room. But all this was just the beginning of the horrors she went through. In a week's time she was close to starvation and completely dehydrated. Baba Santokh Singh then walked in one night and unleashed his bestiality on her. He horsewhipped her till the cuts showed and when she was close to losing consciousness, he raped her. He performed the most perverse sexual acts on her.

That then became his routine for the next few days. Greta would wait in terror every day for when he would come in the night to give vent to his bestiality. Every night he would spring up some new perverse act. He would always rape her at that instant when she was close to losing all consciousness. Then one day all that stopped. He left her alone. She was still a prisoner in the underground cellars but she was given enough to eat and drink. She marginally recovered and even got some colour in her cheeks. But he was fattening her up like a tethered goat. He was saving her up for his most perverse and inhuman act.'

Simran stopped the narrative and trembled violently. She looked into the distance, her own agony now fully coupled with Greta's story. She continued: 'Then one day they bought down her eleven-year-old daughter to the same room where the mother was imprisoned. Baba Santokh Singh followed his armed sentries. The young girl, still not a teen, looked horribly malnourished. Her bones showed and her golden curls fell on her face like pasted straw. She looked on vacantly, unable to recognize her mother. Greta screamed her guts out continually that night and the Baba smiled and instructed his guards to stand in the room and watch him closely. Then he raped the eleven-year-old girl before her hysterical mother and the laughing guards.'

Baba left after the outrage and the guards forcibly took away Greta's daughter to an unknown location in the cellars. Greta almost committed suicide that night. But the haunted look on her daughter's face as she was being taken away gave her the courage to go on. The Baba did not violate them after that. He felt that Greta had been taught a lesson for a lifetime because she had dared to question the scheme of things in the dera.

But Greta developed a great will to pull her daughter out of that hellhole. To do that she required help and she knew that she would have to escape and come back later for her daughter. Her opportunity came one day when a guard missed his shift and there was a man short to check the linen and stained sheets that would be sent out for cleaning once a week in trucks. Greta tucked herself in one of the containers crammed with filthy laundry. The trucks carried her out of the forbidden gate and somewhere on the highway she made good her escape. Her daring escape was discovered in the evening headcount. An enraged Santokh Singh sent one of his most vicious thugs, Rana, who we had encountered, after her. You are aware of what happened after that.'

Simran stopped speaking and became completely still. She looked at Suvir and asked him, 'Tell me Suvir, what is the tipping point at which a man becomes a beast? The Baba raped the little girl and the rest stood and watched and laughed at the act. You are a tough but just and sensitive man. You are the kind of man who is completely different from this god-man. So let me ask you this question, Suvir. Have you ever felt the urge that these men have felt?'

Suvir got up and walked to the balcony and faced Simran. 'Simran, I cannot be a hypocrite and apologize for my gender, at least for some of them and the things they do. That would be cozening those who condemn all this. I find the club hypocrisy of such elements no less dangerous than the deeds of the Baba and his henchmen. The fact is that for all our sophistication and awareness, life is still intensely brutal. The world we live in becomes a primeval jungle in an instant for the victim.

'In that light, it would be fair to let each and every man speak for himself. All my life I have fanatically pursued what is right and tried to stay away from what is wrong. It is only the space in between that has always confused me. What this god-man has done and continues to do is heinous and evil. He must be stopped, incarcerated, perhaps even be sent to the gallows. The real problem, Simran, is that many of us have stored the sum total of what this man does in a little corner in our minds. Some men entertain fantasies of great cruelty in their minds but stop short of realizing them because they are afraid. This god-man has no such fear. He realizes the misogynistic fantasy of men in real time, in the real world. That is why he is so dangerous. That is why he must be stopped.'

Simran eyes flashed again with great anger.

'You sidestepped the question, Suvir.'

Suvir never took his eyes away from Simran when he answered her. 'I really don't know, Simran, and that is the truth. There have been episodes in my life that have been very violent. Did I channel my perverse fantasy towards inflicting violence against those I thought had been wrong, all those who had conspired against the state? I will never know. All I know is that no man can certify himself as being immune to such an influence. You horsewhip a woman or rape her or even abuse her mildly with your tongue—all these acts exhibit similar features belonging to the same family. Like a dormant virus, these features are present in my gender. That is the harsh truth.'

A light shone in Simran's eyes. 'At least you were honest. What you say is cold comfort for the girl behind this door but it does give perspective. What do we do next?'

'We follow procedure. We go the police right now. If we delay this then we are bound to lose this case. Speed is of the essence. I intend to file a complaint and seek Santokh Singh's immediate arrest. Can you get the girl to testify to the police against him?'

31

The station house officer (SHO) of the district, Satvinderpal Singh, came out of the anteroom in the dera and placed a call on his cell phone. Gunvir Randhawa's man Friday and personal assistant, Khurana, took the call on his satphone. Khurana and his boss were seated in a Learjet aircraft flying back to Amritsar from the United States, the trip a farewell present from Ralph Ramsey Jr. Satvinder briefed the man who controlled the network of senior police officers in charge of law and order in the state.

'How do you want me to handle the situation, sir? The evidence against Santokh Singh looks pretty strong and the girl is prepared to testify in front of a magistrate.'

'I will get back to you,' replied Khurana tersely. A short while later Khurana called up the SHO.

'Boss says it's a God-given opportunity, Satvinder. Arrest the man and slap all kinds of charges against

297

him. And later in the quiet of the night do an encounter and eliminate the army man, the girl and that foreigner. That way you can pin the rape case and the murders on Santokh Singh. We will have an airtight case against him. That should be enough to finish his movement completely and send him to jail for the rest of his life.

The line went dead and Satvinder pal Singh walked to the anteroom. Suvir, Simran and a terrified-looking Greta sat on one side of the table. The other side of the table was occupied by a smooth-talking public relations officer (PRO) of the dera. None of Santokh Singh's security detail was visible on the premises. The persuasive PRO smiled and calmly defended the Baba against the police officer's charges.

'Officer, there has been a big mistake. The charges against the Baba are blatantly false. The Baba is a saint and an ascetic. Everyone knows that. Thousands visit him every day. No doubt Greta met the Baba along with the tens of thousands who meet him every day. The Baba blessed her but unfortunately she suffers from a mental disorder. The Baba's team of doctors examined her and found her to be a schizophrenic. She imagines a lot of things. As a policy, children are not allowed inside the dera so where is the question of rape and abuse of a child? If you wish, I can get you testimonials from our team of doctors. These are well-reputed doctors, eminent specialists in their field.

As for your other charges, let me say that one can only feel amused at the nature of the allegations levelled. There are no cellars, slaves and malnourished children running around on these premises. The basement is used for storage purposes and if you get a magisterial search warrant we will gladly open our basement for inspection. It is a cold and wet night. We should all be on our way.'

Satvinderpal began to laugh. Then he put an arm around the PRO, his face animated with a cop's sneer. 'Mr PRO, do we look stupid to you? The new rape law entails a life imprisonment sentence for the offence. Your boss is gone for good. The complainant sitting in front of you has registered an FIR against him. Will you bring him out or shall I beat you up and drag you to him?'

The PRO licked his dry lips. 'There is no need to lose our civility, Inspector. I have a small request. Can I have a separate word with you and Mr Suvir Suri?'

Satvinderpal thought about that for a moment and then nodded in Suvir's direction. Both joined the PRO outside the anteroom.

The PRO spoke quickly, 'Look Inspector, the Baba is not an ordinary individual. Only a court of law can decide if he is guilty. You will have a massive law-and-order situation on your hands if you humiliate him and arrest him in front of his followers by the strong-arm methods your force is well-known for. The grounds have to be prepared if you are to arrest him. If you give me permission, can this sensible man, Mr Suri, meet the Baba in private to discuss the modalities of his incarceration? We will cooperate but we also need some flexibility from your end.'

The SHO thought about it for a moment and gave his assent. 'I will accompany Suvir Suri in this meeting,' he said.

The PRO shook his head. 'No, that defeats the purpose of this meeting. No one else can be present during the meeting.'

'Okay, let's make this quick then,' agreed Satvinderpal. 'Either way, the Baba goes to jail tonight.'

The Baba sat waiting for Suvir in the meditation centre, next to the anteroom. It was a vast hall with floor-to-ceiling French windows and low-hung fans. He sat on a silver throne kept on a marble dais. The Baba's sartorial sense at this time of the night did not really surprise Suvir. He had read somewhere that the man loved to play mind games, especially with his opponents. The Baba had tied his hair in a ponytail, he wore a Nike tracksuit and loafers, and an iPod was plugged into his ears. He sat casually on the throne, his feet propped on the armrests, a picture of rock-star coolness and disdain. The Baba flashed a sixties' peace sign when Suvir was shown into the meditation centre. He also pulled out the iPod earphones and smiled broadly.

'Come in peace, my friend,' he welcomed Suvir. 'I have come to know you have lodged some kind of a complaint against me. I believe that there is a police party waiting for me in the next room. I thought we could have a chat about all that. Part of my job is to calm people down and give them hope. Why should you be any different?'

Suvir kept quiet, not responding to the opening the Baba gave him. He had a sense he was dealing with a highly dangerous and calculating man. The Baba discarded the iPod and took out a smartphone and held it out to Suvir. 'I took the liberty to google you to find out more about you. I have to say I am most impressed. You are a genuine war hero, a commando who went all the way to Pakistan to strike fear in the heart of the enemy, a man who broke the back of terrorist teams. The Internet says you are a rare breed of a man, one who thinks on his feet, acts swiftly and ruthlessly and yet is strangely compassionate.'

Baba Santokh Singh's voice dropped a little, masking the sarcasm. 'You know, I like to think of myself the same way . . .'

Suvir looked around him and noticed there wasn't a chair in the room. The setting, the casual approach and the scene was designed to confuse and intimidate him.

Suvir then decided to level the playing field. He spoke up forcefully, 'I don't think, Santokh Singh, that you understand the meaning of the word "compassion", though you have built a career and an empire around that word. I don't waste my time talking with people who sit on thrones five feet above the ground. You can keep your feudal act for the gullible; if you want to engage with me, step down.'

The Baba with a beatific smile walked down the elevation and tried to put his arm around Suvir's shoulder. He wasn't ready to give up the facade.

Suvir shrugged him away. He came to the point: 'Actually, you are dressed appropriately for a night in a jail cell. Such preparation is wasted on me. I am a cut-and-dried kind of a man. Once I have made up my mind about something, nothing can persuade me not to do it again and again, a million times. And that would be to put you in jail for ever, for the rest of your natural life.'

Baba Santokh Singh dropped the expansive, larger-than-life act, withdrew and held up his hands.

'You are good, I will admit to that. Please understand, I deal with hundreds of different kinds of people each day. Part of my charm lies in becoming something different for different sets of people. So let me come to the point and negotiate.'

'Negotiate for what?'

'Come, come, Mr Suri, we are both men of the world. Why would you want to trouble me at this time of the night with these frivolous complaints? What is it that you really want?'

Suvir looked at what lay beyond the large French windows. Something troubled him. It was as if something had awakened the combatant in him. It cautioned him of approaching danger, and he steeled himself to face it. He spoke harshly, 'Well then let's cut out the games, Santokh Singh. You are going to prison. What is there to negotiate? This is an open-and-shut case.'

'Really, Mr Suri, is it? Let me tell you that we have a lot to talk about and negotiate. I keep tabs on everything that goes on around me, especially in my area of influence. You have recently purchased a large tract of land. I am ready to purchase it from you at five times the price you have paid.'

Suvir laughed at the suggestion. 'I think you can be a little more sophisticated than that. But then again, this is you, is it not, Santokh Singh? You have a profile larger than life but where do you really come from? I think I know about that. But leave that aside. You expect me to persuade Greta to drop the case against you after you have just made a crude attempt to bribe me? All your act has done is to give me proof of your guilt.'

The smile disappeared from Santokh Singh's face. His appearance altered and the persuasive tone in his voice vanished. 'Mr Suri, you have no idea how my mind works. Let me make myself a little bit clearer. I think you did not hear me correctly the first time. I know of your interest in the Chardi Kala village. I know about your plans to build a cancer clinic on the land you have purchased recently. I have known about this for quite some time. I keep an ear very close to the ground; I have my eyes on each and every activity that goes on in places where my interests are at stake.

'So you pick a fight with me and you build your clinic. Even if that clinic comes up do you seriously believe that my men and followers will allow you to work in peace even for a single day? Who do you think you are? Indiana Jones on an expedition in strange lands, dispensing your fucking morality and justice to people you know nothing about? This is not your ecosystem, Mr Suri. You would be best advised to disappear while there is still time. There is a storm that is coming and you have been warned to stay out of its path.'

'Well, I have some bad news for you, Baba. I stay put and you go to jail.'

Baba Santokh Singh dropped the role play and he climbed on the dais and claimed his throne. His face had darkened. His eyes shone with an unnatural light.

'Understand this, Suri. I am not an individual but a symbol of the aspirations and hopes and dreams of a million people. You can't cage a million peoples' hopes in a jail cell. People like you and Greta and your girlfriend go to jail, not me. My fame and my charisma have transformed me. I am beyond the reach of mortals. Last chance—withdraw the complaint, spare yourself and your fellow travellers the grief and we can all go back to sleep through what is left of the night.'

Suvir looked at the man straight in the eye when he answered.

'Santokh Singh, if I strip you of your tracksuit and force you to look in the mirror, especially the sight of your hideous genitalia, which you forced on Greta's underage daughter, and if I squeeze your balls hard enough, then I promise you will squeal and feel the pain like any ordinary man. There is nothing immortal about you. You are low scum, a paedophile and a charlatan. You deserve to be locked up for ever in prison, and this discussion is now over. If you don't come down from your throne, I will drag you down as you weep and plead. The choice is yours.'

Santokh Singh stared at Suvir and then a chilling smile flitted across his face. The unnatural light in his eyes shone more brightly.

'Have it your way, Mr Suri,' said Santokh Singh

as he descended from the dais. Suvir walked him to the door and suddenly he felt compelled to look at the large French windows. Something was not right, he knew. It was almost as if a trap had been sprung.

Suvir was still trying to figure what was tipping him off when the Baba and Greta came face to face in the anteroom. Greta shrank from his stare and Simran held her hand to give her the courage to confront Santokh Singh. But the god-man seized the initiative. He shocked everyone with his words.

'Greta, you stupid little cunt! When will you ever learn? I raped you and your daughter to teach you a simple little lesson. Don't go around interfering in other people's affairs! Now you have done it again! You are not even bothered that your little girl is in our keep!'

Suvir then knew that something was completely wrong with the scene, the words and the sequencing. He realized a little late that a completely different script had been written beforehand for them. Greta broke away from Simran's protective grasp and rushed to the Baba, who claimed her. He began to laugh like a maniac and Satvinderpal also felt that something was terribly amiss. He flipped open his holster to take out his sidearm. The PRO had disappeared and Suvir moved the quickest, his instincts saving him. Instincts he had developed working his entire life in the deadly theatre of uncertainty and extreme violence. He dived towards Simran to take her out of the line of fire. Armed sentries led by Rana raced in through the French windows from the other room. They came into the anteroom and sprayed it with machine-gun fire. Satvinderpal's chest was torn open with repeated bursts.

A searing explosion outside shattered the still of the night. A second team had thrown a grenade at the four-man police team waiting in the police jeep outside. No one survived the attack. Suvir and Simran dodged a hail of machine-gun fire as they ran through the narrow passage leading out of the anteroom. The passage opened out near the perimeter fencing and the fields were not too far away. The clatter of machine-gun fire receded in the background as they made their escape into the nearby fields. But the hyena laugh of the god-man hung like a shroud over the entire area. A thought struck Suvir as they sifted their way in the dark through a jungle of elephant grass. The denouement in the anteroom was not an accident. It was a deliberate, well-planned attack. Baba Santokh Singh was quite capable of turning Greta's story on its head to fulfil his nefarious designs. Perhaps he was planning something bigger.

32

The anatomy of a riot hides more than it reveals. No police force or justice-delivery system anywhere in the world has ever been able to pin down the backroom perpetrators and their motive in a riot. This is especially true in a country like India. The nature of a riot is such that the heinous deeds of men and their conspiracies are consumed in large-scale disturbance and the truth is buried for ever. Only rumours, conjectures, gossip and allegations comprise the detritus left behind after a riot. Truth more than human misery is the real casualty in a riot.

In the early hours of the morning, Baba Santokh Singh's core team began working their cell phones after the incident in the anteroom. They sent a simple message to Baba Santokh Singh's point men positioned in every village, *taluka* and district in the state. These men were told to fan out and galvanize the entire legion of the Baba's followers in the state and whip them up into a frenzy. That would be done by pedalling the following story: The chief minister of the state, his largely upper-class constituents and the landlords had hatched a conspiracy deep in the night to humiliate the Baba and arrest him. False charges had been slapped against the Baba that he had raped a foreigner and her daughter. A particularly notorious SHO called Satvinderpal Singh, also known as the 'encounter cop', was assigned to the case. His job was to drag the Baba in the night in front of his followers and beat him senseless in the police station. By sheer providence, a group of the Baba's followers saw the outrage being committed and intervened. The enraged followers lost control and attacked the police party and killed and burnt the policemen. It was all, of course, very unfortunate but the followers had been pushed to the wall. The symbol of their hope and the leader of their caste movement had been deeply humiliated. The Baba was ready to prove his innocence in the matter. The foreigner was the Baba's 'younger sister' and she was ready to testify before an impartial judge that the Baba had been framed in the conspiracy.

The job of the point men was to let the story gain traction swiftly and enrage the Baba's followers. To step up the offensive, the Baba also issued a call to his followers; he urged them to leave their homes and march to the dera, without wasting a moment. The

Baba would address them at nine in the morning. He would give the call that enough was enough and that the revolution had started. The vast multitudes of his followers would paralyse the state and not leave the dera until the central government agreed to their demand for a separate state.

The subtext of the mass-action plan was a little different. The Baba knew very well that the Gandhian efforts of mobilization could only achieve so much. A heftier push was needed to realize the dream. Subtly, the followers would be encouraged to start rioting as they marched to the dera. A state teetering out of control would either have to give in to the threat or impose president's rule. Either way, Baba Santokh Singh would emerge a winner.

It was a high-stakes poker game and Baba Santokh Singh had made up his mind to cash in all his chips and take his earnings home before the end of the day.

The point men began fanning words of dissent and rage among the faithful. First light had still not spread across the sky before the first riots broke out in the villages around the dera. Santokh Singh's enraged followers clashed with the Jats and soon houses had been set on fire and blood had been shed in the fields. Columns of smoke rose in the early-morning sky and the riots spread with unimaginable speed across all the districts in the state. Bands of people armed with spears, rods and double-barrelled guns assembled near their farmhouses while many others marched to prime economic targets to destroy them. The marginalized fled their homes to escape the fury of marauding mobs. A paroxysm of hatred seized the state in the early hours of the day.

Suvir and Simran, fleeing from the dera, reached Lovely Hotel—the only hotel in the district. Suvir looked at the early-morning sky. Vultures were wheeling in the sky above and many barns and cowsheds had been set on fire. In the far distance, the cries of men clashing with each other could be heard. Someone had activated the loudspeaker at the gurdwara and men were screaming a call to arms. Suvir looked at his watch. He held Simran by her shoulders and looked her in the eye.

'He's done what I had feared he would. To cover his tracks, he has set the whole state on fire. He had planned all this. He's moving towards a big push. The results could be catastrophic. It's very worrying but also too much for you. How are you coping with all this? You must be exhausted?'

Simran managed a weak smile.

'I am okay. I thought I had seen everything but every time the cruelty of men surprises me. I feel awful for Greta. She was forced to make the wrong choice. He will use it to perpetuate his reign.'

'Yes . . . he will,' replied Suvir, looking a little distracted. 'Look, he has unleashed a wave of madness. I have seen too many conflicts and let me tell you that when you enter the eye of the storm, people lose all reason. I have a sense we will be targeted. It makes sense to leave this place and come back later when all this has settled down. There is an early-morning eight o'clock feeder train that we can board from the local station. It will take us to Amritsar city. We can take a flight from Amritsar to Delhi, where I have a house.'

'That's okay, Suvir, but I want to check on Aranjit first. I fear for her safety in this situation.'

Suvir nodded and Simran worked her cell phone but received no reply from Aranjit's phone. Suvir looked into the small cabin next to the reception. The hotel manager, Somnath, was talking excitedly on the phone with someone. He was sweating profusely. Suvir gestured to him to take a break from his conversation. Somnath looked up. The urgency in Suvir's voice was unmistakable.

'Somnath, I am leaving. The situation does not look too good. I will pay by cash.'

Somnath excused himself on the phone and looked worriedly at Suvir. 'Suri saab, I would advise you to stay put here. I am talking to a close friend of mine who tells me that the situation is out of control. Mobs are patrolling the highway and looting and burning anything that moves over there. Another mob has set the district railway station on fire. All trains have been cancelled. There are rumours that the army has been called in.'

Suvir shook his head and swore under his breath.

'Saab, the hotel is still relatively safe,' urged the hotel manager. 'I am asking for some security for the hotel and our guests from musclemen who belong to the local *akhara*. We will do the best we can.'

Suvir could not help but retort, 'You think your local toughs can stand up in front of a maddened mob? That's never going to happen, Somnath. But I see sense in waiting this one out.'

Around the same time the Learjet carrying Gunvir Randhawa landed at Amritsar international airport. A government vehicle escorted by heavily armed Punjab police commandos took the chief minister and the welcoming party from the airport to a government circuit house in the city. The streets were deserted and curfew orders had been given. Signs of vandalism and looting could be seen in the marketplaces. At traffic intersections and main roads, rioters had set up blockades of burning tyres to slow down the advancing police units. Many shops had been set on fire. The police, armed with self-loading rifles, patrolled the streets warily.

The official escort reached the circuit house; a posse of police officers then escorted the entourage from the airport to a private room in the circuit house. Khurana signalled to the police officers and all of them left the room. The entourage accompanying Gunvir Randhawa comprised key members of his cabinet, men fiercely loyal to the chief minister. They were privy to Randhawa's deepest secrets, except one. And that secret was about to be revealed to them today. They were all meeting to discuss a possible solution to the crisis gripping the state. Khurana had enigmatically told them that they would be introduced to a man they had never met before—a man who held the key to the crisis.

Khurana closed the door to the private room and after the men had taken their seats he went to a small room attached to the main room. He emerged a moment later with a man who walked with a slouch, his turban tied untidily. The man had a deep furrow running down his forehead.

The older loyalists in the group stared in horror at the man who had walked in like a ghost. They instantly recognized him, even though the years had not been kind to him. The younger loyalists frowned, wondering what the fuss was all about. Khurana took it upon himself to introduce the man.

'Gentlemen, let me introduce all of you to the man

who has been presumed dead all these years—the man who was Sant Jarnail Singh Bhindranwale's most trusted aide and popularly called "Commander" by the then rank and file. He was the man who planned each and every hit with unerring military precision. I give to you, Avjeet Singh, the man who very nearly crippled the Indian Army's Operation Blue Star thirty years ago!' he said with a flourish.

The breath of the younger lot was taken away. They had all heard about the legend, read about his exploits and how he had marshalled Bhindranwale's fighters holed up in the Golden Temple to blunt the attack by the Indian Army units in 1984. It was widely reported that he, along with hundreds of others, had perished in the fierce battle. But he stood before them, alive and well, a man from a different time and age, a man who was going to make history come full circle and complete the unfinished business of 1984.

Gunvir Randhawa nodded to Khurana who withdrew into the shadows. He clasped Avjeet's hand and invited him to sit with the rest of them. He then addressed his senior cabinet: 'We are brothers here, brothers who have fought many political battles, brothers who have crushed the opposition by fair and foul means, brothers who have tasted the sweet rewards of power. All of us set out on a journey and in the course of that journey we have known and shared each other's secrets, some of them too terrible to be told.

'But none of those secrets are as dark and fearsome as this one. I had good reasons for not sharing this secret with you. I had to make sure I chose the right time, the right moment to tell you about this, after you had given me proof of loyalty, which all of you have done.

'Avjeet survived Operation Blue Star because Santji wanted him to do so. He knew he would not survive the Indian Army's assault and it was important for someone to be around for the future generations to guide them in the changing times. Khalistan has receded in the pages of history but the struggle for a robust Sikh identity is a relevant and live issue. This is all the more important in the present times, when our identity faces a serious threat from the likes of Santokh Singh.'

The chief minister got up, crossed his arms and looked at his men.

'Avjeet Singh has stayed in the shadows and has been advising me for a long time. But now, since all of us are bound to each other by vested interest, I thought it was time to introduce you to him and listen to his advice. What is our vested interest? Do I need to tell it to you? Santokh Singh has awakened the aspirational desire in the man who had never dared to look up at his master. He has changed the entire equation for us. We can no longer reap votes and riches merely by advocating the cause of a uniform Sikh identity. He laughs at the idea of a uniform identity. He says it is a ploy by the upper castes to perpetuate their rule. In his vision of things, caste is directly linked with economic interest and if there is one great idea then it is that caste should form the basis of a uniform identity. Santokh Singh, with his rock-star coolness, has sold his idea well. With each passing day, he is making people at the bottom of the heap aware that behind the slogan of a Sikh identity there are men like us who have used the slogan to deny them justice and fill our coffers.

'The irony is that Santokh Singh is exactly like us. He is ruthless, cunning, a killer—a man who is completely debauched, someone who loves the good and perverse things of life at the same time. Such a man needs to be stopped because he is a threat to our existence and to our way of life.'

Gunvir Randhawa then looked towards Avjeet Singh.

'The man who will help us stop Santokh Singh is right here with us. Avjeet, we are all ears for what you have to say.'

Avjeet, with the impression of great fatigue, got up and looked at the expectant faces in the room. He spoke slowly, with great emphasis, 'I have always been a man of few words so I will keep this short. As I look at it, all of you face an existential problem. You are barely a few hours away from losing the state of Punjab to Santokh Singh. To give the man credit, he has moved well on the chess board. If his followers collect at the dera and you give the go-ahead for police action, then there will be innumerable casualties and you will lose the state for generations to come. This is what he wants. A Blue Star in which hundreds are killed will not work in 2014. But a targeted assassination of a single man might turn the tide back in your favour.

'Understand that Santokh has unleashed the mother of all riots because the sheer pressure of dealing with the situation will cloud all your decision-making abilities. He is also using the riots to put a veil on all the filth that is hidden in the cellars of the dera. Thirdly, he is sending a message to you: "Don't mess with me. Choose to look the other way when you see my excesses." We cannot accept his proposition because we are both fighting for the same cake. If we ignore him he will ultimately render us redundant. He knows that and he has precipitated the crisis because he is a man in a hurry.

'In the old days, satraps used to deploy this strategy. It can still work. Governments, courts, the law-and-order machinery have been known to run into a brick wall against fanatical mandate.

'So how do we neutralize such a man? The only way to do that is to turn the objective of this riot on its head. Let me explain. Santokh Singh has created a large-scale disturbance almost like a smokescreen to conceal his hideousness from the world. He will use the confusion and mayhem to realize his political objectives. What if we also use the same confusion and mayhem to assassinate him? No one will know who did the deed.'

A younger minister spoke up, 'There are police commandos who will do anything that we ask of them. We just have to give the word and they will do the job.'

Avjeet Singh patiently heard the minister and then he whispered, 'No. That would be the most thoughtless action we could agree to. The objective of a political assassination is to smooth out the road to power and not create a roadblock by creating a doubt in the minds of people about the legitimacy of your action. Mrs Gandhi, throughout her political career, could never justify the storming of the Golden Temple. It turned an entire generation of Sikhs against her. A show of force from our side will turn the tide against us. Some new Baba will emerge and channel the anger and disgust of the people against us. We should be telling our police units to delay reaching the dera slightly and let the mayhem continue for some more time. Let the confusion, the killings and the rioting go on unchecked till the time we give the signal. Then a person chosen by me will make good use of the confusion and assassinate the Baba. It would appear as if Santokh Singh had been inadvertently killed in the rioting or, worse, one of his own faithful had killed him.

'Some time after the deed is done, our police units will reach the scene. No one then can lay a finger on us. If we plan this carefully, we could finish him and his movement once and for all.'

Avjeet Singh stopped speaking and there was complete silence in the room. A senior minister then asked the question they all wanted to ask: 'Who is this man who will do the job for us?'

Avjeet Singh, fatigued from speaking at length, sat down and addressed the group looking at him keenly. He could barely whisper: 'It is not a man but a woman who will do the job for us. I trust her with my life. But she will do it when the time is right.'

33

10 p.m., 5 June 1984, Golden Temple—the final hours of Operation Blue Star

The time was out of joint. The hands of the watch of the giant clock tower stood still. In a sense, time stood still—the world outside had been shut out from the temporal seat of authority of the Sikhs. All that mattered was that two sets of combatants faced each other on either side of the *parikrama*, or the outer perimeter around the Akal Takht, the sanctum sanctorum. One set was making its last stand and the other was relentlessly pushing in to destroy the resistance once and for all.

There was a deep rumble at the entrance leading to the parikrama and Aranjit positioned high up, next to the water tank, with her bolt-action rifle, knew that the tanks had been given the green light to move in. Her eyes watered and she knew that the Akal Takht would

come into the line of fire at any moment now. They had
thrown in everything, including special troops dropped
from MI-4 helicopters, into the parikrama. But their
ingress had been ferociously repulsed. When it had
really mattered, the commander had given evidence
of his genius in organizing men and materials to blunt
the attack. His network of men, manning machine-
gun nests ten inches above the ground, was spread
out all across the parikrama and the *darshan deori*.
Others were strategically holed up in the Akal Takht,
the langar rooftop and Ramdas Serai. They controlled
both the commanding heights and ground zero, where
the action would unfold. The generals had thrown in a
mix of troops, many of them from Para Commandos,
10 Guards and the Special Frontier Force. The first
wave had come in, lambs to the slaughter. Withering
machine-gun fire from above and the ground had cut
them down. Scores had been killed and those who
survived writhed on the ground with bloody, torn
kneecaps. The generals were in no mood to hold back
and they pushed in a second wave and then a third.

The ground under Aranjit's feet was littered
with shell casings. From her vantage position, she
worked tirelessly, inserting clip after clip into her rifle,
shooting, maiming and killing troops rushing into the
temple. The successive detachments of troops thrown
into the middle of the pitched battle learnt from the

mistakes of the men who had gone in earlier. They changed their tactics and slowly many machine-gun nests around the parikrama were neutralized. But the sniper fire from the langar rooftop and the heavy machine-gun fire from the Akal Takht area were still taking a heavy toll. Finally the generals, unnerved by the heavy casualties, decided to send in the tanks to cut their losses.

Above her vantage position, Aranjit heard the rumble of tanks preparing to force their way into the parikrama from the main entrance. And then in the next instant, the rumble of tanks died down. The men spearheading the resistance around the parikrama sweated through the brief respite, waiting for the assault to begin again. Aranjit knew that the army was playing with their minds. It was sending a message: "Surrender or else." She smiled grimly. They had no idea of the workings of the Sikh mind. It worked best when pushed against the wall. She saw a movement near the entrance gate. A probing party of four commandos, dressed in black dungarees, had crept in. She brought up her rifle in a flash and fired four rounds, splitting open their skulls. They collapsed in a heap and then it was quiet once again.

She looked at the Harmandar Sahib. Then, for the first time since the battle had begun, she lost her composure. What if the firepower reached the Guru

Granth Sahib, their holy book? It would be sacrilege of the worst kind! Her eyes watered at the thought and then she once again heard the rumble of tanks on the move.

The army first sent in an armoured personnel carrier (APC) before the heavy metal action of the tanks would begin. The words of the commander flashed through her mind: 'There are no half measures for us. A river of blood runs through our fate and history. It has happened before and it will happen again. We always pick ourselves up and face up to whatever is thrown at us. That is who we really are.'

Aranjit's mouth tightened and she threw away her sniper rifle. There was one rocket left in the launcher resting on the ground. She knew she could not miss it. She composed herself and positioned the launcher on her shoulder. The APC had begun to fire but she was in no hurry. She had entered a world of transcendence which every sniper hopes to step into, at least once in a lifetime. It is a world where nothing else exists but the marksman and the target. The APC had launched a brutal assault but Aranjit knew she would have the last word. She slowly pulled the trigger.

The top of the APC exploded and it was the defining moment of the battle. The enraged generals watching the battle from a building near the clock tower gave the permission that they had been holding back so far. They gave the green light to the tank commanders on the ground to begin the assault. The entire complex was suddenly lit up brilliantly with flares. The tanks pushed aside the APC blocking their way. They began to fire straight at the Akal Takht without preamble. Three tanks entered the parikrama. The turrets of the other two Vijayanta tanks turned towards the Ramdas Serai and their main guns began to blast the rooms and the fighters holed up inside. Aranjit knew it would be her turn next. There was no time to climb down the staircase. From the corner of her eye she could see that the turret of one of the tanks had begun to turn towards her. She uttered a short prayer and leapt off the building. A shell came for the water tank from the opposite end and blasted it, spraying gallons of water all around.

Aranjit landed hard on the ground—stunned from the fall. The whine of shells slamming the temple and the screams of injured men filled her ears. In a daze she looked around her. Hundreds lay dead around the parikrama, crater-sized holes had appeared in the Akal Takht and innumerable fires had broken out in the langar area. Men, women and children tumbled out of the langar area, many walking aimlessly in the last few seconds of their lives, their skins peeling off from the burns and deep gashes. A horrible stench rose up in the night sky and muted screams and whimpering cries for water from the dying filled the complex. But all the water had seeped away, spilt on the ground, and the water of the holy tank encircling the Akal Takht had turned red from the blood of the dead and the dying.

Aranjit picked herself up painfully and hobbled her way to the labyrinth of rooms below the temple. The corridor below was littered with the bodies of the fighters while many others still manned their positions, holding their Sten guns, 303 and assault rifles. There was a gloom in the corridor and it was full of choking smoke. A group of fighters, torn and bloody, came out of the gloom. The commander trailed behind them, weapon in hand, his turban opened up. He looked up at Aranjit and both embraced and she wept and he held her tight. He finally broke away from her and she collected herself.

'I need a weapon to make my last stand,' she told him.

He looked up, his eyes glazed, his inherent quiet confidence completely eroded. He guided her to a room nearby. In the relative seclusion of the room, he held her face in his hands and kissed her on the forehead. She tied his turban firmly and told him with a deep conviction in her voice, 'We will make our last stand together. It would be the fitting end, would it not?'

Above them, the tanks had resumed their shelling

and the edifice of the temple shook. Both knew the endgame had begun. The generals would send in the troops to mop up after the tanks had blasted their resistance to bits. Most of the hundred-odd fighters had already been killed. It would not be long before the remaining stray pockets of resistance would be plugged.

He again held her face in his hands and for the first time in her life she saw in his eyes unquestioning love for her.

'Aranjit, I have something important to tell you. You will not be taking your last stand. You will get out of here and live for another day. They have trucks parked outside where the bodies of men, women and children are being thrown in indiscriminately. It would be easy for you to lie still with the corpses and make your escape.'

Her body was racked with sobs when he said that. She then wiped her tears and fiercely looked at him. 'No, never!' she said. 'I will never betray the cause. I will die along with you and Santji and the rest. There will be no discussion on this.'

He breathed deeply, 'He only told me to let you go. This should not be the end of what we had dreamed of. There should be others to carry it forward. You were chosen for that.'

She looked into his eyes and she knew the truth.

Her voice was choked when she asked him, 'He's dead, isn't he? He has been martyred. You made it up, did you not?'

He took a step back and he looked completely drained. She moved towards him quickly and they both embraced and wept bitterly. He then again held her face in his hands and spoke urgently, 'You are right. Santji is no longer with us. I want you to go. It is my decision. I will tell you why I want you to go.'

'No, no, not like this,' she moaned and wept bitterly. 'I can't listen to this. You prepared us for this moment. We all knew what we had chosen. I will not be the Sikhni who turned her face away when it really mattered. I will not do it, Avjeet, never . . .'

He shook her and slapped her. Then he embraced her and apologized. He took her face in his hands. 'Focus, focus, Aranjit! We don't have much time. The troops will be moving in shortly. It will come down to a man-to-man fight. Did you see the faces of the dead lying there in the open? Did you see the mangled bodies tossed like pieces of meat into the trucks outside? Did you see the men lying on the ground with shattered kneecaps, knowing full well that they will never walk again? Were you there when the bodies of so many innocent pilgrims, caught in the crossfire, were thrown into the trucks? Aranjit, there is no dignity in dying with your face half blown up and the skin peeling off of you. It is a tale told by bad writers, poets and illusionists. There is only the gruesomeness of death and nothing else.

'I was looking for an answer when I had seen those bodies pile up in a mound outside the gates of Dacca. I thought of the answer when I fought along with my men this last battle. Aranjit, I finally know what I have been looking for a long time. And the answer has come only here, in this place, next to the Guru Granth Sahib.

'Can I save even one life when everything is coming to an end? Can one of us walk away and live a full life, carrying the hope that we do what we have to do to live and to not die? We make plans and we fight bloody wars but we don't aspire for the obvious. And that stares us in the face. It is the sheer joy of living. And this revelation can only come when one is so close to death. Aranjit, if you could walk away from all this then it would have been worth it. Our sacrifices would not be in vain. Now go to the end of this corridor. I have a man waiting there who will take you to the trucks.'

Aranjit looked at the face of the man who was like no other man she had ever known. She knew that despite his military genius he was at his most brilliant now, when he had said those words to her. She did not want to disrespect him by contradicting him. This was the moment of truth for both of them.

'I will go,' she whispered, looking at him calmly. 'And what about you, Avjeet?'

Above, the tanks launched a terrific barrage. The ground beneath them shook and a blast of choking mortar dust swept through the corridor, reducing visibility to zero. The remaining fighters, taking their last stand, responded ferociously with whatever they were left with.

Death was raining all around them and unexpectedly Avjeet began to laugh. He patted her cheek and turned his back to her and walked away into the gloom, into the line of fire. She was sure he had said these words before he disappeared into the gloom: 'Aranjit, I am a ghost. And ghosts have a way of resurfacing, don't they?'

34

Present day

Suvir locked the hotel room from inside and drew the shades. He looked at Simran standing in a corner of the room.

'We will have to wait it out,' he said. 'The rioters are moving from place to place. If we are lucky they will leave us alone. I will sit on the chair. It has been an ugly night. You must be exhausted. Why don't you prop your feet on the bed and take some rest? We could have a long day ahead. I will keep vigil.'

Simran looked at him and it was at that moment that she realized that she had been on the run ever since the night Ash Kool and his gang had raped her. There had not been a moment when she had felt really settled. She suddenly felt completely exhausted from the effort of running away and deciding all the time. Was there anyone in her life who had truly loved her? She thought of her brother and her eyes stung with tears. Her body shook with emotion as she remembered the time she had shared with her brother, a time when she had been truly happy.

The song of her life had never been articulated or put down on paper, and she had a premonition that this was her life and she would always be on the run. Sweet, sweet Simran lost in a brutal, uncaring world. She wept, sensing a huge loss for a world that could not be hers, that had once existed only in her thoughts. She felt violated once again and she knew then that she was condemned to live a life on the run.

Suvir, looking worried, got up and sat next to her by the bed and took her hand.

'It's okay, you know,' he said. 'I understand. I can't think of any other person who could have put up with what you have been through. Hold my hand. We are in this together. This will also pass.'

She felt she could suddenly breathe more easily. A draught of cool air had blown in from nowhere, into her arid life. She tightened her grip in Suvir's hand. She blocked the hundreds of questions swarming into her mind and listened to her emotion, which had suddenly overpowered her. She could no longer hold it back.

'Suvir, we could both be killed in the next hour. It is a possibility. But that does not frighten me. What really terrorizes me is the feeling that the time when I open up and talk about what moves deep inside me may never come. I think it would be an utter waste of one's life if one went away unsung, unheard of. Not even Aranjit knows what really agitates me inside. Suvir, I have been putting up this brave, stoic face for far too long. And I know I am carrying responsibility beyond my years. I will tell you, Suvir, what I really want. I want a mother who loves me unconditionally. I want to come back from work and sit next to my father, my head resting on his shoulder as he reassures me that he will always be there for me, protect me and love me, his little angel. I want someone who can inspire a poem in my heart. I want to be swept away by that someone when I look at the blue in the sky and the violet shade of the lilac. I want all those ordinary little things that any girl my age desires.

But all this has been denied to me. I have been forced to grow up in such a short span of time. Why do I say all this to you, Suvir? Because I am a lost little girl at heart, Suvir. I crave for someone to lift my face in the morning sun and tell me he cares for me. I say this to you, Suvir, to ask you if you will, if you will be the man who wakes up by my side in the morning.'

Suvir's hand loosened in Simran's grip. She undid her shirt buttons and her white bra stood exposed.

'There might not be a tomorrow, Suvir. Can you love me in this moment?'

There was a moment of quietude between them. Then Suvir buttoned up her shirt. He turned his face away and said, 'I cannot do this, Simran. I am not the man you have thought about. I have nothing to give you. I am completely emptied of all emotion. After what I have been through with Kalpana and Naazish, I have nothing more to give to anyone in life. You are the bravest, smartest and the most humane person I have ever met. I cannot defile you with a moment of passion in this bed. It would be wrong.'

Both didn't know what they felt for each other after the truth between them finally came out. Simran got up and walked to the door and opened it a crack. In the distance she could see a mass of people moving towards the hotel. She closed the door and looked at Suvir, eerily calm.

'I forgot to tell you something, Suvir. The desire to love and be loved, howsoever uplifting, is still a transient emotion. It comes and goes like the need to eat and drink. I think I can survive without it. No, no Suvir, I am not being cynical about it. Actually to meet a genuine man, an honest man, is also a high, perhaps the second-best option and emotion; I will have to do with it for the moment. The world is littered with men who are cruel, who exploit. Perhaps I should be grateful for small mercies, for being with you, right now, my friend.' Suvir shook his head. 'I am so sorry,

Simran. I know I have hurt you badly.'

'No, Suvir, you have not hurt me. You have introduced me to myself. I am a poet at heart and I forgot for a moment that life is prosaic. I was not running away from the exhaustion but from myself. Actually, my real self is quite spectacular. I have been refusing to admit it to myself. Your denial has given me the wings to accept myself. Who knows, perhaps I can fall in love with myself?'

She winked at him and smiled. He came up to her and put his arm around her and kissed her on the forehead.

'You are a hell of a girl, Simran. I am nothing but an interruption in your life. You would not want to wake up in the morning with a burnt-out case. There is no dignity in admitting to yourself that you made a mistake. I would rather be your friend than a mistake made in the heat of the moment.'

Simran kept her own counsel and slightly nodded her head in agreement. She then became all businesslike. 'We have to get out fast. There is a mass of people heading our way. Any bright ideas?'

They opened the door and both ran down the staircase to the back of the hotel where Suvir had parked his motorcycle. Simran sat pillion and Suvir turned the ignition key. The engine sputtered but it would not start. They heard the buzz of a swearing and slogan-shouting mob as it came up to the hotel facade. Suvir, in desperation, turned the ignition key again and again but the motorcycle would not respond. Simran got down from the bike and offered to give it a push from the back. Suvir gave the handle bars traction and Simran pushed from behind to force-start the bike. The bike sprang to life and a cloud of blue smoke escaped the exhaust.

'Quick!' Suvir urged Simran. 'They will be upon us any minute now!'

Simran straddled the bike at the back and Suvir raced through the passageway that turned all the way to the entrance gate. The enraged mob saw both of them making their escape and ran to block the gate leading out of the driveway. In a second the mob of screaming men surrounded them from all sides. A multitude of clubs, pickaxes, swords and traditional lathis were raised in the air, ready to strike. Fearsome slogans rent the air. Some of the younger lot caught hold of the bike's handlebars and many others slapped and punched Suvir. Simran was dragged away from the bike and then someone shouted from the back, 'These two complained against the Baba. I saw them going into the compound with the SHO. Tear them to bits!'

Both Suvir and Simran were dragged away by the maddened crowd. A seething man forced down two hollow truck tyres around their necks and filled them with gasoline.

'A match, a match to teach them a lesson!' the man screamed.

There was a roar from the crowd and Suvir shouted at them, 'Kill me but release her! She has nothing to do with this . . .'

A man hit him with a club and a loud cheer went up in the crowd. A matchbox was found and both were firmly held by the crowd, their arms pinioned behind them. A match was struck but suddenly a man managed to cut through the screaming crowd and reach the centre. He gave the man who had lit the match a hard slap. Hardev pushed back some of the youngsters holding Simran and Suvir. He spoke, forcefully addressing the crowd, 'Have you gone mad? Is this why I agreed to become your leader? These two are innocents. Move back, move back!'

Hardev removed the truck tyres from around their necks. The crowd howled, deprived of their kill. A furious young man pushed back at Hardev, who fell on the ground. He got up and told the man, 'Why don't you kill me first? Satisfy your bloodlust. Come on, do it.'

The young man stepped back and screamed, 'Hardev bhai, you are defending these two against the Baba?'

Hardev addressed the young man and the crowd, 'Let me tell you about these two. I know of Simran. I know her story. If there is a brave girl in this village, it is she! I have heard of this army man. He has defended the country with honour. If we burn them, what kind of an example will we be setting up for our movement? Who will ever take us seriously? We are oppressed people. To seek justice should we become like those who have oppressed us? Then what will be the difference between those who have oppressed us and our movement? If you do this, you will be no more than animals and it will be the end of the movement. Go ahead and lynch them! Finish the fight even before you begin!'

The screaming and shouting suddenly died down and a low murmuring swept through the crowd. Hardev continued, 'Look, I promise all of you that we will get to the bottom of this. While you attend the rally I will have a word with the Baba in private. I will ask him about this FIR filed against him. Let me be the judge of what really happened in the night. Have faith in me. If these two have conspired, we will punish them. Till then we will set them free.'

The sullen crowd parted and made way for Suvir and Simran. Hardev came up to Suvir and whispered in his ear, 'Go now before they change their mind.'

Suvir picked up the bike and this time the engine

did not give him any trouble. They sped away from the mob and Simran asked Suvir to stop the bike near a clearing. She got down and went near a tree and dry-retched. Suvir came up to comfort her. He noticed the odd, eerily calm look in her eyes again.

'We can rest somewhere if you want. It's been a close shave.'

She replied in the negative. 'We can split up here, Suvir,' she suggested. 'I know you don't particularly like Aranjit. But I am going to her place. I will not leave her alone in this crisis. She's not responding to my calls.'

'It's okay, you know. I will come with you.'

He turned and Simran kept a restraining hand on his shoulder. 'Answer a question for me, Suvir. You have seen the face of death before. I experienced it for the first time in my life. After one has seen it, does one change?'

Suvir looked at her young face, which looked animated with an emotion he had never seen before in her. 'You are already changing, Simran. We all do. When you look back at your life, you will remember this day and this time. You will understand then that you had a life before this and another one after this. At any given point of time, we will always be a small club of men and women because of the exclusivity of our experience. I just hope for your sake that whatever you change into does not take away your humanity.'

In a short time they reached Aranjit's cottage. There was no response when they rang the doorbell. Simran opened the door with the spare key and as soon as they stepped in, both knew that something was terribly wrong. A quick search revealed that Aranjit had left the cottage in a hurry. She had not bothered to switch off the TV set when she had left. A news channel was breaking the news that the Baba had given a call for his entire following to assemble at the dera at 9 a.m. Riots had broken out all over the state and hundreds of people, defying curfew orders, were marching towards the dera.

Suvir looked at his watch. There was a little over an hour to go before the Baba would make his dramatic speech for a separate state. His combatant instinct once again alerted him. Something was amiss. He looked around and he noticed the rug in the centre of the room. He knew it had been disturbed. He flung the rug away and his eye picked out the spring lever in the floorboards. He turned the lever and a trapdoor opened, revealing a flight of stairs leading to the basement below.

They went down the staircase, feeling their way in the dark. He explored the walls and found a switch. It lit a light bulb connected to a string. They stood stunned, as the bulb illuminated the basement. It was an armoury for all kinds of weapons. There were handguns, assault rifles, crates of ammunition strewn all over; there was even a box of grenades kept in the room. Suvir rummaged through the entire collection but what really got his attention was not what was in the room but what had been taken away from it. He saw the half-open, empty case of a Winchester Model 70 sniper rifle. He opened the case fully and ran his fingers along its interiors. He frowned deeply and looked up at Simran.

'Your friend is out in the open with a sniper rifle. This is an early eighties' sniper rifle which is very accurate; it releases five rounds every clip.'

Suvir looked at Simran and he lifted her face up in the weak bulb light.

'Simran, I have no proof to back me up, but instinct tells me that your friend has gone to the dera to assassinate Baba Santokh Singh. The state is already on fire. If she does that, she will unleash a caste war that will carry on in the state for decades. Answer me truthfully. You were her closest friend. Did you know about all this? Did you know about her plan? Do you even know who this woman is?'

Simran looked at Suvir and the eerie calm that had been claiming her finally settled deep within her. She knew then that she had crossed the bridge. There was no going back for her. She had, as she had joked earlier with Suvir, fallen in love with herself. She now knew completely who she was and where she was headed.

She lied smoothly to Suvir, 'I had no idea, Suvir, about all this. All this is a great shock to me.'

35

They walked out of the cottage in the crisp winter air and Suvir told Simran, 'We have to make a choice out here, Simran. We can both walk away from all this and continue with our lives. After all, what does Baba Santokh Singh mean to us? Nothing. Or else we choose to do something about this.'

'Can you walk away from all this, Suvir?'

'No, I can't, especially not after what I have seen last night. I cannot set up a clinic dedicated to young girls in the shadow of his dera, knowing what he does to women there. It would be too much irony for me. I cannot shut this man out of my mind. If Kalpana and Naazish had been around, they would not have forgiven me if I chose to walk away.'

Simran looked up at Suvir. 'Greta could be me. Our violation was along the same lines. I have a conscience, Suvir. We cannot walk away from this man and let him be. And then there is Aranjit somewhere on his campus. I feel responsible for her.'

'So then it is settled,' said Suvir. 'We go after him. That's half the battle won.'

Simran laughed. 'Sure—the two of us against his men armed to the teeth and a million of his followers collected in the grounds. And just over forty minutes to achieve all this. What would the odds be, Suvir?'

Suvir smiled but did not answer. He broke off a large twig and sketched a crude diagram of the dera in the soil. The sketch was based on his remembrance of the dera premises when he had visited the place during one of his exploratory walks.

'We can do it if we stumble across a magic bullet. You had once told me that you and Aranjit had thoroughly explored the dera. The women are probably locked up in the cellars below. How did you know all about that?'

'Well, we stumbled on to this separate tower; they have a master control room on the sixth floor. The MCR harbours the controls to the screens outside the estate grounds, all the propaganda films and the scores of robotic cameras set up inside the dera . . .'

'Hang on! Did you say robotic cameras? Has he installed them in the cellars?'

'Yes, he probably has—one in each room to keep track of his slaves or to indulge in audio–visual deviant games.'

Suvir knelt on the ground and prodded the twig at the base of the tower.

'It could be done, Simran. You just gave me the magic bullet. We will have to do a repeat of Operation Black Thunder once again in the state.'

'What exactly is that?'

'It was one of the most famous counter-insurgency operations carried out successfully in Amritsar at the Golden Temple by the Special Forces. I will explain the details to you on the way.'

'Just the two of us will be doing a repeat of this operation?'

'Three would be a crowd,' answered Suvir firmly. He jabbed the stick at the tower once again. 'I will take on his army in the cellars and rescue the women. But the key lies in this tower, in the MCR. You will have to take control of the MCR. Once I rescue the women and you take control of his TV workstation then we will broadcast live an event that will expose him completely. Would you be up for this task, Simran? Without your effort, there can be no magic bullet.'

'Don't be patronizing, Suvir. You can test me out only on the battlefield.'

Suvir backed away. 'Sorry. Some "man" habits take a lifetime to get rid of. Wait here. I have to go back to the cottage and pick up some hardware.'

Suvir disappeared inside and emerged carrying a tennis bag crammed with an MP5 sub-machine gun, spare magazines and a few grenades. He slung the bag across his shoulder and took out a Glock. He gave it to Simran.

'No disrespect to you, Simran, but I am asking a lot from you. I know you have never handled a handgun before in your life. But you would need to use it or, at the very least, use it to threaten and incapacitate the technicians in the MCR. Here, hold it.'

Simran took the gun and with a straight face listened as Suvir showed her how the safety catch worked in the handgun.

Suvir held her face in his hands. 'We are running against time. A lot of people get overawed when they handle a weapon for the first time in their lives. The gun is just another tool to help us—like a hammer or a crowbar. You remember that and I promise you that you will come out good from all this.'

Simran replied with a straight face, 'I will remember that, Suvir. Now, let's get the bike up and running. Remember, we don't have time? '

At the dera, Baba Santokh Singh lay sprawled on a sofa in his personal chambers, nibbling at black grape. His advisers stood at the foot of the sofa, waiting for further instructions.

'So how does it go?' he asked carelessly. 'Has the

hysteria got to them? Would they be willing to do anything for their Baba?'

The Baba's personal assistant lowered his head in deference. 'Sir, on a scale of 10 we are already at 9. You have to see their passion and the love they have for you. The scenes outside the grounds are unimaginable.'

The Baba cut him short, 'Are you getting a little deaf in your old age? I asked about hysteria and not about love and passion. Do you know the difference between these words? I will have nothing less than a 10.'

'Sir, to achieve what you want we will have to push them over the edge. I might just have an answer for what you want.'

The personal assistant came up and whispered something in the Baba's ear. The Baba nibbled at another grape and smiled. 'Good thinking. I like it. Let's get on with this.'

The personal assistant accompanied the Baba, along with the Baba's chief security officer (CSO), to an adjoining room. Hardev and three of his followers stood up and touched the Baba's feet. The Baba embraced him and asked all of them to be seated.

'So what brings you here, Hardev? I thought you would be out on the grounds with your followers. What is it you wish to ask me?'

'Baba, please don't misunderstand me. But can you

truthfully tell me what happened last night? There are a lot of rumours floating around. We look upon you as our God. But sometimes even the gods have to descend to earth. Is there any truth in the allegations levelled against you by that German woman?'

The Baba looked at him as if he had been struck across the face. Then he began to laugh hysterically. He quietened down and looked at Hardev, a sly smile playing on his face. 'It's my mistake, Hardev, that you challenge me so. It is because your education is incomplete. Do you understand the meaning of the word sacrifice? Everyone has to make a sacrifice when they come into my fold. That is the basic tenet of my teachings. People make sacrifices for me and I partake of what they do for me. Today it is your turn. Security, teach him the meaning of that word.'

The Baba and his assistant walked out of the room and the CSO quickly slammed the door shut from the inside. Then he took out his handgun and before any of them could even figure out what was going on the CSO had shot all of them to the ground.

36

Baba Santokh Singh's dera, Pind Jhalan village

Suvir looked at the hands of his wristwatch. He looked up at the dera's clock-tower watch, which stood next to a turret on the top floor. He turned to Simran and told her, 'Synchronize your watch with that of the clock tower. The time is 8.45 p.m. In the next fifteen minutes we will know whether we can save this state or not. Are you prepared?'

She looked at him and smiled. He could not help but wonder at the transformation that had come over her in the last hour. She had the calm of a veteran, as if she had been doing the job she was about to do all her life. He frowned slightly, unable to understand it, and then somewhat unlike his usual self, he kissed her lightly on the cheek. He whispered in her ear, 'Don't take any unnecessary risks. Stay in touch with me via your cell phone all the time. Both of us will come out

349

of this alive—I'm sure of that.'

She smiled again and then she enigmatically told him, 'Thank you, Suvir, for everything. I will never forget it.'

He wanted to hold her hand and ask her what she meant but she turned her back to him and disappeared in the throng moving towards the main stage on the grounds. He focused on the task ahead and broke into a light run towards the rear of the dera. Hundreds of thousands were streaming into the grounds and a cloud of dust hung in the air; the noise from the slogan-shouting and hysteria was deafening. As Suvir came up to the rear, he saw the giant screens flicker with life. The screens showed the bullet-ridden bodies of Hardev and his comrades being brought out in the open on the stage. A voice-over, along with the visuals, inflamed the crowds even further.

'An hour ago one of our very own, our beloved Hardev, and his followers were butchered in cold blood by the landlords of Kasba Chardi Kala! Look! Look! How he bleeds from his wounds! Look at his innocent face! He smiles even in death!

'He will be avenged! We will show no mercy! The day of reckoning for those who have oppressed us for centuries has come! Show your solidarity with the Baba!'

The crowd went wild when they saw the visuals

of the bullet-ridden bodies on the screens. There was more uproar when volunteers carried the bodies out of the dera and placed them on the stage. A roar grew in the crowd and chants for revenge resounded through the estate. Many broke down and cried and many women beat their breasts to show solidarity with Hardev and his followers.

Suvir, grim-faced, focused on the task ahead. The crowd had thinned at the rear side and he saw a row of trucks lined at the back entrance. Two armed sentries were checking the trucks with special mirrors to see if any bomb had been fixed to the undercarriage. It was easy for Suvir to climb on top of one of the trucks as it went in. A massive iron-grilled gate was open and a couple of men with clipboards stood near the gate, ticking off inventory items from the trucks going in and out. Suvir's eyes adjusted to the cavernous area at the back and he realized that boxes with materials were being moved from the cellars to clear out incriminating evidence. He would have to act fast if his plan were to succeed.

The truck came to a stop in an assembly line and he noiselessly climbed down and melted into the dark patches. Up ahead he saw a massive open-air cargo elevator leading to the cellars, transporting men and materials up and down. A guard armed with an AK-74 assault rifle stood near the elevator. Suvir unzipped his tennis bag and slung the lightweight MP5 sub-machine gun around his neck. He took a number of spare magazines and wedged them in his belt. Then he took out a more basic weapon for the sentry guarding the service elevator. He reconnoitred the area around the trucks and stealthily came up behind the sentry. He took out a garrote made from guitar string and looped it round the sentry's neck and pulled hard. The sentry went down and Suvir stepped into the elevator; he then pressed the button for the cellars. He looked at his watch. Ten minutes to go before the broadcast would begin.

Around the time Suvir climbed the truck's top to get to the landing leading to the basement, Simran reached the tower area. She jabbed the buttons in the elevator that would lead her to the master control room on the sixth floor. The elevator would not respond. She tried again and then she remembered that the floors were accessible only with an elevator key. Time was running out and she prepared herself for the only other option she could think of. She inserted the Glock into her waistband, tore her chunni into strips and tied the cloth around her hands. She looked outside the elevator area and found what she was looking for. Coils of wire netting and other construction material was strewn around to strengthen the perimeter fencing. There was a pile of welded, one-inch thick, two-feet-long iron strips lying in a heap. She selected three strips and picked up some bricks kept near the construction material. She carefully balanced the strips between her teeth and created a pedestal with the bricks, climbed on it and then pushed at the roof of the elevator. The service hatch gave way and opened outwards.

She climbed on to the elevator roof and began the arduous task of climbing the steel pylon holding the elevator all the way up to the sixth floor. Her hands were blistered and bled but she continued to climb to the top with manic energy. The closed shaft of the sixth floor came up and she found a foothold below it. She balanced one foot on the steel pylon and jammed her other foot into a crevice in the dark passage. She inserted an iron strip between the doors of the hatch but they remained shut. She continued to push the strip in till she found a leeway. The partition between the doors opened just a crack. She stuck the strip into the crack just as it was about to close again. She quickly looked at her watch. She had lost close to eight minutes and she knew she was running against the clock. She was drenched with sweat and her arms were on fire with pain.

She willed herself to the task again. She stuck the tips of her fingers into the tiny opening and pulled on both sides with all her strength. The veins on her neck stuck out and she had difficulty breathing but she had made up her mind not to let go and try again. It was now or never. The hatch doors opened and she quickly inserted two strips into the opening to jam the open doors. Then she climbed in between the partition and rolled on to the ledge outside. The elevator doors opened out to a landing. She saw a glass cabin ahead of her and a lone technician sitting on a chair, his back to her. He was operating the console in the master control room and on the preview monitor she saw the frenzied crowds and the bodies of Hardev and his followers placed on stage. She heard a sound that vibrated through the room. The clock-tower watch had struck 9 a.m. She knew she was out of time. An incoming call from Suvir on her cell phone vibrated in the pocket of her jeans.

In the meditation room, Baba Santokh Singh finished a glass of sweet buttermilk and wiped his moustache. He smiled and his core group of assistants and personal bodyguards responded with even bigger smiles.

'Is the crowd charged up?' he asked, the disdain in his voice unmistakable.

'Sir,' said one of the assistants, 'the women are beating their chests and the men are frothing at the mouth. Scores have fainted. The volunteers have dissuaded many who were prepared to set themselves on fire to show their protest and solidarity with you.

But despite all that, many in the state have jumped into wells and drowned and others have flung themselves from the rooftops on live electric poles to be electrocuted to death. The state is in the grip of complete madness, like nothing anyone has ever seen before. It was not so bad even during the insurgency thirty years ago.'

'Good,' he answered with satisfaction. 'And did the sacrifices of my dear Hardev and his band of followers go in vain?'

'No, sir,' said the assistant. 'They did more for your cause in their death than they could have ever achieved if they were alive. The scenes of their death, dutifully relayed by the electronic media, have pushed the crowds past the tipping point. Everything is in free fall.'

The Baba rubbed his hands. 'Excellent! Everything is falling into place just as I had planned. In our celebrations, though, we must not forget to exercise caution. What is the situation in the cellars?'

'Sir, even as we speak, men in trucks are removing all materials and incriminating evidence from the cellars. We will start moving out the women and children late at night. We don't want to move them out just yet in this madness. By tomorrow morning you can invite a press and police party to inspect the basement and the cellars. They will find nothing there.'

Another assistant in the party interrupted the conversation, 'Sir, it is time for the address. The crowds are restive. It would not be wise to delay the broadcast.'

'In a minute,' said Baba Santokh Singh. He got up and preened himself in front of a full-length mirror. He said to no one in particular, 'The turban and the peacock feather are a nice touch. They match the solemnity of the occasion and yet they are striking enough to look at. Well, that settles it. Everything is lined up. Let's go and get them, boys!'

A high priest, clothed in saffron attire, came running towards them from one end of the meditation hall.

'Sir,' he shouted. 'A thousand apologies, sir! Please delay your broadcast by ten minutes. Nine o'clock is not an auspicious time by my calculations!'

Baba Santokh Singh yelled at the swami, stumped by the unexpected delay. He lost a bit of his good mood. 'I make my own destiny, swami, don't you know that?! The stars and the constellations move in accordance with what I have dreamed and willed.'

The Baba stopped to ponder; then he smiled and recovered some of his good mood. 'But then again I am a slave to what my people want from me. Your wishes will be respected, swami! While we wait for planetary realignment and the right time, someone fetch me a glass of cold buttermilk with a liberal dose of premium Belvedere Vodka. My thirst just seems to be insatiable.'

Suvir stood behind a column in the large basement complex and looked at the narrow passage stretching in front of him. It was lit with white fluorescent lighting. To his right side he saw a row of similar-sized rooms locked from the outside. Each of the rooms had an eyepiece through which someone from the outside could look in. At the end of the corridor, two men armed with assault weapons emerged from a room, carrying boxes stuffed with clothes, basic toiletries, food wrappings, aluminium plates. He heard the ominous crunching sound of more boots against the floor. From his end of the corridor, towards the left, he saw two more men, armed to the teeth, turn and walk down the corridor towards him. He wondered how many more men were there behind the partitioning wall and the corridor snaking to the left and beyond. There were close to twelve rooms on the right side of the partitioning wall. He thought about it and came to the rough estimation that if there were twenty-four rooms on either side of the wall then there would be a shift of two men for each corridor and a spare one to patrol either side.

There could be an equal number of men or perhaps less on the landing. He looked at his watch. It was a little past nine. He was running short of time. He would have to eliminate all of them in less than a minute if he were to have a chance at completing the mission. The only way he could do that was to get them all to converge at one point. Till now he had been lucky in that he had made ingress without detection. The landing had been dark and he had skipped the arc of the cameras looking in. But the corridor was well lit. The technician in the MCR above would be keeping an eye on things below as well. He wondered whether Simran had neutralized the tech.

The two-man patrol came right up to where Suvir was hiding behind the column and then turned and marched back down the corridor.

Suvir called Simran again and this time he made the connection. 'What's your status?' he whispered on the phone.

Simran looked at the tech lying at her feet. She had knocked him out hard with the butt end of the Glock automatic. She replied to Suvir. 'I have taken care of a tech supervising the MCR. There is a console in front of me. I have to make sense of it.'

'I will guide you in a moment. Give me a minute to clear the corridor.'

Suvir hung up. He quickly moved back to the caged elevator. He brought up his MP5 and fired a burst in the air towards the elevator. The whine of machine-gun fire reverberated in the elevator shaft a hundred times over. It would appear to someone on the landing that the entire basement was under attack. Then Suvir turned the MP5 and swung it in an arc and fired a burst at the base of the corridor. He heard frenetic shouting in the corridor and terrified screaming from the rooms. He saw that somebody had called the elevator up to the landing. It had begun to move up. He positioned himself behind a protrusion in the wall from where he could see the men in the corridor come towards him. He knew a greater threat would be coming down the elevator. He saw two men take position behind a column in the corridor near the row of rooms. One of the guards fired a warning burst.

He ignored the burst and his lack of response encouraged the other guards to move up the corridor, behind the two men. Suvir sensed the guards in the corridor had exposed their flanks. In their panic, they were all collected behind the column. They had all begun to fire towards him but he was not in their line of fire. 'Poorly trained,' he thought to himself. But he knew that excessive confidence had undone even the best in many such instances. He kept a sharp lookout for any movement behind the column but his ear and his focus was on the noise of the descending elevator. His ears picked up the hum of the elevator coming down and then in a swift manoeuvre he took two sets of actions simultaneously. He rolled a grenade towards the column and turned and met in full face three guards coming down in the caged elevator.

It all came down to who fired first. The grenade exploded in the corridor and Suvir fired burst after burst towards the three-man guard party in the elevator, shredding them to bloody bits. He took out his emptied magazine and slapped a fresh one into the MP5. The corridor was full of smoke and the guttural screams of dying men. Suvir knew this was the most dangerous moment of the fight. He heard the elevator going up again and a burst came at him from the corridor. He took evasive action but he had no choice other than to step into the corridor. The smoke cleared just in time for him to see a single guard, limping badly, disappear at the end of the corridor. The others lay dead, strewn in his path, their bodies mutilated beyond recognition. He raced down the corridor and he calculated in his head the time it would take for the elevator to go up and come down at the other end.

Then he cast a quick look at the corridor to the left. He saw a trail of blood lead to one of the rooms. He shouted, knowing full well that the wounded guard could hear each and every word.

'Come on out now, with your hands over your head. I promise I will spare your life. All your friends are dead. You have no chance. Even if you take a hostage I couldn't care less. I will bring you down!'

There was no response from the room. Suvir looked at his wristwatch. He was desperately out of time. It was nearly 9.10 a.m. The cell phone in his pocket had been buzzing urgently. But he could not take the call. He still needed twenty seconds more to wrap things up below. He started a reverse countdown in his head: 20, 19, 18, 17 . . .

Suvir knew that the elevator would be coming down in the next two seconds. He knew the time it would take whosoever was coming for him to reach the left end of the corridor. It would all go down to the wire. He shouted to the guard in the room, 'Okay, I am going to lob a couple of grenades in the room. That will put an end to it.'

'Don't do that, please! I want to live,' begged a voice from the room. 'I am coming out.' Before the guard stepped out, he kicked his assault weapon out of the door to show good faith. The terrified guard emerged with his hands behind his back, one leg bloated with shrapnel injuries. Suvir recognized the threat that was right behind his back.

He shook his head at the limping guard and said, 'I take no prisoners in a battle.'

Suvir shot the guard in the head and turned and went down on his knee and fired a burst; at the same time a guard, freshly emerged from the elevator, fired at him. The burst of gunfire from the guard's weapon went above his head while his ripped open the guard's chest. Suvir knew it was all over down there. There was no one left at the landing to call the elevator up again.

He got up and fired at the locks of the closed rooms. The doors opened to perhaps the most gruesome sight he had ever seen in his life. His hands shook as he called up Simran.

A few minutes before the battle had raged in the basement, Simran had established control over the MCR. The tech had been incapacitated and she took stock of her new surroundings. The room had been fixed after the intensive damage caused by the dust storm. The room was essentially small, more like a control area in a turret. The editing-console area looked to a bay window that was large enough for a man to come through. Beyond that she could see the clock tower and the gable roof of the dera. The roof was oddly broken up into a number of turrets with crenulations. She wondered at the incongruity of the term 'dera'; in fact the structure resembled an Indian nouveau-riche version of a medieval castle in Europe.

She once again took a close look at the odd-looking turrets and a thought struck her. She tried to reach Suvir again but he was not responding. She had a sudden impulse to open the bay window. But it refused to budge. She felt the sill of the window and she noticed that a particular piece of bad craftsmanship was the culprit. A badly inserted jamb had closed the window.

She tried to connect with Suvir once again. This time he answered.

'Are you all right?' she asked. 'Is the situation down below under control?'

'Yes,' he gave a terse reply. 'What's happening on the stage?'

'He's still not come out. It gives us some elbow room. The console set is in front of me. Tell me what to do.'

A little after 9.10 a.m., Santokh Singh left the meditation room along with his security detail of four men and a couple of assistants. As he walked to the stage he asked his chief security officer, 'I hope you have the security net in place. We are facing an incendiary situation. You never know what could happen with an out-of-control crowd. Give me a quick recap of your arrangements.'

The CSO gave the Baba a preview of the arrangements: 'No need to worry, sir. There will be four of us guarding you with our lives on the stage. We will be keeping a hawk's eye on the crowd. There are at least six other security personnel spread out on the grounds. Plus, we have a team of at least thirty volunteers who will be keeping a watch and controlling the crowds. All these personnel are in radio contact with me. In the basement, we have at least ten men guarding the cellars. In addition I have radioed three men to go to the roof. I have plugged all the weak areas. The place is impenetrable, like a fortress. Rest assured, sir.'

Baba Santokh Singh came out to the stage and the crowd erupted. People began to shower rose petals on him, hundreds of others swooned and a sonorous chant of 'Baba! Baba!' grew till it drowned all other sound and seemed to fill up the senses of everyone and everything around the stage. Baba Santokh Singh raised his arms and looked heavenwards; he then began his address: 'My dear brothers, sisters and all my fallen comrades, the revolution has begun . . .'

Simran's cell phone crackled again. Suvir was at the other end. He began to instruct her as to what to do next.

'Simran, you will break in a little before he makes his big announcement. Remember what you told me. You are a poet at heart. The visuals and your voice-over will have to be far more powerful than the horror show he has put on. You words will have to match his; they will have to be better than his. You will have to convince a million people out there and many more watching the live telecast. It will all come down to you. He will rave and rant and take his time to build up the expectations of the crowd, whip them into a frenzy. You will cut in to deflate whatever he has built up. Timing is everything.'

And then in an instant it did not matter to Simran what Suvir was telling her and what was going on down below. Her heart leapt and she quietly cut the line when she saw the snout of a Winchester 70 sniper rifle emerge behind a turret. She saw Aranjit's head come up behind the rifle. It was all happening so fast—as if a film on a projector was running at twice the normal speed. Aranjit had exposed herself behind the turret; she had taken her stance, with one knee bent and the rifle balanced perfectly on her shoulder. The stage below was less than fifty feet from the building facade and her shot, when fired, would traverse a perfect triangular slope, covering a distance of eighty feet, to split open Baba Santokh Singh's head from behind. There was no way she could miss the shot. Simran could see her clearly through the bay window but the sun was in Aranjit's eyes and she could not see Simran diagonally opposite her. Neither could she see the three men come up behind her. Simran screamed at Aranjit to take evasive action, she pummelled the jammed window, but Aranjit was lost to the world in that unique space and time that only a sniper knows. The window would not open and a single shot was fired; no one heard it amid the din and the hysteria.

A bullet pierced Aranjit in the neck and she fell on the gable rooftop sideways and tumbled all the way down and came to a rest on a ledge projecting out underneath the bay window of the MCR. The guard who had shot her leapt over the turrets and ran towards her, and the other two followed.

For less than a second, Simran's world completely collapsed. Then she opened her eyes and the fury raging inside her claimed her. The Glock was out in a flash and she fired at the jamb, which broke free. She pushed against the window and it swung open. Aranjit lay collapsed below her on the ledge. She still held on to her rifle and blood was spurting out of the wound in her neck. The three guards saw the new entrant in the game of death being played out on the roof top of the dera. As he jumped over the precarious roof, Aranjit's assailant's last thoughts were that he had never seen anyone in his life move and fire a weapon as fast as the girl who stood framed in the open bay window. Three shots rang out and all three men toppled backwards, felled by clean headshots. The magic of Simran's marksmanship and death danced over the rooftop.

Aranjit was drawing in painful lungfuls of air as she gasped with pride, 'That's my girl!'

She held her rifle out and Simran caught the snout and pulled at it, dragging Aranjit to the bay window.

She came up and Simran dragged her inside and embraced her.

'Child, I am gone!' said Aranjit, the blood filling her mouth. 'You do what you have come to do.'

'Never!' wept Simran, as she tore a piece of her chunni and tied the cloth firmly around Aranjit's neck to stop the bleeding.

Aranjit smiled despite her great pain. 'Come closer, Simran,' she whispered. 'There are things I have to tell you before I go.'

Below, the show on the estate grounds continued uninterrupted as Baba Santokh Singh came to the most important part of his address. He did not mince any words as he came to the nub of the matter. He gave the call for the setting up of a separate state. A convulsion went through the large crowd. The world media picked up his dramatic announcement.

In the MCR, Aranjit was done speaking with Simran. She was out of breath and did not have the strength to say another word. Still, she managed to tell Simran, 'Do what you came to do. Let me take a back seat for a change.'

Simran finally responded to Suvir's calls. She quickly came to the point: 'I will do it. Don't ask me for an explanation.'

She used the switcher on the console and stopped the transmission of the tape showing the dead bodies of Hardev and his followers. She then directed on to the main screen the feed coming in from the robotic cameras installed in the rooms below, in the cellars. She previewed the feed on a monitor. Satisfied, she brought the mike closer to her and prepared to broadcast the ugly truth—not the tissue of lies that was being peddled around.

Thousands below suddenly saw the giant screens go blank and the propaganda broadcast fall silent. Baba Santokh Singh also stopped mid-flow and looked up at the giant screens. A voice had begun to address the vast crowds. Someone was stealing his thunder.

'My name is Aranjit Kaur. Even as I speak to you I am dying. I have been shot in the neck by Baba Santokh Singh's guards. I will be dead in the next couple of minutes. All of you know that a dying person speaks only the truth. In the last few minutes of my life I want to talk of a lie that you have been told. You have been fed this lie for decades. I want to show to all of you a truth that lies buried deep in the cellars of this dera. I have such little time left and there is so much to say. Let the visuals I am about to show to you tell their own story. A picture, they say, tells a thousand words. What you are about to see is a live feed coming from the cellars of this dera. Look at these visuals and then think of the words that come to your mind.'

Simran switched on the feed from the robotic cameras. The giant screens broke up into four boxes and each box showed visuals that took the breath away from the vast multitudes thronging the grounds. The cameras showed white women completely naked, their ribs sticking out, many of them chained to their beds. The doors to their rooms had been opened but they sat shrivelled in corners, refusing to come out, faces pale and stricken with terror. Some stared vacantly into space while others walked around aimlessly, looking deranged and lost. The cameras shifted focus and showed faeces piled in the corners. There were puddles of urine spread all around and the bed sheets were stained with blood. The cameras picked up little children, many among them girls, moving around in a daze, clutching straw dolls, completely naked, many of them malnourished, their stomachs unnaturally bloated, some of them scratching their hair infested with lice.

As the visuals ran on the screen, Simran reinforced the imagery with a short voice-over.

'These pictures tell you the thousands of atrocities committed by this Baba on these women and children. All the women and children shown in these pictures have been repeatedly raped by the Baba, night after night. They have been raped so brutally that their vaginas have been ruptured permanently and they shed blood all the time. The Baba particularly enjoys starving them and then raping them to enhance his pleasure. Most of these women have lost their minds.'

The transmission ended with one of the robotic cameras zooming in on the face of an eight-year-old girl looking vacantly into the camera, chewing at her straw doll.

The voice-over came back one last time over the frozen shot of the girl.

'The Baba's entire life is a lie. He is a predator who must have his fill of helpless women and children night after night. You have looked at these visuals. This is the truth. Now you have to decide whether a beast will lead you in the future or you will decide your own destiny. Whatever you decide, remember the face of this little girl shown on the screen. I rest my case.'

The sweating, swearing, slogan-shouting crowd went completely quiet. They all continued to look in stunned disbelief at the larger-than-life frozen image of the starving eight-year-old girl on the giant screens.

A sixty-year-old woman suddenly got up and raced to the stage, shouting at the top of her voice, 'We have built up a monster! He preys on our women and daughters!'

Another woman in the crowd stood up and beat her breasts in agony.

A third got up and screamed in pure anger, 'I

brought my little girl to touch this sinner's feet the other day. I have defiled my little girl with my thoughtless actions. I have to wash her repeatedly to clear the stain!'

Another woman got up and turned her back to the Baba and the stage. She looked at the men in the crowd.

'Look at all of you!' she screamed. 'He has taken away your manhood and you sit here and listen to him. Shame on all of you!'

That was the trigger that fired up the vast crowd. In an instant they all turned against the Baba. People got up in great rage and hundreds of shoes and slippers were thrown at the Baba. Ferocious calls erupted among the crowd to lynch the Baba. Men with murder in their hearts raced towards the stage. Baba Santokh Singh's four-man security detail took out sub-machine guns and fired in the air to disperse the crowd. Complete chaos overtook the grounds. People ran in all directions to escape the automatic fire, many were trampled in the confusion and still others ran to the dera to ransack it.

The guards and the volunteers in the crowd disappeared, fearing for their lives. The four guards protecting the Baba forced him off the stage, urging him to make a run for it.

Completely out of breath, the Baba looked at his

chief security officer. 'Where are you taking me?'

The CSO replied rudely, 'It's all over for you, Baba. The moment we exhaust our ammunition they will string us all up from the nearest tree. There is a car waiting outside that will take us to safety. Baba, you better put some juice in your legs and make a run for it. Otherwise it will all be over for you.'

Baba Santokh Singh began to run like he had never run before. He could not help but turn his head one last time to see men enter the dera and ransack it. He ran away stung by the thought that in less than a minute an unknown girl from nowhere had brought him down along with his empire built over decades.

In the MCR, Aranjit had begun to vomit but she was also smiling as she lay cradled in Simran's embrace.

'I am so proud of you. It was all worth it in the end. I can now go away in peace. I might have failed but you took up the challenge. And look how you delivered.'

Simran's face was utterly calm as she stroked Aranjit's hair over her forehead.

'You did not teach me to leave a job half done. Hang in there for some more time and watch me complete it.'

Simran carefully rested Aranjit's head on the floor and then cradled the Winchester rifle and kissed it. Then she went to the bay window and looked out.

Baba Santokh Singh and his four security guards were running across the estate grounds and they were almost out of sight. The distance between the bay window and the fleeing party was almost eight hundred metres. It would have to be a once-in-a-lifetime shoot-out if the fleeing target were to be brought down from such a great distance. Simran knew it. The challenge gave her wings.

Simran brought up the rifle and looked through the scope. For a millisecond, the world ceased to exist for her. The sounds of chaos and tumult all around her died down. Her blood song had floated into her head like a revelation. She knew she was a poet at heart. Her heart was full of her song. She was singing her own song. She knew then that she would carry her blood song forever in her heart. It would always guide her, stand out for her. She smiled and slowly pulled the trigger. Greta and her child were running in the estate grounds. She suddenly saw the Baba and four of his men running towards her from the opposite end. She was terrified out of her skin. And then the most incredible thing happened right before her eyes. The heads of the four guards exploded in a blood shower right before her eyes. Baba Santokh Singh was the last man to go down. He went down on his knees after his skull had split open and his brains had tumbled out on to his face. He continued to look at her intensely as he went down.

Simran placed the rifle by Aranjit's side and put the dying woman's head in her lap.

'It's over. Everyone is accounted for. You did not fail. We won,' she whispered.

'My girl,' Aranjit managed to say her last words. Simran looked at her mentor and then a tear flowed from her eye.

'Did I tell you how much I love you, Aranjit?'

She knelt down and kissed her friend on the lips one last time. When she broke away, her friend was smiling at her with the calm that comes to a few at the end of their lives.

37

Avjeet Singh stood up, wrapped a muffler around his neck and buttoned up his wool overcoat. He looked out of the window in the chief minister's office at the parking lot. His ride for the airport had arrived. It was cold and blustery outside.

'I should be going,' he told the chief minister. 'You can get in touch with me through the usual channels if something else comes up. I think I have wrapped up just about everything out here.'

Gunvir Randhawa looked up from his desk and pushed back his spectacles.

'Indeed you have,' he agreed. 'Well, thanks are in order. Your woman removed the single biggest threat I have faced in quite some time. I am sorry for your loss. But life continues. The way ahead is clear now politically but we still need the money. So it's a job half done. I have made commitments in Virginia. I hope you are working on the case.'

Avjeet seemed preoccupied as he grasped his briefcase. He stood looking out of the window and then put down the briefcase. He looked at Randhawa and told him what was on his mind, 'Randhawa, sometimes I wonder if Santji had been alive today what he would have said about the work I do. I had set out to discover a brave new world and look what I have descended to. I have become a hitman for people like you who gain from profit. Is this how revolutions and insurgencies finally end? Is there no glory in the endeavour of humans to reach for the stars, to dream of a different world? Do we all have to collapse into the ordinariness of living, where we live only to profit and prosper?'

Gunvir Randhawa chose his words carefully. 'I don't possess your sensitivity and genius, Avjeet. I am a very basic kind of man. But I do know something that has stood the test of time. All paths in one form or the other lead to this. Perhaps the highest endeavour of a human being should be to step up the standard of his life and of those he cares about. The rest of it, if you may pardon me for saying it, is excuses and intellectual excess.'

Avjeet looked at Randhawa closely as he picked up his briefcase. 'The woman who assassinated the Baba and died in the dera for you—I loved her, you know.'

Avjeet walked to the door and turned once again. 'I

will be moving between Montreal, Kitchener, Ontario and Victoria to shake off anyone following me. This will be the last job I do for you. Santji taught me never to leave a job half done. Goodbye, Randhawa.'

Intelligence Bureau office, Delhi

The room was full of cigarette smoke as the three-man panel finished their debriefing session with Suvir. The senior investigator Srivastava crushed a cigarette in the ashtray and looked at the two other panellists for their assent. They shrugged their shoulders and Srivastava collected his papers and put them in a leather briefcase. He had an urge to take out another cigarette from the pack but he resisted the temptation.

He spoke to Suvir, 'I think we should wind it up. We have put you in the clear regarding this affair at the dera. The country owes you its gratitude for what you have done in the past. You have many admirers in the home ministry. Even the prime minister is one of them. Now this affair at the dera—you killed more than ten men. But we are all inclined to take a view that you cleared vermin for us. You also resolved one of the biggest headaches for us—what to do with this Baba. He was on the verge of creating a caste conflict that could have spread fire not only in the state but all over the country. A lot of people are breathing easy in

South Block after all this has come to an end.

'Look Suvir, this is a messy affair. Punjab Police wanted to keep you in the can and grill you but we intervened. The orders to go easy on you come right from the top. We suspect that wheels within wheels are turning in this case. The complete truth might never come out. But there is a huge hole in this investigation and I want to plug it. We now know that an ex-Khalistani terrorist Aranjit Kaur was involved in the imbroglio. But we also have unconfirmed reports that there was another girl called Simran who was involved in the matter. We have been told she was a good friend of yours. But she seems to have disappeared. Where can we find her?'

Suvir pointed at the cigarette pack kept on the table. Srivastava picked it up and offered a cigarette to Suvir. 'Want one?'

'No,' said Suvir. 'I thought you might need one after what I am about to tell you. You are right, Srivastava—there are both confirmed and unconfirmed reports circulating about this affair. Let me first tell you what is confirmed in this matter. Reports of this Simran girl being involved in this entire affair are complete nonsense. Simran was a girl in her early twenties who had come from England to recuperate in the village of Kasba Chardi Kala. She had suffered a terrible personal ordeal in England and she was on medication for depression. She was a complete nervous wreck. She did not even have the confidence to walk from her uncle's house to the village square. She was a nobody, really. Indeed I helped her but it was more out of pity. The girl is a mouse at heart. Ask the people in the village and they will verify to you what I have said. I am not surprised she has disappeared. She is perhaps hiding in a hole somewhere. It is best to leave her alone. She has no bearing on this case.

'As for the unconfirmed reports—I think you might want to light up your cigarette now. Like you, I have also lived in the world of shadows. I have heard whispers in this world that Aranjit was not alone when she planned her mission against Baba Santokh Singh. She was assisted by a man, rather a ghost who had risen from the past. Thirty years ago after Operation Blue Star ended the army was confident that they had killed Bhindranwale's right-hand man, Avjeet Singh, in the operation. Well, they were wrong. Avjeet escaped and he has stayed in the shadows all along. He teamed up with Aranjit to assassinate Santokh Singh. We in the army have studied this man closely. After all, he was one of us. He is a man of exceptional genius. The problem for you is that this man is still on the loose. You should be really worried about that because this man never leaves a job half done. The job did not end with the elimination of the Baba. It will end with the assassination of the prime minister.'

There was a stunned silence in the room. Srivastava's hands shook as he fingered the lighter to light up his cigarette. Suvir got up to take his leave. Srivastava's voice had a rasping, fearful edge to it.

'How the hell do you know this, Suvir?'

Suvir stopped at the door and looked back. 'I told you, Srivastava. I have lived in the world of shadows. Some of those shadows still speak to me. They call it unconfirmed reports in the bureaucracy.'

38

Forty-eight hours ago, Baba Santokh Singh's dera

After it was all over, Simran called up Suvir.

'I know you have been trying to reach me desperately. So here I am. Ask me anything that is there on your mind.'

Suvir looked at the shattered skulls and scrambled brains of five men lying on the estate grounds.

He spoke softly, trying to get a sense, a kind of reassessment of the person he thought he knew rather well.

'Even the best sniper in the army could not have done this. I am looking at five men shot from a distance of half a kilometre. Who did this? Was it Aranjit or was it you?'

'Who do you think it was, Suvir?' replied Simran.

Suvir was stunned at the reply. He thought about all the training and the preparation it would have taken for her to get here. The revelation for him was overwhelming.

'Bravo, girl! You have come of age. You fooled me completely. I feel stupid giving you a handgun and explaining its features. I am thoroughly confused about you, Simran. What should I do with you?'

'Nothing. I am not in your keep. I never was. You met me at a turn in my life when I was changing. You were the last man standing that I believed in. I doubt there will be another. I am going to disappear for ever, Suvir. You will read of my exploits from all over the world. They will not mention my name but my signature will be there for you to know.'

'Is there some way I can hold you back?'

'I doubt it. I will treasure the moments we spent together, walking in the evenings to the tea stall. But you hold no ownership over me. No one does. If someone attempts to do that, and that includes you, then I will respond in my own unique way. Even as we speak I have locked you in my rifle sight. There was a Simran who opened her shirt buttons for you. There is a Simran after that.'

Suvir stood up and looked at the tower. He smiled.

'You think you can get me at this distance?'

'Do you want to bet on it, Suvir? Trouble is, if I gun you down, from whom will I collect my bet winnings?'

Suvir laughed and said into the cell phone, 'I believe

you, Simran. You are a big girl now.'

'There's just one more thing, Suvir. It's the exit line of the time we spent together. Despite your detachment and the ennui you carry around as a badge of honour, you are at heart a traditionalist. And I despite my quiet, introverted self am a rebel at heart. Before Aranjit died she was exhausted of all that she had been carrying within her for years. She wanted to unload it all. She told me of her husband, Avjeet Singh. He was Bhindranwale's right-hand man during the insurgent years. Your army believed it had killed him during Blue Star. They were wrong. He has been working all this while with the CM of this state to assassinate the prime minister of the country. That is the real job these men have set out to do. Santokh Singh's killing is just an added bonus.'

'Why are you telling me this, Simran?'

'I told you that because you are a traditionalist. Like in the movies of old, you are still prepared to die for your country.'

'And what about you, Simran? Who are you really? You just told me you are a rebel at heart. And now you tell me this, knowing full well that I will stop this event from happening.'

Simran spoke to Suvir for the last time in her life, 'Like all other men, you also cannot understand the way a woman thinks. In that hotel room all alone with you, I loved you as I had never loved anyone before in my life. Then you changed all that. I refuse to be in debt to anyone in my life. I have released you from my rifle sight, Suvir. You are free to go.'

39

One month later, Avignon, France

The EU trade commissioner signed on the dotted line and his Indian counterpart, seated next to him, also completed the protocol. Standing behind the two men the Indian prime minister, Avatar Sidhu, politely clapped along with the rest of the Indian and Franco-British delegation. The trade commissioner then stood up to make a short speech.

'Ladies and gentlemen, this agreement provides for the transference of cutting-edge European farming technology to our Indian counterparts. In return, we look forward to the opening of Indian agricultural markets for our produce. We thank the Indian prime minister, Mr Sidhu, and the Punjab chief minister, Mr Randhawa, for taking this initiative.'

The commissioner ended his speech and a round of applause broke out among the select gathering in a suburban hotel in Avignon city. Drinks were served. Avatar Sidhu chatted with the commissioner and looked from the corner of his eye as Randhawa made his way in the gathering towards them. The prime minister introduced Randhawa to the commissioner and later, when the two men had a moment to themselves, Sidhu told Randhawa, 'I think we wrapped it up quite nicely, Rummy. The deal will really bring great benefits to Punjab and the agrarian states. Actually, more than the deal, I am happy we broke the ice. We have been estranged for far too long.'

'Couldn't agree with you more, Sid. We have been sulking with each other for no reason. We actually go back quite a bit. I have to say, these are good beginnings.'

'Well, here's a thought, Rummy. Before the official dinner tonight, why don't you come to my room? The mayor of this beautiful city presented me with a great bottle of Rothschild red. We could share it—just like the old times.'

'Yeah, I would like that. They have dinner early in these parts. So shall I call upon you at 6.30 in the evening?'

'Sounds like a great idea.'

The two men shook hands and broke up. The day was spent sightseeing and exploring the ramparts of the historical city with a couple of courtesy calls to dignitaries thrown in. By early evening the Indian delegation had retired to their hotel rooms. At 6.30 p.m. sharp, Randhawa knocked on the door of Avatar Sidhu's official suite. Sidhu welcomed his old friend with great bonhomie and fixed drinks. Both sank in the plush sofas and sipped their wines. There were reminiscences of times past, the days of struggle, even talk of their first dates in college when they had gone out together as a foursome.

'Those were good times, Rummy,' said the prime minister, finishing his drink and fixing some more for his friend and himself. 'Days of innocence, as I would call it. And then we grew up and fell apart.'

'Yeah, the world came in and separated us. But Sid, as they say, shit happens. Can't we put the acrimony of the past behind us?'

'I don't see why not. Once we are back in India, why don't we catch up again with the wives? That's the best way to bring back the spark in our relationship.'

'Yes, that's a thought. The wives dictate the agenda . . . The days of doing things on your own are gone.'

Both men laughed and then Avatar Sidhu's face looked pensive. 'You know, Rummy—why do we have to wait for all that? You know how it will be once we head back: the same routine of party meetings, schedules, official courtesies and all that. It could be months before we meet again. So here's an idea. We are both headed to Paris for official meetings before we finally fly back home. Why don't you and I skip the flight from Avignon to Paris and instead take the TGV to Paris? I believe it's less than three hours by train from the station here to Paris. I could ask someone to book an entire carriage for us. We could send the others by flight to Paris. It would be just you and I and a couple of the Special Protection Group guys. We could drink wine all the way, admire the French countryside and talk of old times. There will be no one to disturb us. I am really keen to get our relationship back on track. We should spend quality time with each other. So what do you say to that? We can arrive at Paris drunk as lords!'

Gunvir Randhawa laughed heartily and slapped his knee in good cheer. 'Ah, finally there speaks my friend of old! The Punjabi by nature had to surface one day! Of course, I am game for this. But can you organize an entire carriage to be booked?'

'Small change, my friend,' replied Avatar Sidhu. 'Call it the perks of the job.'

Both men laughed and after a few more drinks broke up for the evening dinner.

A short time later, the prime minister's official itinerary was changed and the necessary changes were put in place. An entire carriage was booked on the

Train à Grande Vitesse (TGV) which would depart around noontime from the Avignon Train Station the next day.

Later that evening, when the entire Indian delegation sat down for dinner at an official meet, a taxi made its way up the steep mountain road through the hill resort of Gordes which was less than fifty kilometres away from Avignon city. The occupants of the taxi got off at one of the budget hotels in the inner part of the hill town. The small hotel had a restaurant on the ground floor and by the evening it was packed with tourists. One of the occupants of the taxi, carrying a large duffel bag, began to climb the narrow staircase that led from the side of the restaurant to the reception on the first floor. The second man, with a deep furrow down his forehead, fell back a bit to check on the tourists packing the restaurant below.

Avjeet Singh was in full operation mode and he did not want to leave anything to chance. He had decided to become personally involved in the operation because his accomplice was long on fiery rhetoric but a little short on operational capability. But he was still the best he could tap into. Bachitter Talwandi was a veteran of a Khalistani cell that operated in Montreal. He had been active in the years after 1984 but in the last few years there had not been much action. He would once in a while join the protests, along with others, in front of the Indian High Commission when an important minister or dignitary from India came visiting. But he usually stayed in the shadows and rarely came out into the open. His real usefulness lay in the network of connections he had developed with extreme right-wing white nation groups in Canada, the United States and Europe. For the current operation he had used that network to purchase MP7 sub-machine guns from a dealer in Marseille.

Both men closed the door in their hotel room behind them and then proceeded to unzip the duffel bag and check their weapons. After a thorough, satisfactory inspection they called up room service and placed an order for a light meal. Some time later, Avjeet pushed away his half-eaten cheese sandwich and sipped strong black coffee. He had a few things on his mind.

'Bachitter, I would be lying if I told you that I don't worry about tomorrow. You are still young. You have a life ahead of you. There will be opportunities in the future. I am still not clear on why you want to go ahead with this. I could have done this on my own.'

Bachitter scraped the last few crumbs off his plate and smiled at his senior wolfishly. 'I find it strange, Bhaiji, that my appetite has come back so strongly in the last few days. For a man suffering from an incurable disease with only a few more months to live, this is nothing short of a miracle. Perhaps it is the expectation of what we will be doing tomorrow that invigorates me. But sorry for having digressed. I think I am clear in my head on why I want to do this. I know my reputation in the gurdwaras. They say I am good at bluster but I am a man of no action. I want to change all that. I want to exit this life with a flourish. I want people to remember me along with the likes of Beant Singh and Satwant Singh. That would be glory, wouldn't it?'

'And you know full well that I have no exit plan in all this? Unlike in the movies, we cannot jump off a train sealed shut, speeding away at over two hundred and fifty kilometres per hour. After we assassinate the prime minister, we have no choice but to take our lives. I ask you again. Are you prepared for all this?'

'Absolutely, Bhaiji. You have my word on this. There will be no going back for me.'

'Good, that settles it then. It's important to get a good sleep before tomorrow. I am hitting the bed. I would advise you also not to sleep too late.'

'Absolutely, Bhaiji.'

Bachitter took the plates and the cups and deposited them outside the room in a tray. Avjeet switched off the bedside lamp and both men turned in their beds in the double room. Avjeet looked at the sliver of moonlight that was streaming in through the parted curtains of the window.

Bachitter coughed apologetically and asked Avjeet Singh, 'Bhaiji, if I may ask why are you doing this? You are still healthy for your age. You can still mentor the movement. Why end your life like this? What is it about Avatar Sidhu that you dislike so much? After all, he is a fellow Sikh.'

Avjeet Singh spoke in the dark after a moment's hesitation. 'And that is why I hate him so much. He is a fellow Sikh and he has always defended the party that massacred the Sikhs in the country. He has not even once apologized for Operation Blue Star. Every year he ritually garlands the portrait of that woman who ordered Operation Blue Star on us. I could have forgiven a non-Sikh for these lapses but not a fellow Sikh.'

There was silence in the room and Bachitter wondered if his mentor had gone to sleep. He still ventured to ask, 'Bhaiji, is that the only reason why you are set on this suicidal mission?'

Avjeet turned his back to Bachitter.

'You won't understand it, Bachitter. Your time here is short and you have still not seen and experienced the agony of life. I have seen it all. I feel so exhausted of it. Now I have no desire to experience it any more. There is nothing to look forward to, no more new worlds to conquer. If only someone could put me to sleep so that I never wake up again. But I always wake up and my persuasion claims me. But soon, very soon, I will break this never-ending cycle.'

40

The eight-carriage TGV pulled out of a rail shed outside Avignon city and came to a halt on an elevated platform in the city's main station. It was a brief five-minute halt. The guards opened the turnstile gates and allowed the commuters from Avignon to board the carriages, bound for Paris. It was less crowded than usual and a sparse line of people streamed into the carriages. At the turnstile for boarding-gate number five, Avjeet and his accomplice deliberately fell back in the line and allowed the other passengers to get through ahead of them. Security was lax in the touristy city and it was easy for both men to walk in unchecked, carrying their deadly cargo.

Avjeet kept a sharp lookout for the prime ministerial party which he knew would board the train at the very last minute. There were a couple of minutes left for the train to depart and suddenly there was a flurry of movement. Avjeet saw the prime minister and a couple of Special Protection Guards (SPG) personnel escorted by French officials walk towards the first-class carriage attached next to the engine. Behind the entourage he saw the Punjab chief minister walk up briskly to the same carriage. He saw the French officials extend the usual courtesies and then the prime minister, the Punjab chief minister and two SPG personnel boarded the carriage. That was the cue for Avjeet and Bachitter to board carriage number five of the train at the very last minute.

The prime minister's overcoat's lapel was drawn across him and he was wrapped in thick woollies and a muffler. He was coughing repeatedly, his voice had gone hoarse and he had put on dark shades to protect his red-rimmed eyes from the glare. His nose was running and he clutched at a box of tissues for comfort. One of the SPG personnel held his briefcase. Worry lines creased Gunvir Randhawa's face.

'My friend, you look very sick. And that looks like a very nasty cold. I feel guilty about all this. You could have hopped on a plane and spared yourself this discomfort.'

The prime minister shook his head. 'Don't be silly, Rummy. I would not miss this trip for anything. I think I caught a cold when I was strolling in the balcony early morning. You know how it is in these parts. The chill can come in from nowhere. And I guess the wine last night did not agree with me. So instead of wine, shall we drink some brandy? It would be more agreeable with me.'

'Of course, Sid,' smiled Randhawa. 'The idea is to get the circulation going and arrive in Paris in high spirits.'

One of the SPG personnel laid out a table for them and then both SPG men sat a few seats away in the empty carriage to give the prime minister and his guest their privacy. The train glided out of the station and in a matter of minutes it picked up speed well over 200 kilometres per hour. The fabled south-of-France countryside flashed past. Both men drank their brandy and Randhawa, in high spirits, made small talk. But his host was strangely uncommunicative, the coughing bouts not helping matters.

In carriage number five, Avjeet nodded to Bachitter and both men made their way to carriage number four through the vestibule. The pantry was set up in the fourth carriage and already a small knot of tourists had collected around the bar-cum-eatery. Both men ordered tea and stood near the pantry, making small talk. Avjeet fingered the cell phone in his pocket, awaiting the signal. He stole a quick look at the vestibule at the end of the pantry carriage. They would have to go through two more first-class carriages after the vestibule before they could reach the last carriage.

It would be a short run to the target area and there he would not allow anything to come between the target and him. He looked sharp and waited for the signal that would come any minute now.

Gunvir Randhawa, for old times' sake, wanted to have one last decent conversation with his friend before the endgame began. But his friend and host was hardly able to talk. He kept fussing with the tissues and he looked as if he was completely out of place. Randhawa nevertheless tried.

'Sid, there is a lot of history between us and we are trying to put behind some of the ugly episodes that have dogged us. That's all good but we need to revisit the past to move ahead. There is this one instance that I find hard to forget. You remember the Rolex I gave you as a gift when I became the general secretary of the party opposed to you. You wore the watch for a couple of days. Then you returned it and told me you could not accept anything that was bought with 'corrupt money'. I was deeply hurt, Sid. I had especially got a few words engraved on the watch to seal our friendship. Do you remember those words? Can you tell them to me so that I know you cared for me?'

Avatar Sidhu broke into a coughing bout that did not seem to end. He looked choked and Randhawa waited for him to settle down but it was of no use. He finally gave up and took out his cell phone and pretended to make a call. There was something troubling him greatly ever since the time he had boarded the train with Avatar Sidhu. He could not identify what was agitating him but he knew it had something to do with the man noisily wiping his nose. He knew it in his bones that something was amiss. The man had refused to answer a question asked of him, even if the question in essence was a lie. No Rolex watch had been given by him to Sidhu. So why then had his friend not repudiated his lie? He asked the question again but Sidhu had begun to wheeze with discomfort. He accidentally spilled his brandy.

Gunvir Randhawa stole a look at his wristwatch. He was running out of time. Avjeet would be getting impatient. He had to make his move now and hope for the best. The prime minister looked discomfited, the SPG men were distracted and perhaps this was the ideal moment to send the signal. Maybe Avatar Sidhu's head was so clouded with the effects of the cold that he could not think straight.

Gunvir Randhawa stood up, pretending he had to go to the men's toilet wedged next to the vestibule. The cell phone was in his hand; he pressed a button on it and sent the signal. Almost in an instant the entire scene in the passenger car changed instantly.

The man sitting at the table had seen Randhawa press the switch. His bout of coughing ceased and the man took off his shades. Randhawa looked in horror at the man. He looked like the prime minister but it was not him. It was a body double.

From the other end of the vestibule, Avjeet Singh pushed Bachitter to action. Both men tossed their styrofoam cups in a bin and raced out of the fourth carriage towards the carriage attached to the engine. They had taken out their MP7 sub-machine guns from the duffel bag and even as they raced across carriage number three and two, Avjeet knew he had walked into a trap. Both the carriages were empty save for some dummies kept on the seats. The small knot of people standing in the pantry car had dived to the ground after receiving their cue. Avjeet knew he was trapped from both ends but he had made up his mind to go down in a hail of fire.

Gunvir Randhawa also knew that he was in the firing line as he stared in shock at the stage actor sitting on the chair. He turned to run towards the vestibule attached to the engine. The toilet door opened and Suvir Suri emerged holding an MP5 sub-machine gun.

The action that followed barely lasted for ten seconds. Both Suvir and Avjeet were separated from each other by Gunvir Randhawa, who was caught in the middle. Avjeet's burst lifted Randhawa off his feet and slammed him against a seat at the back, his chest torn open with gunfire. Suvir's burst found its mark and Avjeet went down. One of the SPG guards was slow to react and Bachitter spilt open his head with repeated gunfire. The second guard's MP5 jammed and two sharpshooters from the French government agency—the General Directorate for External Security—swiftly emerged from the second carriage and shot Bachitter in the back. Avjeet had collapsed near the vestibule and his stomach was torn open but he was still breathing. Suvir, cradling his MP5, came up to him.

'I know who you are,' gasped Avjeet painfully, as he spat out blood. 'We both served in the same army. Don't let me die like this. Give me a soldier's death. I deserve it. Please.'

Suvir nodded and then he shot Avjeet in the head. The stage actor couched in the seat began to scream and cry at the same time. Suvir walked up to him and patted him on the shoulder.

'You are in shock. It will pass. You did really good in a situation like this. It's all going to be fine.'

The train made an unscheduled stop on the tracks and more officials from the French agency came up to the carriage to take stock of the situation. Bachitter Talwandi survived the shoot-out and shortly afterwards a French army Alouette III helicopter landed near the train. A medical team airlifted the wounded terrorist for an emergency procedure in a nearby hospital. Suvir retrieved the cell phones from the slain terrorist and the chief minister and sealed the vital evidence in a plastic bag. His cell phone had been ringing incessantly for quite some time. Finally he took the call. An intermediary connected him with the prime minister sitting in a hotel room in Avignon city.

'Mr Suri, are you safe? Do we have the situation under control?' asked the prime minister.

'Yes, Prime Minister, we have the situation under control. The main assailant, Avjeet Singh, has been killed and his accomplice is seriously wounded but he will live. As soon as he recovers we will interrogate him for more details. The cell phones are in my possession. We have evidence to show that the chief minister was directly in touch with Avjeet Singh.'

Suvir sensed that the prime minister had begun to breathe a little easier.

'It goes without saying, Mr Suri, that the cell phones hold the key to this extraordinary operation. I would have never been able to justify to Parliament and the Indian public why we undertook such a risky operation without the evidence now in our possession. The cell phones will also give us a look into the other conspirators in the state cabinet as well as the terrorist cells operating abroad.'

'Prime Minister, the operation has been realized at some cost. Unfortunately, the chief minister and an SPG officer were killed in the crossfire. We are mopping up what remains of the operation. The French agency and the TGV authorities are also assisting us.'

There was a moment's silence and then the prime minister spoke firmly, 'My thoughts will be with the family of the young officer who died in the line of duty. Well, it was a hell of an operation. An entire train and intelligence staff from two countries had to be brought in for this operation. I will be calling up the French prime minister to thank him for their extraordinary assistance. Please extend my thanks to the stage actor who agreed to risk his life for this operation. And, of course, I cannot thank you enough for pitching in and planning all this. My intelligence agencies had initially shot down your idea of a pre-emptive strike. I am glad I listened to my gut instinct and placed my trust in you. You sprang the bait and Avjeet took it. And I would not worry about the chief minister if I were you. The man had it coming. My heart, though, goes out to his family. I have known them for quite some time. I will find a way to break this news to them.'

There was a moment's hesitation in Suvir's response and Avatar Sidhu picked it up.

'There is something on your mind, Mr Suri, is there not? You can tell me. Please don't hold back.'

'Very well, Prime Minister, here is what I have to say. I know what I am about to tell you is outside my remit but then who cares. I speak to you as a concerned citizen now. I have two men lying dead at my feet. One is an SPG officer killed in the prime of his life and the other is a dreaded terrorist who has waged war against the state. Both have served in the army. You might not believe it, Prime Minister, but at our counter-insurgency courses we studied Avjeet Singh's tactical and strategic moves in a conflict situation. He was a brilliant officer. Why would a man like Avjeet take part in a suicidal mission against the state and a young SPG officer fearlessly lay down his life in the line of fire? The SPG officer never got to see and experience the extent to which a politician will go to consolidate his power base. Avjeet Singh saw it all. He saw his entire community be branded as traitors and pushed against the wall. And it was your party, Prime Minster, that did that. Thirty years after Blue Star and Woodrose and no one from your party has really stood up and apologized, straight from the heart, to an aggrieved community. There have only been half apologies and attempts at denying what really happened during those years. Prime Minister, you can only go forward if the past sets you free. Otherwise, we will continue to stumble. Men like me will continue to defend the state and put in place such operations. But only heartfelt words can prevent the next terrorist from picking up the gun and defying the state. The choice in this matter lies entirely with you, Prime Minister.'

41

The Banga residence, Southall, London

There was a knock on the front door and Nirmal Kaur opened it. Suvir stood outside the door, the light raindrops glistening on his black overcoat. Nirmal folded her hands in the traditional 'Sat Sri Akal' greeting and asked him to come in. Balwinder Singh, standing behind her in the gloom, offered him a seat. The house looked as if it had frozen into lifelessness— everything stood still. Nirmal Kaur excused herself and went up the staircase and left the two men alone downstairs. Balwinder Singh offered Suvir a drink but he politely refused.

Suvir closely looked at Simran's father who sat in an easy chair, wrapped up in woollies, looking shrivelled. The heating was not working properly and the house looked as if a layer of blue frost had claimed it; everything was cold, damp and inert. Suvir struggled to find the words to begin with.

'Mr Banga, I sought time with you but honestly I don't know why I wanted to meet you. I have known Simran and she was a good friend during the time she spent in the village at Kasba Chardi Kala. Perhaps what I am trying to say is that I want you to feel proud of your daughter. She is an exceptional girl. Perhaps she is the toughest, kindest person I have ever met, a contradiction in a way but ultimately an individual who knows her mind. I have nothing but admiration for her, the way she has evolved into something completely different after her personal ordeal.'

Silence then ensued between the two men and Suvir felt at a loss for words, not knowing what to say next. He saw Balwinder Singh's eyes brimming with tears.

'Mr Banga, I hope I have not distressed you.'

Balwinder wiped his tears and looked up. 'You are listing the virtues of a child to a parent who abandoned her. You cannot distress me, Mr Suri, any more than what I and my conscience have to answer for. In a sense I killed my son and then let go of my daughter. I sometimes wonder if I will ever be forgiven for what I have done. Nirmal and I are nothing now but two broken individuals, condemned to spend the rest of our days in regret and loathing.'

Silence ensued again and Suvir looked up at a framed picture in the room showing Sant Jarnail Singh

Bhindranwale ringed by the most trusted advisers of that era including Avjeet Singh. Suvir wondered at the irony of the situation. Balwinder caught him looking at the picture.

'Simran hated me for espousing the Khalistan cause. She considered my support to the cause an anachronism. Perhaps she was right. Men like me had ossified in a time and place that cannot coexist with the present. We refused to acknowledge that the world has changed. And now I have to bear the brunt of it.'

Suvir gently chided the senior citizen: 'And yet this picture finds pride of place in your house?'

Balwinder's face looked ravaged with despair. 'Mr Suri, I am a man who has lost both his son and daughter. There is nothing to look forward to in my life. I know this cause is dead but I keep it alive because men must have their illusions to go on. Otherwise life would be so stark.'

Suvir had restrained himself till then but he was forced to respond.

'Mr Banga, all children mimic their parents. It does not matter whether the parents have been good or bad. Simran might have hated your cause but the poison of your beliefs seeped into her system. She is now a girl who will always be on the lookout for a cause. And there will be nothing to hold her back when she takes up her cause. She will let her rifle do the talking. Your little girl has grown up to be one of the most feared markswomen in the world. She will not be a moderate in her dealings. She will be extreme about everything.'

A fearful look crossed Balwinder's face. 'Sache Padsha, what have I done? Is there a point of return in all this, Mr Suri? Please give me some hope. Are you in touch with my daughter? Tell her all is forgiven. Tell her to come back and be with her parents in their old age. Can you do that for me, Mr Suri?'

Suvir got up and brushed off some of the raindrops scattered on his overcoat. He now regretted having paid a visit to Simran's parents. He understood that his visit would only end up causing them more hurt. Perhaps it was best that they coped with their loss in their own unique way of grief- and self-denial. Perhaps a further laceration of self-inflicted wounds can give relief to some people. Such people could go blind when led out of their gloom to the bright light of the truth outside. But the truth was out in the open and there was no way he could hold it back. The parents had made their child; they were entitled to know how their progeny was faring in the world.

'Mr Banga, we cannot recreate the past. I am not in touch with your daughter. She has disappeared for ever and she will only resurface of her own volition. I will always wait with bated breath to see what she does next. And when she does that, I promise you it will be nothing less than extraordinary. Good day to you, Mr Banga.'

42

An abandoned warehouse near the docks, East London

The fog, like a twisted, forked entity, swept into the warehouse and licked and scraped at the edges before finally settling down. It hung low and enhanced the sinister look and feel of the warehouse. Heavy-metal rock sounds pounded away in the basement and the walls were a riot of racist graffiti painted in the style of the New York artist Zephyr. A gang of five were sprawled on deadbeat sofas and easy chairs whose coil-and-sponge innards had sprung out. They were all taking heroin shots intravenously, living it up in the night before they headed back to Southall in the morning. The basement was dimly lit and rats scurried around; they were all at home.

Andrew Hall heard it first—the clack of a woman's stiletto heel on the stairs leading down to the basement.

He looked up and through the fog's haze he made out a woman standing on the stairs. She was dressed in black leather pants; she wore a shiny black overcoat that came up to her knees. She sported a saffron band around her forehead. He stopped the tape belting out the heavy-metal sounds. The girl stood there on the steps, arms akimbo, looking at them. Hall looked closely and caught his breath. It was the same Indian girl they had gang-raped some months back. He stood up and burst out laughing.

That drew the attention of the other four and they all closely examined Simran standing a few feet away from them. They all joined in the raucous laughter. Only Ash Kool kept his own counsel and shrank away in the shadows. Hall made an obscene gesture and unzipped himself.

'You came back for more, Indian bitch! Well, here I am! Why don't you come down the steps, bitch, and make my night?'

Klute looked up lazily and joined in, 'Welcome back, bitch. Where were you all this time?'

Tattohead began to laugh hysterically, the spittle forming at his mouth. 'Cunt's come back for some bondage stuff. I can swear on that. It can't be anything else. Look at her—she looks desperate for it. Man, I thought I had seen everything. But she takes the cake.'

Sam the Nazi looked at her sceptically. 'What's

with the saffron headgear, raghead whore?'

Simran smiled but the smile never reached her eyes. Her eyes were stone cold. She walked down a step. She spoke with a lilt in her voice: 'A little bit of colour never hurt anyone. So grandpa, you want to do it, eh? At your age you might need some help. How about I give you a teaser first? It will get you in the mood. What would your preference be, grandpa? A slow strip followed by a dance? Let your imagination run wild, grandpa!'

The announcement was greeted with catcalls and more raucous laughter. Sam the Nazi had been hit with a heroin spike in his bloodstream and he was in no mood for seduction. He quickly came to the point.

'Let's gang-bang her again, chaps, before I start tripping. Spare me the strip and the seduction talk. Let's fuck her like a hard-working yeoman—the Englishman's way—and dump her near the docks.'

'Hey boss, I bet she's wearing black lingerie under that overcoat. Give us a real slow strip, babe!'

A difference of opinion broke out in the gang. Ash Kool had by now completely melted into the shadows at the back of the basement. He knew that something was completely out of place. Simran killed the argument by slowly unbuttoning the top of her overcoat. She suddenly stopped midway.

'Oops! So sorry! I wrote a song for all of you. I call

it my blood song. I want to sing my blood song. The song is dedicated to all of you, especially grandpa!'

They were all taken by surprise at the change of mood. A thought entered Hall's head that the raped girl was acting in an absolutely bizarre manner. His survival instincts kicked in. If something did not make sense to him then he would always nip it in the bud, before it could bloom. Hall was still struggling with his thoughts when Simran began to sing her blood song full-throated, lustily. Her song soared within the confines of the basement and stunned Hall's gang members. Her voice was strong and sonorous but it was the lyrics that chilled them. Simran never took her eyes off them as she sang her song.

I sing a song of blood and waste
Of eternal youth and mad love
Dreams speckled across a blue sky
A greening of my young life
The name of the rose
Riotous and unchecked
Fertile earth, soft earth, moist earth, the good earth
I could lie on it
Ear to the ground
Hearing the world heave and move in my favour.
I sing a song of blood and waste
A whirlwind coming my way

Held down by the weight of the world
My legs parted
Wasted in my prime
Defiled, staked and burnt to the ground
Fertilizer to the good earth
I sing a song of blood and waste.

Simran paused and her face showed so many conflicting emotions. There were tears welling up in her eyes but her look was icy and strong. She looked stretched and taut like a wire and suddenly everyone in the room felt the tension of the moment. Simran had quietly unbuttoned her overcoat but she had not yet revealed what was underneath.

'End immediately what you do not understand.' The thought finally settled into Hall's head. His hand moved quickly to his back pocket to bring out the .38. And it was then that all the men in the basement saw the fastest draw of a weapon by a human being.

Simran in less than a blink of an eye had brought up her bolt-action rifle, strung across her shoulder, to a firing mode. Five shots rang out. Two shots shattered Hall's kneecaps, a third went through Sam the Nazi's spleen, the fourth shot broke the fibula in Tattohead's leg and the fifth shot smashed the femur bone in Klute's leg.

All four men collapsed on the floor as cripples,

completely unable to move. Their repeated cries of unbearable pain resonated in the derelict basement. Simran inserted another clip into the rifle. She fired again and the .38, which was just beyond Hall's grasp, went spinning away. A second shot burned a hole and took a chunk of flesh, along with the switchblade, out of Klute's upper leg, right below the waist. Another shot smashed the knuckleduster along with all the knuckles on Tattohead's right hand. The men continued to scream as they scraped the floor painfully, lying in a pool of their own blood and piss.

Simran came down the stairs and reloaded the rifle. She began to sing another stanza of her blood song to an audience of crippled men.

> I planted a demon seed
> Lay still on the soft earth
> And watched it grow insidiously.
> It looks like me
> But it is not me
> The world is too big for a single girl
> A zillion shoots coming up
> But I am unique, all of me.

Simran stopped singing. She went up to Tattohead and took out her own switchblade and thrust it into Tattohead's left hand.

'You want to live, Tattohead? Nod your head if it's a yes.'

Despite his great pain, Tattohead vigorously nodded his head.

'Good. So here's what you have to do for me, Tattohead, if you want to live. I don't like the tattoos all over your body. You will scrape all the tattoos off your body with the knife. Get cracking!'

'No! Please!' begged Tattohead. 'Not this, please . . .'

Simran lifted her rifle and Tattohead began to peel the skin off his chest with the knife in a frenzy. He screamed and cried at the same time from the pain and collapsed, the knife dropping out of his hand.

Simran lifted her rifle again and shot him in the face with a line of regret: 'So much to do, so little time.'

She then turned her attention to Klute. He mustered all the strength left in him to scamper away from her. Simran went up to him and took his hair by the roots and pulled it.

'I like it, Klute, that you are showing initiative. It shows that you have a great will to live, unlike your friend Tattohead. So we are going to play a little game. I know you are unable to move but surprise me. If you can pick yourself up and move one feet away from me, I will let you live. Your time starts now, Klute. Haul up your ass and get moving.'

Simran lifted her rifle and the veins on Klute's head and neck became strained as he put in a supreme effort to inch forward. But he was unable to move an inch.

Simran watched him struggle and then she spoke slowly, 'Haven't got all day for you, Klute.'

She shot him in the back and his spine exploded into pieces.

Sam the Nazi spat blood at Simran as he saw her come near him.

'Fucking bitch, no games with me. Shoot me, I don't care.'

Simran caught him by his hair and dragged him near a wall.

'Sam the strong. We shall see.'

Simran slapped him hard and made him look at her.

'Okay, no games with you, but you have to do something for me. It can't be too difficult for you. If you do that I will let you live, perhaps even call an ambulance when I leave this place. Kapish, Sam?'

Sam looked at her through a sea of pain. Perhaps the woman was soft in the head. Perhaps there was a remote chance he could survive this nightmare.

'Okay, bitch, tell me what I have to do,' he agreed.

Simran walked away from him to the opposite end of the wall.

'Okay, Sam, dip your finger into your intestine and write a message with your blood for me on the wall.

I will dictate the message to you.'

Sam looked at her as if she had gone mad. Then he painfully inserted a finger into his ruptured intestine and scrawled Simran's message on the wall. He collapsed from the effort and Simran waited for him to revive. When he opened his eyes Simran told him, 'That's a job well done, Sam. Now read the message for me.'

Sam began to read what he had written on the wall: 'I raped Simran. Do I deserve to live?'

Sam stopped reading and turned to look at Simran. He knew he was looking at the face of death. Simran lifted her rifle and asked him, 'Do you deserve to live, Sam?'

She shot him in the head and his brains scrambled over the message he had written in his own blood.

Simran turned and slowly began to walk towards Andrew Hall, singing moodily:

I sing a song of blood and waste
Looking through a glass
What a sight!
My finger brushing a man's penis trigger
Pulling back the glans skin of the penis
The pain and the ecstasy flooding me
The blood vessel rupturing one by one
Soft, popped and crackled, the noise

I hear it! I hear it!
My ear to the ground
I hear my song of blood and waste.

She stopped in front of Hall, knelt down and whispered, 'Grandpa, it's been so long.'

There were tears in Simran's eyes. She kindly stroked Hall's face, as he writhed in agony, and then she kissed him on the lips. She held up his chin and spoke soft words to him.

'Grandpa, how would you like to die? Should I shoot you in the penis or the head? Actually, why not shoot you in both places? You thought through it all with your head but you used your tool to rape me.'

Simran looked at his face again and lightly smacked him.

'Dirty old grandpa. Look what you have made me do. Some men never learn, do they?'

She got up and walked across to the extreme end of the basement. She lifted her rifle and positioned it carefully on her shoulder.

'Look at me, grandpa. Say cheese.'

Two shots rang out. In the last millisecond of his life, Andrew Hall felt the most excruciating pain of his life in his groin. But that was nothing compared to the pain of his realization—what the girl must have experienced when her vagina was forcibly torn open and ruptured by men like him. His head exploded and he knew before dying that Simran's pain had transferred to him. It was like no other pain in the world.

Simran brought down her rifle and out of the corner of her eye, she saw a movement towards the stairs. Her rifle was up in a flash and she fired a warning shot above Ash Kool's head. He slipped and tumbled down the stairs. She slowly walked up to Ash Kool, who was shaking with fear, as if in convulsion.

'Open your mouth,' she told him tersely.

He looked at her wide-eyed, in complete terror, and then he opened his mouth. He pissed in his pants.

She inserted the barrel of the rifle in his mouth and asked him, 'How does it feel, Ash Kool? How does it feel when there is forced entry?'

Ash Kool's eyes had frozen with the horror of his situation. He desperately wanted to close his eyes and not see Simran press the trigger. But he was unable to do that. Simran made sure that he saw and experienced every moment of his agony. She finally took out the barrel of her rifle from his mouth and held him by the hair and forced him to look at her.

'I have a worse fate in store for you, Ash Kool. I will let you go for now. But I will come after you. Whatever time you are left with, you will always be looking over your shoulder. You will always wait for the silent bullet coming your way. You will not enjoy a single waking or sleeping moment of your life. Now go. Be sure that I will be coming after you.'

Ash Kool collapsed on the staircase, shuddering with shock and tears. Then he painfully picked himself up and climbed the stairs. Simran sat down on the steps and looked at the bloodbath she had let loose in the basement. Then she slung her rifle around her shoulder and climbed the staircase.

The fog had lifted and the night was cold and clear. She buttoned up her overcoat and felt hopeful and connected with the world. She began to walk across the deserted dock area, singing the last stanza of her blood song lustily:

I sprang new wings overnight
I flap them around, prepared to take off,
The world pulls me back as it must
What will you survive on?
A blood song and a prayer?
I take wing
A shadow falls between the earth and the heavens
Half the world is lit, the rest dark
They all look up at the bird that flew
I sing a song of blood and waste.

Acknowledgements

It is said that the best films are produced when the director is in complete sync with the lead actor. The director almost second-guesses what the actor will end up doing in each and every scene. The actor also feels secure that he or she is in the safe hands of the director. Now that can only happen when the director has a rare talent for drawing out the best from the actor. Vaishali Mathur, executive editor at Penguin Random House, has that rare directorial/editorial talent I have been talking about. While working with her again on this latest book with Penguin, believe me, I have seen that rare talent at close quarters.

Speaking of editing—what does it mean when the writer asks for a particular copy editor by name to hammer and mould his creation into the best possible shape? It simply means that the editor is really good at her job. Full marks to Tanvi Kapoor for doing a fabulous job in trimming the fat and the excess and shaping *Blood Song* into the compulsive read that it is today.

And it would only be in the fitness of things to say a word to acknowledge the unsung heroes who contribute so much to spreading the word of the writer to the masses. A big thank you to all the wonderful sales staff at Penguin Random House for pushing my books in bookstores all across the country with so much energy and enthusiasm.

And last but certainly not the least, there is everyone else and then there is Amrita Talwar—the marketing whizz-kid at Penguin Random House. One senses that Amrita adopts a book as one adopts a cause. There is a messianic zeal to her taking up the cause. And all that is done with that big, infectious smile of hers that is her trademark. Don't ever change, Amrita!

And finally, this is not to acknowledge but to admit that I would not have set sail for this wonderful journey as a writer had it not been for the encouragement, support and absolute conviction of my wife, Sonu. It would not be an exaggeration to say that she knew before me that I had it in me to put words to paper. But then that's Sonu for you—calling a spade a shovel and telling you to keep digging and digging with that shovel till you have finally reached and hit the mother lode.